Salern
alerni, Dianne K.,
he Morrigan's curse /
16.99

W9-BTO-579

HARRIS COUNTY PUBLIC LIBRARY

WITHDRAWN

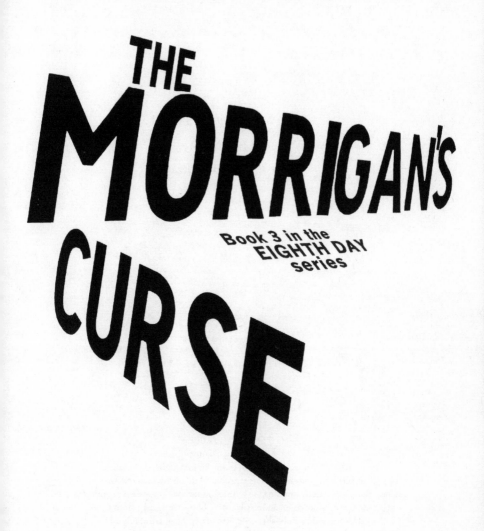

THE MORRIGAN'S CURSE

Book 3 in the EIGHTH DAY series

DIANNE K. SALERNI

HARPER
An Imprint of HarperCollins Publishers

The Morrigan's Curse
Copyright © 2016 by Dianne K. Salerni
All rights reserved. Printed in the United States of America.
No part of this book may be used or reproduced in any manner whatsoever without
written permission except in the case of brief quotations embodied in critical articles
and reviews. For information address HarperCollins Children's Books, a division of
HarperCollins Publishers, 195 Broadway, New York, NY 10007.
www.harpercollinschildrens.com

Library of Congress Control Number: 2015950812
ISBN 978-0-06-227221-8 (trade bdg.)

Typography by Ellice M. Lee
17 18 19   CG/RRDH   10 9 8 7 6 5 4 3 2
❖
First Edition

To the teachers at the Avon Grove Intermediate School
who kept telling me, "You can do this."
Sorry about all the snow days.

FAMILY REFERENCE CHART FOR THE MORRIGAN'S CURSE

TRANSITIONER FAMILIES WITH A SEAT AT THE TABLE
Bedivere
Bors (vassal to Dulac)
Dulac
Kaye (vassal to Pendragon)
Lyonnesse
Morgan
Owens (recently deceased)
Pellinore
Pendragon
Sagramore

A PARTIAL LIST OF TRANSITIONER VASSALS
Ambrose (vassal to Dulac)
Aubrey (vassal to Emrys)
Balin (vassal to Wylit)
Crandall (vassal to Pendragon)
Ganner (vassal to Dulac)
Morder (half-Kin, vassal to Dulac)

A Partial List of Independent Transitioners
Carroway
Donovan

Kin Families Allied with Transitioners
Corra
Emrys*
Taliesin

Adversary Kin Families
Aeron**
Arawen (formerly confined to Oeth-Anoeth)
Llyr (formerly confined to Oeth-Anoeth)
Mathonwy
Wylit

* Elwyn Emrys betrayed the traditional loyalties of his family when he conspired to break the Eighth Day Spell.

**Aerons were briefly allied with Merlin Emrys to avoid incarceration in Oeth-Anoeth when the Eighth Day Spell was cast. They are adversaries in the present day.

1

NORMALLY, ADDIE EMRYS DIDN'T like heights, but in this case, the view was worth it. Leaning on the wooden railing of a second-floor balcony, she watched waves crash against rocks on the shore below, blasting themselves into wild sprays of foam. Addie had never seen an ocean before today. Lakes, yes. Her Transitioner foster parents had taken her to lakes, but even Lake Champlain was a puddle compared to this.

She found herself mesmerized by the motion of the water. In Addie's experience, natural bodies of water were always caught in the moment between two Normal days. Trapped within a single second that stretched over twenty-four hours, lakes lapped listlessly like water in a bathtub, streams lay as still as ponds, and waterfalls dripped like leaky faucets.

The waves she was watching now were abnormal for the eighth day and roused by wind, which was also new to her. Addie raised her face, exulting in the cool air that brushed against her cheeks and rustled her ponytail. This was *weather.*

Only magic could create weather on the eighth day, and for the last fifteen hundred years, the weather-working Llyrs had been confined to the bowels of Oeth-Anoeth, an ancient Welsh fortress that suppressed magical talents. Two days ago, an armed military force had broken into that fortress, releasing the only surviving descendants of the half dozen Kin families originally imprisoned there.

Two Llyrs. One Arawen.

Now free of their physical and magical constraints, the Llyrs were creating the first eighth-day weather since their ancestors had been captured centuries ago. Addie was on her way to watch them work their magic in person, but she had stopped here for a moment to enjoy this panoramic view: the vast ocean, the thin line of land in the distance that marked the coast of Maine, and the endless sky where dark clouds now swelled.

Droplets of water struck her skin, but the sudden prickle of gooseflesh on her arms had nothing to do with the cold sea spray. Someone was trying to spy on her through a scrying spell again. Whoever it was, he was persistent. Turning around, Addie stared at the white stucco exterior of the house and imagined herself surrounded on all sides by walls like that one, hidden from view.

The scryer could have been someone from her foster home, but Addie doubted it. More likely, it was the Dulacs, a ruthless Transitioner clan who'd imprisoned Addie and from whom she'd escaped only yesterday. Unfortunately she'd left plenty of herself behind that could be used for scrying: Hair. Bitten-off fingernail scraps. Blood.

I am invisible behind my wall. Addie concentrated on her pulse, the rhythm of her blood rushing through her veins— the blood of an Emrys carrying the Eighth Day Spell through time. After a few seconds, her goose bumps subsided.

"Again?" asked a voice from behind her. She turned to find Kel Mathonwy watching her from inside the glass balcony doors. "I didn't want to break your concentration," he said. The wind rustled his silvery hair, and he smoothed his side-swept bangs back into place, copying the famous style of a Normal pop star whose music neither Kel nor Addie had ever heard.

"They've given up. For now." Addie smiled at her old friend. Well, really, her *new* friend, who she'd known briefly a long time ago, back when *his* father had worked with *her* father on a daring and rebellious plan to countermand the Eighth Day Spell. As children, she and Kel had played games in the woods behind her house, in spite of her sister trying to keep them apart.

Meeting Kel again a few days ago had been more than a coincidence. Addie thought it was a sign that she was destined to follow in her father's footsteps. Getting captured by Dulacs immediately afterward had interrupted that destiny, but only until Kel came for her with the most astounding rescue party imaginable.

"You should tell my father that someone's been scrying for

3

you," Kel said, holding the glass door open for her. "And stay in the house, where you're warded." Kel's father had a knack for protective wards, which were tricky to master.

"There's no reason to. I have a blocking spell."

"You're going to exhaust yourself, casting a defensive spell over and over."

"No," Addie said confidently. "I won't." She flashed Kel a grin.

"Come on. You don't want to miss the show, do you?" Kel led the way downstairs and through his house. *His mansion,* Addie corrected herself, admiring the spacious rooms with white carpets, suede furniture, and floor-to-ceiling windows facing the sea. Bookshelves were filled with classics as well as recent best sellers. Newspapers and magazines were stacked on end tables, and expensive artwork adorned the walls. During Addie's years at the way station run by her foster parents, she'd seen fugitive Kin pass through homeless and destitute. None of them had used their extended lives to amass such wealth by Normal means the way Kel's father, Madoc Mathonwy, had.

Of course, it helped that the Mathonwy magical talent was *prosperity.*

She and Kel exited through the ground floor by way of patio doors and hurried along the path to the airplane hangar. On the tarmac, a group of people were watching three figures at the end of the runway. Kel's father stood among the larger group, calmly smoking a cigarette and looking smug.

It was Madoc's long-term planning and wealth that had brought this cabal of powerful Kin together. Addie supposed he had every right to be pleased with himself.

With him were members of the Aeron clan—the muscle behind Madoc's brain. The Aerons were gifted with a talent for invoking havoc and mayhem. The day prior to Addie's rescue from the Dulacs, the Aerons had manned military aircraft purchased by Kel's father to break the Llyrs out of Oeth-Anoeth in Wales. In the gloom of the gathering dark clouds, their faces seemed ghostly and devilish. The Aerons made a habit of adorning their faces with fearsome tattoos to celebrate their achievements, and all those present had earned new ones for their role in the triumphant assault on the medieval Welsh fortress.

At the end of the runway, Bran Llyr, leader of the most famous family imprisoned in Oeth-Anoeth, faced the sea and shouted ancient words into the wind. In one hand he held a staff, and his long, straight white hair flew behind his head like a flag. Beside him, his son, Griffyn, muttered his own spells, his brow compressed in concentration. Griffyn was eighteen or nineteen years old, and he, too, had long hair, although his was braided like a medieval warrior's. The final member of the trio was a girl, as tall as Griffyn and almost as broad across the shoulders. Ysabel Arawen wasn't a weather-worker—the Arawen talent was darker and more morbid—but she loaned her strength to Griffyn through their clasped hands.

They still wore the clothing they'd escaped in—coarse

cloth trousers and tunics. Griffyn and Ysabel also wore leather jerkins, with throwing daggers strapped to their arms and legs that made them look like they'd stepped out of the Middle Ages. From the little Addie knew, imprisonment at Oeth-Anoeth had been sort of like being trapped in medieval times. Ten generations of the Llyr and Arawen families, along with several others, had lived their lives in that fortress, dying out over the centuries until only these three individuals remained.

Freed from their prison, the survivors had flown from Wales to Greenland to this island—and then, at Kel's urgent summons, straight to New York City to rescue Addie.

Addie was, after all, the most important Kin girl on the planet, the sole remaining member of the Emrys family and the only person left to carry the Eighth Day Spell in her blood-line. If Addie died, the eighth day would cease to exist, along with thousands of members of the Kin race, all of whom existed solely within that day.

Addie's parents had been killed years ago, and she'd recently learned that her brother and sister were dead as well. In fact, according to her Dulac captors, her older sister, Evangeline—the smart one, the *good* one, their father's favorite—had died only five days ago while attempting to break the Eighth Day Spell in Mexico. Addie knew she should feel grief, pain—*something*—but it had been almost half her lifetime since she'd seen her sister. Addie didn't know how to grieve for her.

Instead she watched the growing storm.

Powerful magic came naturally to the Llyrs, even if Oeth-Anoeth had suppressed it all their lives. Addie had seen Bran wield lightning several times during their harrowing escape from New York in the early hours of this morning—at least during the parts when she wasn't covering her eyes in terror. But even that paled by comparison to what he was doing now. Thunderclouds grew into a city above the sea, with black skyscrapers towering heavenward and lightning arching like bridges between them. Rain plunged down in sheets. Addie's clothing clung to her skin.

Then Kel nudged her with an elbow and pointed at a rocky protrusion about a quarter mile offshore—a knobby twist of land not large enough to be called an island. In the rain and darkness, Addie barely made out the figure standing on rocks with black objects circling overhead. Addie's mouth fell open to exclaim that one of the Aeron girls must've gotten herself stranded offshore and needed rescuing—and then it dawned on her that the circling objects were crows. Her warning cry withered on her tongue.

Bran Llyr barked out a final command and thrust his staff into the air. The monstrous storm moved southward, away from the island. He laughed with satisfaction, then turned to look at the rocky outcropping.

Addie looked again too. The girl was gone.

"Did you see her, Madoc?" Bran demanded, in an accent Addie vaguely identified as "British," but which she knew must be Welsh.

Madoc exhaled cigarette smoke. "I did. Closer this time than last."

"You've seen her before?" Kel asked incredulously.

"She was on the hillside above Oeth-Anoeth two days ago," said Condor Aeron, leader of his clan.

"And Ysabel saw her outside the Dulac building yesterday, while you were freeing Addie," Madoc added. The Arawen girl nodded in agreement.

The Girl of Crows was one of the three incarnations of the Morrigan, a supernatural force of chaos and destruction. The Girl was known to nudge events in the direction of chaotic conflict, while her Woman form prophesied death and the Crone changed the fates of individuals.

Addie shivered in her wet clothes. *That makes two of them I've seen now.*

"Where did you send the storm?" Kel asked Bran Llyr.

Bran waved a hand dismissively. "To that city—that nest of Transitioners. What was it called?"

"New York," said Addie, marveling that these ex-prisoners were so ignorant of the modern world they didn't even know the name of New York City.

Just then, she felt the skin on her arms and neck prickle. The would-be spy was at it again, scrying for her mere minutes after the last time. Oh, very clever—trying to catch her off guard. Too bad he didn't know who he was dealing with!

Whirling around, Addie faced the hangar where Madoc kept his personal plane. She pictured herself surrounded on all sides by featureless wooden planks like the painted white boards on this building, creating a fortress of them in her mind. Behind her, she heard Kel tell his father how she'd been repeatedly fighting off this scryer since midnight. Addie tried not to listen, focusing instead on her secret source of strength and her intent to block the spell.

Bran's voice, however, insisted on being heard. "Look at me, child." Addie glanced up, and Bran placed a rough hand on her forehead.

Blinding-white heat shot through her head, ripping a scream from her. Everything went black and spotty, colors winking in the darkness. When sight returned, she found herself lying on the tarmac. She gasped, over and over, trying not to vomit, and looked up with shock at Bran.

"There," the Llyr lord said with pride. "Let's see if the person on the other end of that spell appreciates my little gift."

2

IN A MOTEL ROOM outside New York City, Jax Aubrey watched his liege lady arrange a pan of water, a package of saffron, and torn pages of a letter on the table in front of her. If he was counting correctly, this would be Evangeline's seventh attempt today at casting a scrying spell for her younger sister. She'd made two tries shortly after reappearing last night at midnight and had taken only a few hours' break to sleep before starting again. For Jax, a week had passed since Addie Emrys had escaped from the Dulacs with the help of the evil Llyr clan, but for Evangeline and her sister, who lived eighth day to eighth day, it had been only yesterday.

"Is she hidden behind wards?" Jax asked.

"Today she is," Evangeline replied. "But for the first few hours after midnight last night she was actively blocking me."

"Doesn't she know it's you?"

"She has no way of knowing who it is," Evangeline replied grimly. "And she's got every reason to fight off someone spying on her." Jax nodded. Addie had been held for days in a Dulac basement prison. She probably thought they were the ones trying to locate her. "But blocking my spell will tire her," Evangeline added. "If I catch her outside the wards, I *will* break through. We need to know where the Llyrs took her after they got away from Sheila Morgan's clan this morning."

Jax wasn't so sure Evangeline would break through. Casting the spell was exhausting *her*, too. Her hands trembled as she pried apart the plastic tabs on the saffron container. "I think you should rest first, like you said you would," he told her. Evangeline had promised Riley she would sleep before trying again, but as soon as he and A.J. Crandall had gone out to the motel parking lot to change the fluids in Riley's motorcycle, she'd gotten up.

"I can't sleep, Jax. I have to know if she's okay. She's in as much danger from *our* side as she is from the Llyrs."

Jax understood Evangeline's desperation. They'd come close to rescuing her sister from the Dulacs last Grunsday, missing her by mere minutes. And in the early hours of *this* Grunsday, Addie had presumably been present during a skirmish that ended with a number of Transitioners from the Morgan clan dead and the renegade Kin escaping.

11

Adelina Emrys had gotten out of the frying pan and landed right in a very hot fire.

On the last eighth day, a couple of hours before midnight, the Llyrs and their unknown allies had left the Dulac building in Manhattan with Addie. Since they couldn't have gotten very far before their secret, isolated day ended, Sheila Morgan—head of the clan leading the search—assumed the Kin had a place to hide for the seven days they skipped over. The Morgans had spent a week scouting the area, and on Wednesday, multiple armed teams had positioned themselves to intercept the Kin wherever they reappeared.

On Wednesday evening, a few hours before the eighth day began, Riley had sent his vassal Arnold Crandall to the Morgan headquarters to serve as a courier of information between their clans, since telephones didn't work on the eighth day. Meanwhile, Riley had chosen this motel as a base. It was far enough from the action to keep Evangeline safe, but close enough that they could get into the city quickly if Addie's location was discovered—or if Evangeline saw her through the scrying spell.

However, Evangeline's scrying efforts had failed, and by dawn they'd received bad news from Mr. Crandall. An aircraft had been spotted taking off from a field south of the city, and two planes sent by the Morgans to intercept it had been knocked from the sky by lightning. Transitioner forces had acquired a description of the enemy plane and

the heading it was on, although they suspected those head-
ings were a feint in the wrong direction, because no one
had seen the plane since.

"How does scrying work?" Jax asked as Evangeline sat
down again in front of the pan of water. "Is it like looking
through her eyes, or . . ."

"No. I should see Addie and her immediate surroundings."

"But so far you've seen . . ."

"Nothing when she's warded. Barriers when she's using
a blocking spell." Evangeline rubbed her temples, like she
was fighting off a headache, and took a deep breath.

"Is there any way I can help you?" Jax asked. "I know
I can't cast spells . . ."

"Actually, you can." She looked up.

"Help you? Or cast a spell?"

"Both. Anyone with magical abilities can cast a spell."
Technically that was true. Jax had seen Lord Wylit
cast a spell that nearly ended the world. But spells were
Evangeline's *talent*—which meant she did it with more
variety and more power than other people. "Then why
does Riley say he can't do spells?" Jax asked.

"He *can*," Evangeline replied. "He helped me repair the
Eighth Day Spell on the pyramid, didn't he?" She glanced
toward the window facing the parking lot where Riley was
working on his motorcycle with A.J., then whispered to
Jax. "The voice of command makes him lazy."

Jax grinned. He loved poking fun at Riley, but it was rare for Evangeline to join in.

"I *am* fatigued," she admitted. "If you're willing, I could really use your strength."

"You have to ask?" He sat down beside her. "If I've got this talent for information, let me use it."

They'd recently discovered that Jax was more than an inquisitor. He'd inherited his father's talent for compelling people to answer questions, but through a unique set of circumstances, he'd developed an additional ability to pull information out of thin air. This had earned him the right to claim *Aubrey*, the name his father had used as an alias, as a branch-off Transitioner bloodline.

"Your talent combines the normal inquisition magic with a sensitivity for information," Evangeline said. "It blends two categories of magic, which is pretty rare. With some training, you'd probably be good at scrying, but a crash course is all you need to throw your magic in with mine." She waved her hand at the items on the table. "Symbols are needed to invoke any spell. The pan of water reflects reality. The letter is in Addie's handwriting, so it's a connection to her. Saffron traditionally symbolizes clarity of vision." Evangeline tore a strip off Addie's letter and gently placed it in the water, where it floated.

"I've never seen you use any symbols when you hurl those invisible fireballs," Jax said. She'd thrown quite a number of those fighting a wyvern in the Dulac basement last Grunsday, which was only yesterday for her.

"For that one, I call on the energy of my own body. That's why I can't hold it long or do it very often without . . ."

"Getting weak and pale and tired?" Jax didn't mention the shadowy smudges under her eyes, but she gave him an insulted glare, so he said, "Symbols, got it. Plus, you mumble gibberish."

"I prefer Welsh, because that's the way my father taught me, but English works, too. The words focus your concentration and magic." She held out the container of saffron. "Put a strand on your tongue, but don't swallow it. I'm going to cast the spell and draw on your strength to support me."

She took a strand of saffron for herself and held out her hand, which Jax clasped tightly. While Evangeline whispered her Welsh words, he leaned over the pan, willing Addie Emrys to appear in the water—preferably standing in front of a recognizable landmark.

Adelina Emrys, where are you?

To his surprise, the water grew cloudy, and the reflection of the hotel ceiling tiles above them faded into something else. Jax didn't know what, exactly. It was a rough, white surface that might have been part of a wall. He stared until his eyeballs burned, feeling the buzz of magic transferring from his hand to his liege's. Finally, Evangeline gasped and sat back, letting go of him. The image faded.

Jax blinked and rubbed his eyes. "What was that?"

Evangeline gave him a tired but triumphant grin. "That, Jax, was my sister defending herself. She's not behind wards right now, and what we saw is something she's projecting at us, trying to block our view of her. Give me a chance to recover, and we'll do it again. Let's see if we can wear her out."

Jax was worried about Evangeline wearing herself out, but he didn't argue. Evangeline rested only a few minutes before removing the soaked strip of paper from the pan and replacing it with another. They each took more saffron and joined hands.

When the water clouded and cleared, Jax got a close look at what Addie was using as a mental barrier. It was something different this time: white, painted boards that were definitely part of a building. The image was so vivid, he could see the grain of the wood and the chips in the paint. Elated, he squeezed Evangeline's hand and concentrated on breaking through that wall to the girl behind it.

Then the white of the boards exploded like a supernova searing through his brain.

3

EVANGELINE SCREAMED AND YANKED her hand away from Jax. Blackness rushed in over the blinding white, and something hard struck the back of Jax's head.

He wasn't sure if it was seconds or minutes before he realized what had hit him. *The floor. I hit the floor.* His head throbbed, his stomach heaved, and he tasted blood. Tentatively, he tried to move various body parts and felt a strange tingling in his limbs.

"Jax, can you hear me?" That was Mrs. Crandall's voice.

"Jax?" And Riley's.

He opened his eyes, then groaned and squinted. It was too bright. And he was wet. Remembering the taste of blood, he sat up in alarm. "Easy there," said Mrs. Crandall.

Jax checked himself. He wasn't covered in blood. The pan of water had overturned on him. Evangeline must have knocked it off the table to break the connection.

Evangeline . . . He looked around worriedly.

Riley was kneeling beside Jax, holding Evangeline. Her eyelids fluttered but didn't open, and she looked as bad as Jax felt.

"Take her to her room," Mrs. Crandall instructed Riley. "A.J.'s got Jax."

Jax felt hands under his armpits. A.J. hauled him toward one of the motel beds, while Riley carried Evangeline to an adjoining door.

Mrs. Crandall looked Jax over, but apparently decided Evangeline needed her more, and disappeared through the doorway. Seconds later, Riley was expelled from the neighboring room with a shove, and Mrs. Crandall shut the door in his face. Riley turned to Jax. "What happened? She was supposed to be resting! Why'd you let her get up?"

"I couldn't force her to take a nap, Riley." Jax probed his tongue with his fingers. He must've bitten it when his head struck the floor. "So I was helping her. Then it felt like we were hit by lightning." He sucked in his breath. "That's what the Llyrs do, isn't it? Throw lightning?"

"Among other things," Riley scowled as he picked up the pan and the overturned chairs. He folded what was left of Addie's letter and stuffed it into his duffel bag. "I'm going to keep this for now," he said. "I don't want her scrying again."

Mrs. Crandall returned a few minutes later with a report. "She has a raging migraine and she's exhausted.

I've got her lying in the dark with a cold compress." When Riley headed for Evangeline's door, Mrs. Crandall stopped him. "Leave her be. She needs to sleep."

Mrs. Crandall made Jax lie down too and put a cold washcloth on his forehead. She shut the curtains to darken the room and threw Riley and A.J. out. She told Jax to sleep, but once the pain subsided to a dull ache, he didn't feel like it. Twice, he reached for the TV remote before remembering there was no TV on Grunsday. Nothing with a computer chip worked today, and the only reason they had electricity in the motel was because A.J. had broken into the utility room and fired up the emergency generators.

So Jax stared at the ceiling, wondering how they were going to rescue a girl who didn't want to be rescued. She didn't seem like a very *nice* girl, either. Not just because her Llyr buddies had zapped him, but also because of what Jax had read in Addie's letter to her Transitioner foster parents, the Carroways, before Evangeline started ripping it up for the scrying spell. It'd been three pages of complaints written to people who'd given her a home for thirty-five years. Well, only *five* years for Addie, but it was still a lousy way to say thanks.

Jax threw off the washcloth, which was no longer cold. He hated to admit it, but Addie's letter reminded him of the way he'd complained to his dad about unfair bedtimes, video games he wanted but didn't get, and all the business trips that took his dad away from home and left Jax with a babysitter. He'd said stuff he wished he could take back, now that his dad was dead and it was too late.

He'd had a lot of complaints about Riley, too. A few months ago, Jax might've written a letter at least as long as Addie's, listing all the things he hated about his guardian. But the truth was he was going to miss Riley in the fall, when he went to live with Billy Ramirez.

Riley had made that arrangement last weekend, after calling Mrs. Ramirez and offering to pick up her son from golf camp on the pretense of giving Billy and Jax a day together. In reality, Billy had never been to golf camp. He'd been kidnapped by Jax's relatives, the Dulacs and the Ambroses, and held as a hostage to make Jax turn himself over to them.

Mrs. Ramirez knew nothing about the kidnapping, but she thought Riley was an irresponsible slacker, so he'd had to use his voice of command to convince her to let him drive Billy anywhere. Once they brought Billy home, though, Riley didn't use any magic on the Ramirezes. Instead, he was polite and respectful and explained his dilemma: He was taking a new job that would require him to move around a lot, and he was worried about where Jax would go to school in the fall. Parts of the story had even been true.

As Riley had hoped, Billy's parents immediately offered to take Jax in so that he wouldn't have to switch schools for a second year in a row. Mrs. Ramirez even commended Riley on his new maturity. "Jax has had a positive influence on you," she said.

That remark had left Riley utterly speechless. Jax shook with laughter. Mr. Ramirez hid his smile behind his hand, and Billy had looked puzzled. Billy thought Riley was perfect.

In fact, Billy thought the best thing that had ever happened to him was getting sworn on as Riley's vassal. "Any orders?" Billy had asked before they left, looking up at his liege lord with hero worship. At that point, between the Grunsday when they'd narrowly missed Addie at the Dulacs and this one, they had still hoped to rescue her before the enemy Kin took her from the New York City area.

"Research," Riley said. "I've filled you in on everything we know about the Kin who helped the Llyrs escape Oeth-Anoeth, which I know isn't much. Just the aircraft and weaponry they had, when they arrived in Wales, when they left . . . If you can find clues to any further sightings online . . ."

"Got it," Billy replied briskly.

"Be careful," Jax cautioned him, remembering his own online encounter with a bank robber masquerading as a Transitioner. "There are some shady sites out there and people who aren't who they say they are."

"Duh, Jax," Billy replied, making an *Are-you-kidding?* face. "Everyone knows that."

Riley shot Jax an amused look but didn't embarrass him by mentioning Jax's notorious lapse in internet safety. Jax consoled himself by remembering that this was a bogus assignment. Billy wouldn't find anything about Kin online. They lived off the grid with no access to modern technology. Riley was humoring Billy so he could feel like he was making a contribution.

The unfortunate reality was that they were going to have to depend on the Morgans—or worse, the Dulacs—to track down the Llyrs, and that worried Jax. Not only might Addie get hurt in any resulting conflict between the Transitioners and the Kin, but who knew what the Llyrs would do to Addie if she didn't cooperate with them. He had not forgotten how Lord Wylit had threatened and injured Evangeline, trying to force her compliance with his evil plans.

And now Evangeline's scrying spell, their one hope of locating Addie quickly and efficiently, had proved itself very dangerous.

As Jax stared at the motel room ceiling, the plaster tiles puckered. A small brown-and-white blur fell from above and landed on his bed.

Jax sat up and grabbed his honor blade, waving it defensively at an animal the size of a large rat with a flat face and no tail. The fur on its body was brown, with a tuft of white that stuck up from its head. In its slender hands it held a ball of red-and-white fabric. "You!" Jax gasped, lowering his dagger when he recognized the creature. "What are you doing here?"

The brownie darted forward and dropped a balled-up pair of socks in Jax's lap. Jax picked them up, lifted a foot, and compared the red stripe on the socks he was wearing to the ones in his hand. "Are these mine? Where'd you get—"

Then it hit him. When he'd gone to New York to trade himself for Billy, he'd brought a change of clothes in a backpack. His aunt, Marian Ambrose, had searched that backpack and—because she was the strangest mix of motherliness and villainy that Jax had ever met—laundered all his clothes, balling up his socks in just this way. "Did you use these socks to track me here?"

The brownie's round ears rotated like radar dishes. He cocked his head, and the tuft of white fur bobbed comically.

"You're Stink, aren't you?" Jax's relatives had all complained about the pet brownie his father had kept as a teenager. It had run amok in their building, turning up in people's kitchens and digging through the trash. Jax had felt a connection to *this* brownie from the moment he'd laid eyes on him and released him from the Dulac holding pens.

Jax reached out and scratched the top of the creature's head. "Are you an orphan now, too?" Maybe Stink was looking for a new owner. "C'mere." He held out his arm. Stink latched on with his spidery hands and clambered up to Jax's shoulder.

Outside, the pink Grunsday sky was darkening into a purple evening, and the dim light didn't hurt Jax's head so much. He walked across the parking lot to where Riley was wiping his hands with an oily cloth and staring at the window of Evangeline's room. A.J. saw Jax approaching. "Ugh! Where'd that come from?"

"Meet Stink," said Jax. "He was my dad's pet."

"Don't tell me you inherited him." A.J. made a face.

Riley chucked the dirty rag into his toolbox and addressed the brownie directly. "You want to hang out with Jax, that's fine. But stay away from his liege lady unless you like getting squashed with a broom."

Stink bobbed his head and scurried around to Jax's other shoulder.

Jax narrowed his eyes at Riley. Last Grunsday, Stink had snatched a gun from Jax's uncle before he could shoot Riley. A little while later, a crowd of brownies had lured a wyvern into attacking Ursula Dulac instead of its intended victim—*Riley*. At the time, Jax thought the brownies were out to get Ursula, but he suddenly realized that saving Riley's life might have been their real priority. "Okay. What kind of arrangement do you and the brownies . . ." Then he froze, staring past his guardian and over the roof of the motel. "What's that?"

There was a dark, blotchy cloud in the purple sky. "Smoke?" suggested Riley. "Fire?"

Jax shook his head. Every hair on his body was

standing on edge, and an icy coldness swept over him. "It's a storm. Coming this way."

"Can't be," said A.J. "There's no weather on Grunsday."

"We're dealing with Llyrs, A.J." Riley held up a hand for his friend to be quiet. "Jax? What do you know?"

Jax's fingers twitched toward the honor blade sheathed at his waist, seeking information. "We need to get out of here."

"Let's not panic over nothing," said A.J.

"Pack up," Riley snapped. "This is Jax's talent. If he says we have to get out of here, we get out!"

4

JAX GRABBED ALL THEIR possessions out of the motel room, stuffing them into Riley's duffel bag without any regard to whether they were his, A.J.'s, or Riley's. Then he ran outside just as Riley was helping Evangeline into the Land Rover and A.J. was tying down Riley's motorcycle in the back of his truck.

What had been only a thumbprint in the sky had grown to fill the horizon, with clouds that looked like they'd been finger-painted by an angry preschooler. The temperature had dropped, and a wind was rising.

Jax climbed into the Land Rover beside Evangeline, who recoiled at the sight of Stink on his shoulder. The brownie leaped into the cushions of the rear seat and vanished. Evangeline rubbed her eyes. "I'm worse off than I thought," she said. "I'm hallucinating brownies."

"You're not hallucinating," Riley said, backing the Land Rover away from the motel. "Jax has a new pet."

Jax ran his fingers over the seat cushions. The spot where Stink had disappeared was spongy, and he pushed into it. His hand vanished as if it were cut off at the wrist. Stink had created a brand new brownie hole inside the car. Jax couldn't resist. He shoved his head in.

The hole didn't lead to a tunnel like the ones in the Dulac building. Instead, it was more like a pocket of tunnel material, which was a crinkly, translucent substance that seemed to be made of pure magic. From inside the brownie hole, Jax could see the car all around him, but Evangeline and Riley weren't visible, and through the windows—nothing, just blankness. Jax was inside the car but outside of time. There was no sign of Stink. *He jumped to somewhere else!*

A hand gripped the back of Jax's shirt and yanked him out. "Are you crazy?" Evangeline exclaimed. "We're in a moving car! What if your head got left behind?"

"My head was still inside the car," Jax protested. "I'm experimenting, to figure these things out."

"No experiments that could get you decapitated, Jax," Riley said. "That's an order."

It wasn't, though—at least not a magical order. Riley was too busy concentrating on driving to throw his talent at Jax. Rain pattered against the windows, and a gust of wind pushed the Land Rover sideways. "Is this what storms are usually like?" Evangeline asked.

"Regular storms don't move this fast. And the main

part of this one hasn't hit us yet," Riley said. "When it gets here"—his eyes met Jax's in the rearview mirror—"it'll be like Hurricane Sandy, except without any warning for the Normals."

"Any chance it'll vanish at midnight along with the Kin who made it?" Jax asked.

"There hasn't been weather on the eighth day since the Llyrs were put into Oeth-Anoeth, so who knows?" said Riley. "We can hope."

He didn't sound hopeful, though, and neither was Jax. *Why should things start going our way now?*

Evangeline wrapped her arms around herself, shivering. "I read the newspapers," she said. "I know what Hurricane Sandy did."

Jax rummaged in the duffel bag to find her a sweatshirt. While he was searching, the bag began to vibrate, and a muffled burst of music came from the bottom. "Is that your phone?" Jax asked Riley incredulously.

"Get it," said Riley. "It'll be Deidre."

Jax dug for the phone. The screen was dark, showing no incoming call, but the ringtone inexplicably continued. Jax stabbed the answer button. "Hello?"

"That you, cutie?"

Nobody but Deidre Morgan called Jax *cutie.* Thankfully. It wasn't something he wanted catching on. "Yeah, it's me," he said. "Making the phone work on Grunsday? Pretty impressive." Jax knew the Morgan talent was working with machinery, but he'd never really thought of phones as *machines* before.

"Tell Riley you guys need to leave that motel *now*," Deidre said. "Head inland as fast as you can."

"We already are." Jax held the phone out so Riley and Evangeline could hear too.

"Arnie said he'll meet you at the mountain house," Deidre continued. "Transitioners are leaving the city as fast as they can. I'm sure the storm was meant to attack *us*, but it's the Normals who are going to get clobbered. Three airplanes that were frozen en route to JFK or LaGuardia have been knocked out of the sky already."

"Thanks for the warning, Deidre," Riley called out.

"I'll add it to the list of things you owe me for, sweetie." Deidre's reply faded away, and although there was nothing visible on the phone to indicate the end of this magical call, Jax knew she was gone.

He looked out the rear window. A.J. and Mrs. Crandall were behind them in the truck. The black cloud of doom hovered over the New York skyline like bad CGI in an apocalyptic movie. Jax wondered what the Normals were going to think when they reappeared at 12:01 a.m. on Thursday. Seconds ago, by their own timeline, they'd been enjoying a clear summer night. An instant later, they were going to find themselves in the middle of a massive storm—or, at best, in the aftermath of one. Some of them wouldn't have time to register the situation before they were, as Deidre said, *clobbered*.

Riley drove west, heading for Pennsylvania, where they had a cabin in the middle of the Pocono Mountains. He made good progress at first, matching the storm's speed and staying on the outer edge of wind and rain. He steered the Land Rover around stationary vehicles on I-80 that were frozen in the moment between Wednesday and Thursday. Only once did he clip somebody's side-view mirror, when an unexpected gust made their car swerve. "Sorry, dude," Riley muttered. Then he looked ahead and cursed, braking.

Construction on a bridge had left one lane open, and it was currently blocked by a line of cars. Neither the Land Rover nor A.J.'s truck were going to fit through. Riley reversed and turned the SUV around. "Holler if you see a way to get past the median and into the oncoming lane."

"It won't do any good," Jax said, pointing. The oncoming lane on the bridge was blocked by two tractor trailers traveling side by side.

"Okay then." Riley turned the wheel hard. "We're going off road." The Land Rover bumped its way over a large grassy stretch with A.J.'s truck following, down a small hill and onto a secondary road.

"Do you know where this road goes?" Evangeline asked worriedly.

"Doesn't matter, as long as I keep *that* in the rearview mirror." Riley stabbed with his finger at the mirrored reflection of the black clouds behind them.

But it did matter, and he'd made a poor choice. This new road took them along the river that the I-80 bridge had been crossing and wound its way through a heavily wooded region. They had to cut their speed, and the storm caught up with them.

The sky had grown darker as evening fell, but it suddenly became pitch black. Trees whipped back and forth. Torrential rain sheeted down. What was probably a shallow, slow-moving river on a normal day now overflowed its banks. Riley's hands gripped the steering wheel tightly. "Keep your eyes peeled for a better option," he said.

Jax pressed his face against the window, looking for a side road that would lead them uphill, away from the water. It was hard to see anything except darkness and rain.

Then a flash of white. A face.

"Stop the car!" Jax yelled.

Riley braked. "What is it?"

"There's someone by the side of the road!" Jax threw open the door and jumped out.

"Jax, wait!" Evangeline cried.

Driving rain plastered his clothing to his body. He jogged back up the road toward A.J.'s truck, which had stopped behind the Land Rover. Mrs. Crandall rolled down the passenger window and shouted something, probably asking him what in the world he was doing.

He wasn't sure what he'd seen, but he'd had the impression of someone—a fairly young someone—standing by the side of the road with an arm raised, signaling for help. Had it been a girl? In a white dress, maybe?

Jax heard a loud crack behind him, and turned to see the shoulder of the road collapse into broken chunks. The Land Rover tilted, its right rear tire plunging into river water that gushed into the break. Jax heard the car's engine roar, and the front wheels spun. The Land Rover lurched upward momentarily, but another chunk of asphalt broke away. The Land Rover's second rear tire sank into the water.

Jax watched in horror. The river was going to break across the road and wash away the car. Riley and Evangeline would drown. Just like his dad.

Then A.J.'s truck surged forward and smacked the back end of the Land Rover, propelling it out of the gully. Riley gunned the engine; the back wheels came up onto the road, and the car sped away. A.J. reversed and jerked the truck to a stop beside Jax. Mrs. Crandall threw open her door and nearly yanked his arm from its socket, pulling him in. The door wasn't even closed when A.J. hit the gas and spun the wheel, careening into what remained of the left-hand lane.

Jax hauled the truck door shut, then turned to look out

the back window. Around the motorcycle, which was still miraculously tied in the bed of the truck, he saw the river bust across the remaining width of the road.

"That was close!" gasped A.J. "Jax, what'd you get out of the car for?"

Jax trembled violently. "I saw a girl by the side of road."

"In the woods in this storm? Alone?" Mrs. Crandall twisted around to look.

"Forget what you're thinking, Mom," said. A.J. "We can't go back. Unless you expect me to jump that new canyon back there."

"I must have been imagining things." Jax wiped his wet face with both hands. What had he seen? A girl in a white dress?

I've seen her before.

Jax shuddered again, and Mrs. Crandall pulled him close and rubbed his arms vigorously. But he wasn't cold; he was horrified.

The Morrigan.

Last week Jax had seen a dark-haired girl in a short, shapeless dress standing at the edge of Central Park across the street from the Dulac building. He'd seen her from *inside* the brownie tunnels, which should have been impossible, and there'd been crows flying above her head even though there weren't normally any birds on the eighth day. Evangeline had tried to explain to Jax what the Morrigan was, but the explanation was confusing. She wasn't a

Transitioner or Kin; she was the personification of chaos and disorder, three beings in one. The version of her that appeared as a girl with crows was supposed to manipulate events in order to foster the chaos the Morrigan wanted.

Just after Jax had seen the Girl of Crows last Grunsday, a vengeful horde of brownies had set a wyvern on the Dulacs at the exact same time that the Llyrs had shown up to abduct Addie Emrys. Now she'd appeared again, causing Jax to stop the Land Rover at a dangerous place on the road. She'd almost gotten the two people most important in the world to him killed. *Do you know my father drove his car into a river and drowned? Is that why you picked that spot? So I could see my friends die the same way?*

Evangeline and Riley could have been killed by that wyvern last week. Riley almost had been. Was that a coincidence, or was the Morrigan targeting them deliberately?

Jax clenched his jaw. He didn't care what she was—a person or three people or a force of nature, or *whatever.* She was his enemy.

Game on, Girl of Crows.

5

ADDIE'S HEADACHE AND NAUSEA faded quickly. Healing spells had been easy for her to learn, once she'd seen someone else use them. Feeling better, she wandered downstairs, running a hand along the polished banister of the L-shaped stairs to the living room below with its walls of glass.

The sky had grown too dark to see the ocean. Midnight would arrive in a couple of hours, thrusting everyone on this island a week into the future. Kel's father had assured them it was safe here, that no one would find them while they were absent from time and vulnerable. "This is my private island, and the house is warded against intruders," Madoc had told them on their arrival. "No one comes here except by my say-so, and the ones who do are well paid to perform their jobs and leave without talking about it."

Addie heard raised voices outside. She crossed the room and pressed her face against a window. A crowd of younger Aerons had made a bonfire off the patio and were cheering two boys wrestling in the sand, each of them trying to push the other into the fire. From what Addie knew of this clan, if one of them got burned to a crisp, the other would probably be rewarded with a tattoo.

It had been an Aeron who originally enticed Addie to run away from the house of her foster parents, the Carroways. Addie hadn't known that at the time, because sharing family names and talents was against Dale Carroway's rules. The girl, Wren, hadn't known Addie's family name either. She just thought Addie was fun to be with. "Let's leave," Wren had said. "We can have adventures and see the world, and you won't have to put up with these old people and their rules anymore." Addie, who'd recently been punished for breaking a minor house rule, had jumped at the chance.

But Wren had been wild—more than Addie had counted on. She'd *said* she was taking Addie to meet friends. "But there's no hurry. We can have fun along the way." Wren had led them on a meandering path across New England, magically "hot-wiring" the cars of Normals and then, as each vehicle ran out of gas, setting it on fire.

"Why?" Addie had asked, shocked by the wanton destruction.

"For fun!"

Addie had gotten the impression that Normals weren't real to Wren. Their world was a playroom, and Wren liked to knock over the blocks and break the toys. She also wasn't in any hurry to rendezvous with her friends, but in the end, *they* found *her.*

"Hey, cuz! How'd you know I'd be here?" Wren had cheerfully asked the tall Kin boy who caught up with them in an expensive vehicle called a Hummer on a highway in New Hampshire.

"How?" The boy had been irate. "Everywhere you go, you leave disaster behind, you moron! You've made a dotted line marking your trail!"

"I was bringing a recruit to Condor," Wren said. "Well, eventually."

Then a second Kin boy got out of the Hummer. "Kel Mathonwy," Addie said in surprise.

"Addie Emrys," Kel replied, breaking out into a grin. The other boy stopped yelling, his eyes bugging out of his head. Because Wren Aeron, certified moron and pyromaniac, had accidentally stumbled across an Emrys heir.

The *friends* Wren had been taking Addie to were some of her own father's allies, the people he'd included in his secret meetings when she was just a child. They were trying to resurrect his plan to break the Eighth Day Spell, and that was when Addie knew that fate—or something—had brought her to them.

But Wren's cousin had been right to be furious with her. She *had* left a blazing trail of senseless vandalism that had attracted the notice of Transitioners. The Dulacs ambushed the Hummer less than twelve hours after they met up. Even Wren's talent for destruction hadn't saved them. Kel had escaped in the confusion, but Addie had been captured.

Wren and her Aeron cousin had been killed.

Voices drew Addie away from the mansion's windows—quiet, level voices that contrasted with the shouts and catcalls outside. She approached the doorway to a large dining room where Normal owners might've held dinner parties. The Mathonwys had turned it into a war room.

"Elwyn wouldn't allow it," Madoc was saying. "He said it would taint the counterspell and ruin what we hoped to achieve."

Addie pressed herself against the wall, out of sight. Elwyn had been her father's name.

"The rest of you allowed him to have the final say?" Bran Llyr asked. "You trusted an Emrys to lead you?"

"He was the spell caster and the one who knew the most about the original casting," Madoc explained. "We had to. Wylit argued with him, of course. But Wylit was half mad even before he got his face melted off trying to break the spell with a little boy too young to do it."

"You're sure the male Emrys heir was killed?" That was Bran's son, Griffyn, speaking with disdain. "We're left with nothing but this girl?"

"I had no contact with Wylit after Elwyn was killed. Wylit worked alone after that, but I've pieced together what happened. The Emrys boy died in a poorly planned spell-breaking ritual, and the older daughter was killed by Transitioners in Wylit's recent failed attempt on the pyramid in Mexico. That's what the Dulacs discovered when they investigated, and Luis

Morder passed the information on to Kel," Madoc replied. "There's only one Emrys left."

That's me, the leftover. Not as good as my little brother, because he was male, and not as good as Evangeline, because she was always better at everything.

"Elwyn was counting on the power of the Kin Treasures to reinforce his counterspell," Madoc continued. "The Cauldron, of course, was destroyed centuries ago as far as we know. But he acquired the Stone and the Sword, and he believed the final Treasure was located with the Llyrs in Oeth-Anoeth."

"Which was the only reason he had any interest in freeing us." Bran's voice was dry. He did not confirm or deny whether he had a powerful Kin relic in his possession. But Addie had been suspiciously eyeing that staff Bran never let out of his sight. None of the Kin Treasures had been a staff, but there was the Spear of Lugh . . .

"What happened to the Treasures Elwyn Emrys had acquired?" Bran asked.

"They disappeared after his death," Madoc said.

"How could he have the Stone of Fal and the Sword of Nuadu and *not* defeat his enemies?" Griffyn asked incredulously. "The Stone by itself should've protected him!"

"I wasn't there when the attack occurred," Madoc said. "I don't know what happened."

Condor, the leader of the Aerons, spoke up. "I think he must have been taken by surprise and wasted valuable time making sure his children escaped."

"No Kin should consider that time wasted," Bran replied. "We're lucky to have the remaining Emrys heir with us. She needn't lurk behind doors."

Addie stiffened, imagining everyone in the room turning to stare at the doorway. *How did he know?* Then she lifted her chin, straightened her shoulders, and walked into the room as if she hadn't been eavesdropping. As if she'd been *invited* to attend the meeting and take her father's place. She was the Emrys clan leader after all, even if she was the only member of that clan. By rights, she was equal to Madoc Mathonwy, Condor Aeron, Ysabel Arawen, and even Bran Llyr. They didn't outrank her.

Nevertheless, they were an intimidating group for a thirteen-year-old girl to approach. Oddly, Addie was drawn to Bran more than the others, despite the fact that he'd zapped her with his magic a few hours ago. She met his gaze unafraid and sat across from him. Only then did she notice Kel seated beside his father. He'd been silent in the discussion.

"Do you know what happened to the Stone and the Sword?" Bran asked her.

"No," she said. "When Transitioners attacked my house, my sister made me run with her through the woods to escape. We were met by the Taliesins, who separated us and sent us into hiding. I was only eight years old, and nobody explained to me what happened." She'd known her parents were dead, though. No one had needed to explain that part.

Griffyn made an impatient noise. "It's no mystery.

Transitioners took the Treasures."

"Or they were hidden for safekeeping, and Elwyn couldn't get them quickly enough," Ysabel suggested. "That would explain why he was defeated."

"I searched," Madoc argued. "If they were hidden anywhere near the Emrys home, I would have found them years ago."

"Do we really need them?" Condor said. "Human sacrifices would provide the power we need, and Elwyn Emrys is no longer here to object."

Addie wondered who Condor planned to sacrifice and whether it included volunteers from his own crazy clan. Madoc gave Condor a look of disgust. "Countermanding the Eighth Day Spell involves dangerous magic, and we have Wylit's failed attempts as exemplary models for disaster. Locating the Treasures would be our safest bet."

"An oracle might help find them," Addie piped up.

"Wylits are prophets. What happened to Wylit's body?" Griffyn nudged Ysabel with his elbow. "Would he be too far gone for you to talk to?" The Arawen talent was speaking to the dead.

Addie shuddered at the thought. "I know of a *living* oracle," she volunteered. "A refugee who was staying at my foster parents' house. She might not be there anymore, but they'll probably know where she's gone." Addie was so eager to make a significant contribution that the words were out of her mouth before she thought them through. The Carroways had always opened their home to Kin in need, and she'd forgotten for a second that the Kin at this table would not be kindly disposed toward Transitioners.

"What was this woman's name?" Bran asked.

"Aine," Addie said, wondering if she'd made a mistake and how to fix it. When Bran's eyebrows hunched together, she realized he wanted Aine's family name. Her personal name was unimportant. "The Kin who stayed with us always kept their family names secret," she explained, "but I think she was a Corra."

"Having a Corra among us would be useful," Madoc said.

Addie nibbled nervously on a fingernail. Would Aine agree to help them? What about her foster parents? Would they interfere?

"Let me speak to Adelina alone," Bran said.

Everyone else rose from their seats. Kel moved slowly, as if worried about leaving Addie alone with Bran. But she wasn't afraid of Bran. She was too busy trying to figure out a way to make sure her impulsive suggestion didn't bring harm to the Carroways. Addie hadn't forgotten how Bran had killed that half-breed spell caster, Dr. Morder, outside the Dulac building. As awful as that had been to witness, Morder *had* betrayed his liege by helping the Llyrs rescue Addie. He'd expected to be praised and rewarded, but his betrayal only proved how untrustworthy he was. Addie understood why they couldn't take Morder with them *or* leave him behind. *Killing him was unpleasant but necessary.* Bran Llyr was harsh, but Addie didn't think he was unreasonable.

In fact, the first question he asked Addie after everyone had left the room was, "Are you recovered from this afternoon?"

"Yes, I'm fine."

"I didn't warn you what I was going to do because you would've resisted. That would have made the backlash greater. I knew you would be hurt, but not greatly harmed."

There. Perfectly reasonable. Addie smiled. "Well, I didn't think you were trying to kill me."

"I am surprised to see you recovered so quickly." Bran held his staff in one hand and examined her with his eyes. "A healing spell?" She nodded. "What did you use to cast it? Madoc has healing herbs, but he says you didn't seek any from him."

I have my own supplies. That was the smart thing to say. But Addie was squirming in her seat with the desire to show off her cleverness. "I didn't need any."

Bran nodded, as if he'd already guessed, and leaned his staff against the table. "Give me your hands." She did, and he took them in his own rough ones, examining the tips of her fingers and her arms. Addie smirked, knowing what he was looking for and that he wouldn't find it. "You're using blood magic," he said finally. "I know you are. Where are the scars?"

"I don't need to spill my blood," Addie replied. The sacrifice of blood was a ritual that enhanced magic. It was shunned by people afraid of dark magic. Her own father had forbidden it.

"Your blood carries the Eighth Day Spell," Bran said. "It is more powerful than mine—perhaps more powerful than all other Kin combined. A few drops of it—"

"Will help somebody else perform magic," Addie interrupted. "But I can keep all my blood where it belongs and still call on it for my magic."

"Who taught you this?"

Now *that* was a strange story. "Someone passing through my foster parents' way station," she gave as her answer. It was sort of even true.

"Adelina Emrys, do you want to break the Eighth Day Spell?"

"Yes, I do."

That kind of talk wasn't tolerated at the Carroways'. Emma had explained many times why things had to stay the way they were. Dale expected her to accept it. But Addie never had.

"Are you as strong as your father?" Bran asked.

She hesitated. "My father was trying to learn a spell that would put the eighth day back into the Normal world's timeline, but he never mastered it. That . . . frustrated him." Drove him to fits of temper. Made him yell at his wife and snap at his children, especially Addie, for whom he had little patience. "I'm strong," she told Bran, "but I need that spell, and I don't know it."

Bran leaned across the table. "I will personally instruct you in what you need to know, after we speak to the Corra woman."

Addie sat up. Her father had taught all his children the

basics of spell casting, but he'd always singled out Evangeline as his best pupil. Now Addie had the opportunity to learn from the personal instruction of Bran Llyr, one of the most powerful Kin men on the planet. And with this opportunity came her chance to bargain, because even a Llyr couldn't countermand the Eighth Day Spell without the cooperation of an Emrys. "I'll learn whatever you can teach me *and* talk Aine Corra into joining us. But you have to promise me something first."

Instead of striking her dead with lightning, Bran smiled. Addie suspected not many people could make demands of this man and be rewarded with a smile.

"I don't want you to hurt the Transitioners who live in that house," Addie said. "The Taliesins placed me in the Carroways' care, and they gave me a good home for years. They're practically the only parents I remember."

Bran sat back in his chair and retrieved his staff. "I commend your youthful spirit and boldness. I look forward to training you in the proper use of your potential."

Addie grinned triumphantly.

6

RILEY FOUND AN UNOBSTRUCTED bridge across the river, and once they were back on a highway, the two vehicles increased their speed to outpace the storm. The wind and rain lessened the farther inland they traveled. When midnight came, everyone except Evangeline transitioned into Thursday, and A.J. turned on the truck's radio. Reception was poor, but Jax caught references to a freak storm, flash floods, and a coastline ravished by hurricane-force winds.

However, it was raining only lightly when they arrived at their cabin in the Pennsylvania mountains. Jax watched Riley get out of the Land Rover and look back at it unhappily as he closed the door. Evangeline was still in there, sort of, and would remain there till next week. She wouldn't feel the time passing; it *wasn't* passing for her. But that didn't make it any easier to walk away from the car. Jax felt the same way every Thursday, wherever he left her.

Mr. Crandall showed up about an hour and a half behind them, complaining of flooded roads and the long detours he'd needed to get home.

"Anything to report on the Llyrs?" Riley asked him.

"Other than the whopping hurricane they dumped on us? No. They vanished like smoke." Mr. Crandall sounded tired and discouraged. "They might have flown halfway across the country or switched to land transportation at any time. Sheila Morgan says they couldn't have crossed the Atlantic in what they were flying, but they might've changed planes later. We know from the assault on Oeth-Anoeth that they have more than one."

"But if they made that storm," Jax argued, "they couldn't be that far away, right?"

"It was created by magic and traveling faster than naturally possible. We don't know where it came from." Mr. Crandall sighed. "Fact is, they could be almost anywhere."

Jax and Riley exchanged glances. Neither one of them looked forward to sharing that news with Evangeline next week.

By late Thursday morning, the magical storm had dispersed into scattered showers, but New York City and parts of New Jersey and Connecticut were without power. Beach towns were devastated. Dozens of people had drowned in their homes or cars, and a couple hundred were assumed dead, vanished along with the planes that had blipped off the radar map at midnight. Riley got on the phone with Deidre as soon as cell phone service was restored, trying to learn what the Morgans would do next.

Meanwhile, Jax surfed the online news reports on his computer while checking his phone. Billy had texted him, asking him to get in touch, but someone else was on Jax's mind. Twice he picked up the phone and chickened out. The third time, he opened his contacts and punched the telephone symbol next to a certain name.

"Yeah?" That was how his call was answered.

"It's Jax," he said.

"I know who it is."

Friendly as ever. Jax was already regretting the call. "I was just wondering if . . . uh, if you guys were okay. I didn't know if you were still in New York City."

"Are you crazy?" Tegan Donovan said. "We weren't going to hang around for a hurricane."

"Have you thought any more about helping us?" The Donovan family—Tegan, her twin brother, Thomas, and her father—had a highly developed scent sensitivity for magic. They could identify Transitioner and Kin families by smell, which had proved useful more than once.

"We weren't thinking about it at all," Tegan replied coldly. "We told Riley *no* when he asked us last week. I told *you* no. We're not stupid enough to go sniffing out people who can raise hurricanes and tornadoes when they feel like it. We don't owe you anymore. If anything, you owe us."

"Yeah, I know." Tegan had saved his butt from the Dulacs, much as Jax hated to admit it.

"You should take Blondie and get as far away from those Kin as you can instead of going after them."

"I thought you didn't care about Evangeline."

"I don't care about either of you. That was just disinterested advice. Why'd you call me?"

"I dunno. Thought you and your family might be headed into New York to do some looting and wanted to offer my own disinterested advice. Water's high. Try not to drown."

"Jerk." She hung up.

"Same to you," Jax said, even though she was already gone. He shook the phone vigorously, pretending to throttle it. Then he texted Billy.

```
Jax: hey whats up?
Billy: can you get on video?
```

A few seconds later, Billy appeared in a video box on his computer screen. "Dude," he said. "Glad to hear you're all okay."

"Yeah, we are. But how'd you hear it?"

"Riley texted me last night to let me know." It was

kind of weird that Riley and Billy kept in communication now, separate from Jax. "Hey, I've been working on my research for Riley," Billy went on, "and finding all this cool stuff. Have you ever thought about elves?"

"Elves?"

"They're supposed to be gifted in magic, right? They live extra-long lives. And a long time ago they vanished from earth to go live in a magical world humans can't get into. Sound like anybody you know?"

"Evangeline is not an elf, Billy."

"Of course not. But didn't you tell me the Kin are sometimes transported in coffins? Who *else* gets moved around in coffins?"

"Dead people."

"Vampires." Billy grinned. "What if Bram Stoker saw people being moved around in coffins and got the idea to write *Dracula*?"

Jax sighed. This was pure Billy—connecting everything to his favorite science fiction and fantasy stories. "How do vampires and elves help us find Addie Emrys?"

"Now I know where to look." Which made no sense to Jax. Then Billy's grin died away. "But that's not why I wanted to talk to you. Dorian emailed me something a little while ago, and I'm supposed to forward it to you."

"Dorian has your email? Do you think that's smart?" Dorian's dad had kidnapped Billy to get to Jax.

"Dude, your uncle knows where I live. What does it

matter? Besides, Dorian says now that I'm Riley's vassal, messing with me is practically an act of war."

"Uh, the Dulacs assassinated Riley's family. They shot him up with tranquilizers and threw him in their dungeon. They're already at war with Riley."

"That was under Ursula's leadership. According to Dorian, Sloane has the chance to wipe the slate clean."

Jax would be really surprised if his cousin Sloane was interested in slate cleaning. The new eighteen-year-old leader of the Dulac clan had already proved herself as devious as her grandmother. "So, what are you supposed to send me?"

"Scanned pages out of your dad's journal. From back when he was a teenager."

Jax froze. Dorian had told him about this. "A log of the truth," his cousin had called it. Jax's dad had recorded everything that happened to him because his Dulac relatives had used their talent to manipulate his memory.

They'd done the same thing to Jax. Ursula Dulac had gotten into Jax's head and twisted his memories until he hated Riley and Evangeline. If it hadn't been for Tegan's advance planning to protect Jax's mind, the change might've been permanent. Jax would be living with Dorian's family right now, and Riley and Evangeline might be dead.

"I, uh, read the pages," Billy went on. "Hope you don't mind."

"No, it's okay," Jax mumbled. Above the video box on the screen, an email from Billy appeared with an attachment.

"I didn't want to forward it to you without telling you that I'm here for you, dude." Billy made a face. "That sounded girly, didn't it?"

"Yup."

"I'll let you . . . um . . . yeah, bye."

The video box disappeared, and Jax stared at the email notification for a long time before clicking it open. He read Dorian's message first.

Jax,

I'm sorry I didn't give this to you when I had the chance. Later Dad took it away from me and grounded me for like 30 years. But there was a brownie here yesterday before the storm, rummaging in your backpack, and he created a new brownie hole in my bedroom that my parents don't know about. So I'm not as grounded as they think I am.

I stole your father's journal back last night. We couldn't evacuate until after midnight, because of Lesley, and by then it wasn't safe to move. As soon as the rain and wind slacked off Dad got us out of the city, and now we're at our vacation house in the Catskills.

I'm emailing Billy so he can forward these scanned

pages to you. I'll keep the original safe, so you can have it someday if you want it.

Dorian

P.S. Used the brownie tunnels to steal Dr. Morder's notes from his apartment before we left. I'll let you know if I learn anything useful.

Jax was ashamed to realize he hadn't given any thought to his relatives during the storm. *Of course* they couldn't have left without Dorian's sister—a dud with no magical talent. Unless Lesley was handcuffed to a family member, she skipped over the eighth day every week and reappeared at 12:01 on Thursday like the rest of the Normals.

As for Dorian, that was a lot of sneaking around and defying authority for a nerdy prep-school kid. Jax wondered if he'd been a bad influence on his cousin.

Bracing himself, he opened the attachment and began to read.

Jax was still sitting in front of the computer, stunned, when Riley found him a little while later and asked with concern, "Jax, you okay?" Instead of answering, Jax stood up and gestured at the computer screen. Riley sat down. "What am I looking at?"

"My dad's journal," Jax said flatly. "Dorian emailed it to Billy."

If Riley was surprised Dorian and Billy were email buddies, he didn't show it. Riley silently read through the journal pages, which detailed how Jax's dad had found evidence he'd been used to help assassinate a rival Transitioner family—and how the whole thing had been wiped from his mind afterward. "Considering what they did to *you*," Riley said finally, "this doesn't come as a shock." He pointed to a passage on the last page. "See this part, where your dad says he knows who he's going to contact for help? I'll bet he meant *my* dad."

Jax nodded.

"This explains what your dad's problem was with vassalhood—why he stayed independent and was dead set against me swearing you on."

"Do you think he committed murder for the Dulacs?" After Jax blurted out the question, he wished he could take it back. Riley's family had died in an explosion engineered by Ursula Dulac.

Riley hesitated. He'd been present when that bomb killed his family. He'd almost been killed himself—and in official records, he was legally dead. Jax was just opening his mouth to retract the question, when Riley said, "Maybe they only used him to get close to their target."

That wasn't an answer. It was a way out. But Jax recalled how gleefully *he* had betrayed Riley and plotted against Evangeline under Ursula's manipulation. He knew what the Dulacs were capable of making someone do.

"This clears up a lot of things about your father," Riley said.

"Not everything." Then Jax told Riley what Angus Balin had said to him in the Dulac basement—that Jax's father had deliberately driven his car into a river to get away from his enemies. That information had been eating a hole in Jax's stomach for a week.

Sharing it with Riley eased the pain a little, especially because Riley didn't hesitate a second before saying, "Balin lied."

"You think?"

"Your father struck me as someone who didn't do anything without a plan—and a backup plan—and a backup for the backup. Trust me, your father didn't panic and kill himself because he couldn't shake the Balins. It was an accident, and Balin was lying to hurt you." Riley squeezed Jax's shoulder.

Jax didn't say anything. In the end, whether the car had gone into the water by accident or design—even as a part of a crazed, desperate backup plan—the result had been the same for Jax.

7

OVER THE WEEK, THE mid-Atlantic coast struggled to recover from the Impossible Storm. Scientists tried to explain how a category-five hurricane had spontaneously appeared in seconds, while politicians blasted each other for inadequate preparation. Nobody, as far as Jax could tell, was blaming an ancient feud between two magical races.

However, the severity of the crisis convinced Transitioners that a concerted effort was needed to stand against the Llyrs. They'd have to put aside their rivalries and work together.

"How are we going to find these Kin when they could be anywhere?" Jax asked Riley.

"Sheila will have a strategy for locating them," Riley replied. "Guaranteed."

On Saturday, the phones of Riley, Mrs. Crandall, and Jax buzzed with identical texts.

Sheila Morgan: Monday. Table Meeting. 1pm.
Bedivere's mountain house. Be there.

"This is it," Riley said grimly. "I'm officially coming back from the dead."

A.J. checked his phone. "I didn't get anything."

"She only sent it to the people attending," Mrs. Crandall said. "Me for the Kaye seat; Riley for Pendragon."

"Why'd she text me?" Jax asked, staring at his phone. "I can't go." The Table was a council of the highest Transitioner lords—ones who could claim a direct ancestor present at the casting of the Eighth Day Spell. Branch-off lines weren't included, and Jax's line was a branch-off in the newest possible way. He was the first of a bloodline that came from the Ambroses—who were, in turn, only a diverted branch from one of the knights of the Round Table.

"Gloria and I had a great idea, and we warned Sheila in advance out of courtesy. This is going to shake up a few people." Riley grinned at Mrs. Crandall.

But Mrs. Crandall was staring at Riley in horror. "I can't take you to the Table like *that*."

"Like what?" Riley stared back at her.

She turned on Jax next. "Both you boys in the car. Now!"

Mrs. Crandall said she wasn't going to let her liege lord claim Philip Pendragon's chair at the Table wearing a biker jacket and cowboy boots. That was why, on the following Monday, Riley came downstairs dressed in a navy-blue suit with a red tie and black polished dress shoes. Mrs. Crandall had even made him get his hair cut—*short*.

Jax fell down on the sofa laughing. "Shut up," Riley said, tugging on his collar like he was being strangled.

"You look like you're going to a job interview," Jax said. "At a bank. To be an accountant."

"Next time," Riley growled, "I'll let them buzz you."

Riley had scored a reprieve for Jax at the Hair Cuttery on Saturday by convincing Mrs. Crandall that they needed to leave him looking like himself—"a dumb kid."

"Hey!" Jax had exclaimed.

"That way they'll underestimate him," Riley had finished. "Like we all did."

Jax had gotten away with just a new shirt and a half-inch trim on his wavy mop, but he still had to pass inspection before they left for the meeting. Mrs. Crandall straightened his collar and smoothed a loose lock of hair off his forehead. Then she turned to Riley and picked lint off his collar. "You look like your father," she said.

"Then I should be wearing jeans." Riley spoke quietly, not meeting her eyes. He wiggled a finger into the knot of his tie to loosen it.

Mrs. Crandall swatted his hand away. "Philip could get away with that. You can't." Riley winced at the mention of his father's name, and by the expression on his face, it looked like taking his dad's place at the Table made Riley a lot more uncomfortable than the clothes did. Mrs. Crandall put her hand on his arm and spoke gently. "You can't walk in there and try to fill his shoes. Just be yourself, and they'll see the similarity for themselves."

"But this isn't the real me." Riley waved a hand at his attire.

"Trust me on this. Ten years from now, if you want to ride in there on his motorcycle, you can. But today you're wearing a suit and tie."

Jax groaned. For someone who was supposed to have a talent for information, he sure did miss a lot of obvious stuff. *The motorcycle. It was his dad's.* No wonder Riley spent so much time working on it. No wonder A.J. had taken the time to securely stow it in the truck before fleeing a hurricane. Jax got it now.

"So, Sir Bedivere," Jax said as Riley drove the Land Rover along a scenic highway through the mountains. "I looked him up. He had one hand, and he was the knight who returned Excalibur to Niviane after King Arthur died. He's not going to be mad that Riley took it back, is he? Well, not him. He's dead. I mean *this* Bedivere."

"I didn't steal the blade off Niviane's body," Riley said

indignantly. "Wylit did that. I took it from Wylit. Spoils of war. It's mine."

"Sir Bedivere didn't have one hand," Mrs. Crandall added. "That's a mistranslation in the legends. He had the hand of power. It's the Bedivere talent."

"And what is that, exactly?"

"Anything they do with that hand, whether it's wield a sword or a tennis racket or sign a business contract, is magically enhanced." Riley glanced at Jax in the rearview mirror. "He'll use a handshake to evaluate you, and be careful what you say while doing it, because you might find yourself bound to an agreement."

"Is he not trustworthy?" Jax asked.

"Philip thought Calvin Bedivere was a *fair* man," Mrs. Crandall replied. "But most members of the Table will look out for their own interests above anything else. Be wary of all of them."

"Is Bedivere the leader of the Table?"

"Why would you think that?" Riley asked. "The whole point of Arthur's Round Table was that everyone was equal. No one's vote counted more than anyone else's, no matter if you were a king or a knight or a noblewoman. This one runs the same way. Gloria's my vassal, but she can vote against me if she wants to."

"Not that I will," Mrs. Crandall said. "If I disagree with you, I'll tell you privately."

And probably smack him in the back of the head

besides, from what Jax had observed. "Well, the meeting's at Bedivere's house," Jax pointed out. "I just thought . . ."

"The Table usually meets at a neutral location in Manhattan," Mrs. Crandall said. "But the city's still recovering from the storm, and Bedivere's house is a favorite alternative. You'll see why when we get there."

The first thing Jax saw from the highway was a little town in the valley, tucked into a bend in the Lehigh River. Once they left the main road, he spotted the house on the mountainside overlooking the town. Maybe *castle* would've been a better word, because it seemed to guard the town from above. It had turrets and balconies and other architectural stuff Jax had no words for. He figured Bedivere must've signed a lot of contracts with that hand of power to afford this. "Does a whole clan live here?" Jax asked. "Like at the Dulac building?"

"Calvin's a widower," Mrs. Crandall said. "He has three daughters, several grandchildren, and vassals with families of their own. They might stay with him from time to time, but I believe they all have their own residences, and only Calvin lives here year round."

They took a narrow, switchback road to the house, where they were stopped at an ornate gate by three guards who ordered them to get out of the car and show their marks. When they did, two of the men betrayed no reaction, but the youngest one whistled in surprise over the Pendragon family crest.

"We're here to claim our seats," Riley said.

"You and Kaye, perhaps," the head guard said. "But the boy stays outside."

"No, he's coming with us." And then Riley explained why.

The inside of the mansion was as impressive as the outside, but Jax didn't have a lot of time to admire it. A guard marched them to a set of double doors, knocked briskly, and waved them into a banquet room. The table inside wasn't round, which disappointed Jax. It was a regular rectangular dining table with four men and three women seated around it. One of the women was Deidre's mother, Sheila Morgan, and another was Jax's cousin Sloane Dulac.

Jax stiffened at the sight of her. The last time he'd seen Sloane, he'd been fighting to keep himself out of her clan and Evangeline safe from her malicious plans.

A gray-haired gentleman rose from his chair at the head of the table. His smile seemed genuinely welcoming. "Gloria Kaye. Have you come to claim your brother's seat at last?" He offered her his hand, not by showing his mark in the Transitioner fashion, but in the Normal way.

"Good to see you again, Calvin." Mrs. Crandall accepted his handshake. Her maiden name was Kaye, and she was descended from the Sir Kay of legend. Her family had served the Pendragons for centuries, but like Riley, she was the last of her line. Her only child, A.J., had inherited his father's talent, not hers.

Calvin Bedivere turned to Riley, who solemnly showed his mark. "No need, young man," said Bedivere, offering a warm handshake to him as well. "I recognize you. Philip's boy. I'm glad to see you alive and well."

"Thank you, sir," Riley said.

Jax detected a surprised reaction from some of the people in the room—but not many. Sheila Morgan and Sloane already knew Riley had survived the assassination attempt five years ago, and it looked as if word had leaked out to other Table members as well. Too many people had seen Riley at the pyramid in Mexico and at the Dulac building for it to remain a secret much longer.

Bedivere smiled at Jax next. "You, son, I don't know."

Jax showed his mark. "Jax Aubrey, sir."

"Indeed." Bedivere shook Jax's hand with a friendly smile. "Now, Gloria and—Riley, is that right? You're both welcome to take the seats of your ancestors at our Table. And your young friend can wait outside."

It was politely stated but firm. Jax was not welcome in the room.

"Jax isn't tagging along," Riley said. "He's serving as proxy to someone who can't attend the meeting."

"Ah," Bedivere said. "Owens? Is he finally claiming his seat, too?"

"No." Riley's voice was quiet. "The Owens line is deceased."

"I can confirm that," said Sheila Morgan. "Miller Owens died fighting Wylit's vassals in Mexico."

"Another bloodline of the Table lost," grumbled a bearded man, shaking his head. "While the branch-off talents increase like rabbits, snuffing us out."

"Get over yourself, Pellinore," said a wispy-thin, elderly lady with snow-white hair. "Branch-off talents aren't inferior to ours. Back before the spell, nobody cared about such things. It's only an accident of history that our families ended up earning a seat here—and an extra day, as well."

Jax perked up his ears, suddenly wondering how many people with magic talents had not become Transitioners because they hadn't been present at the casting of the spell. He was pondering that when Bedivere cleared his throat to catch Jax's attention. "Who are you here to represent then, Aubrey?"

Jax snapped his thoughts back to the task at hand and said what Riley had told him to say. "I'm here as a proxy for my liege lady, and on her behalf I claim the Emrys seat at the Table."

A number of voices called out at once.

"What?"

"That's nonsense!"

"There are no Kin at the Table!"

Sloane leaned over and whispered to the man sitting next to her.

"The Table is a Transitioner council," Bedivere said to Riley.

"With all due respect, sir," Riley replied, "seats at the Table are owed to clan leaders descended from the people who cast the Eighth Day Spell, which included one Kin lord."

"He's right," said the woman with the white hair. "There used to be an Emrys seat at the Table, although I don't believe it's been filled since the seventeenth century."

"You would know," muttered the bearded Pellinore, who seemed to be stinging from the *Get over yourself* remark.

"We can't invite an enemy to join us," Sloane said loudly. "We're at war with the Kin, and the Emrys line conspired against us in the past. There's an Emrys consorting with the Llyrs right now." The man beside her nodded.

"A child," said Mrs. Crandall. "Who was driven to seek refuge with the Llyrs after being held against her will by the Dulacs."

"It was protective custody," Sloane corrected.

"It was a jail cell," Jax snapped. He looked at everyone else. "My liege lady wants to get her sister away from the Llyrs."

A narrow-faced man with a cross-eyed gaze waved his

hand for Jax to be quiet. "You don't have a right to speak here, boy."

"If the Emrys leader wants to cooperate," Sheila Morgan said, "it would be foolish to refuse her. Let's put it to a vote."

"There's no reason for a vote," the elderly woman said firmly. "An Emrys cast the Eighth Day Spell. The Emrys bloodline is owed a seat."

But they voted anyway. Sheila Morgan and the white-haired woman voted in favor, and so did Riley and Mrs. Crandall, who hadn't even had a chance to sit down yet. Sloane voted against, along with the man beside her, the cross-eyed man, and Pellinore.

The deciding vote fell to Calvin Bedivere, who smiled wryly. "I find myself swayed by historic precedence. The Emrys family is welcome to our council." He looked at Jax. "By proxy."

"Thank you, sir." Jax tried not to look as nervous as he felt. Riley clapped a hand on his shoulder, and together they moved toward the Table to find a seat.

8

INTRODUCTIONS WERE MADE FOR Jax's benefit. The elderly woman was Carlotta Lyonnesse. Ash Pellinore was the name of the bearded guy. Roger Sagramore was the cross-eyed man, and the man seated next to Sloane was Oliver Bors.

Bors. Jax recognized the name, but his visit to the Dulac clan was hazy in his mind, thanks to the fix Tegan had arranged for his memory. It wasn't until Sloane whispered in Bors's ear again that Jax remembered Ursula Dulac had been married to a Bors and some of her sons had inherited her husband's talent. Oliver Bors must be Sloane's uncle.

Jax had expected more people to be here. According to Melinda Farrow, his tutor in all things magical, most of Arthur's knights and a lot of lords and ladies had participated in the casting of the Eighth Day Spell. But, as Pellinore had pointed out, families died out over fifteen centuries—or diverged into new talents in a magical version of evolution. Jax wondered how much further this elite group could dwindle before the branch-off Transitioners stopped allowing them to make decisions for everyone—and whether that might be a good thing. After all, as Carlotta had said, their only qualification was having a direct ancestor present at a specific historic (and magic) event.

I'll bet Mr. Crandall would be a better leader than Sloane Dulac!

The nine Transitioner bloodlines represented here today were the only ancient ones left in the U.S., but there was apparently another group operating independently in the U.K. "They've promised support in the way of money and resources," Bedivere said of the British version of the Table. "None of them have offered to come in person."

"In other words," muttered Roger Sagramore, "'Better you than us and good luck.' They must feel like they dodged a bullet, having the Llyrs come here instead of wreaking havoc there."

"I hardly think they 'dodged a bullet.' Scores of men were killed defending Oeth-Anoeth," Bedivere said.

"Our first task is finding the Llyrs," Sheila Morgan said. "To that end, we need to identify the Kin responsible for breaking them out and transporting them across the ocean—*and* locate their base of operations."

"I can't believe you missed them in New York!" interjected Roger Sagramore. "You had seven days to prepare a dragnet to catch them when we knew where they were!"

"We didn't miss them," Sheila said, her face stiff. "I lost two teams confronting the Llyrs. It was only by chance that my daughter wasn't aboard one of those crafts. What did *you* risk in the search, Roger?"

When Roger Sagramore clamped his thin lips together and said nothing, Sheila looked away with disdain. "From our previous meeting, you already have the specs on the military aircraft that assaulted Oeth-Anoeth." Everyone nodded, including Riley—which made it clear to all the Table members, if they hadn't already figured it out, that Riley had been secretly receiving information from the Morgans while the rest of them presumed he was dead. "We found a hangar in Greenland that served as their intermediate stop before they arrived in North America. I have a squadron stationed there, in case they return to it. Now, this is what we saw them leaving New York with."

Sheila Morgan passed out images she'd printed from Google. "They used a twin-engine prop plane, possibly a de Havilland. We're currently scouring the U.S. for this plane, which must be resting somewhere during the seven days they can't use it, but a de Havilland doesn't need a big runway, and it could be hidden somewhere as small as a barn."

While Jax pondered the immensity of searching for a plane that could be stashed almost anywhere, Sheila continued, "These Kin clearly have a small fleet of aircraft, and there's no telling if we've seen them all. So, if any of you intend to fly on the eighth day, file your plans with me. My people will shoot down unidentified planes and ask questions later."

Jax sat up in alarm, but Sagramore beat him to a protest. "You can't do that!"

Ash Pellinore grunted in amusement. "There go your drug-smuggling runs, Roger."

"Ash, you mangy dog—"

"Go ahead. Deny it in front of Gloria Kaye," Pellinore dared him.

Sagramore shot Mrs. Crandall a wary glance. For the first time since Mrs. Crandall's brother had died, they had a truth teller among them.

"It would make me very, very sad to shoot down fellow Table members by accident," Sheila said, sounding like she meant the exact opposite. "For everyone's safety, notify me if you plan to travel by air."

"What about my liege lady's sister? What if—" Jax began.

"They have more than just planes," Sloane interrupted him. "My clan had a run-in with Kin teenagers in a Hummer the week before the breakout. We tracked them down after they set fire to a number of cars over several eighth days. One of them was the Emrys girl, which is why *we're* convinced she's in league with the enemy." She shot Jax a triumphant look.

He answered her with a glare, then exchanged glances

with Riley. This was the first time they'd heard how the Dulacs had captured Addie in the first place, and even Jax had to admit it didn't sound good. *Whose side is she on?* From the expression on Riley's face, he must have been wondering the same thing.

"Based on eyewitness accounts from Wales, we're also dealing with Aerons," Sheila Morgan said. "They're the only Kin known to tattoo themselves."

"I want to know how Kin got their hands on military aircraft and Hummers," said Ash Pellinore. "Most of them live on the streets or in the houses of Normals, leeching food and shelter. How did these Kin gather the resources to mount an assault on Oeth-Anoeth, and how did they coordinate it? What are they using for communication? Ham radio?"

"Scrying," Jax suggested.

"You can't send a message through scrying," Oliver Bors said. "It's only for observation."

"Unless you schedule it on both ends and bring notepads and pencils," Jax pointed out. "Then it's a video call with a chat box."

Everyone stared at Jax. *Well, duh,* he wanted to say. *Didn't you think of that?*

Sloane cleared her throat. "My father is trying to track down Wylit's heirs in Romania. Wylit led the last two attempts to break the Eighth Day Spell."

"I don't think they're involved," Riley said. "Miller

Owens infiltrated Wylit's clan for me and was observing them for months before the pyramid incident. Wylit had no contact with any other Kin during that time, including his own family. He was working alone. Miller made very sure of this, because we wanted to identify any collaborators."

"So," Pellinore grunted. "You weren't just cowering in a hidey-hole these past few years."

"No sir," Riley said. "I was doing the job my father left me as best I could."

"We can't entirely discount the Wylits," said Bedivere. "I'm not surprised Aerons are involved—we've all had unpleasant encounters with them over the years. But they're a disorganized, unruly mob. I don't believe they could have spearheaded this venture or acquired the resources to pull it off. Nor do I believe a child could lead them, even if she is an Emrys. We're overlooking someone important." Now he turned to Jax. "There *were* collaborators who escaped the raid on the Emrys house thirty-five years ago, which is the last time multiple Kin clans organized against us. Perhaps the current Emrys clan leader can give us the names we're lacking."

"She was only eleven at the time," Riley pointed out.

"Eleven-year-olds have sharp eyes and ears. If she wants to prove her loyalty to this council, she can give us the names of the Kin who conspired with her father."

Jax looked at Riley for guidance and, when he nodded,

answered accordingly. "If she knows any names, I'm sure she'll tell you."

"Finding their base is our number-one priority," Sheila reminded everyone.

"Once we've located it," Roger Sagramore said, "I assume there will be a preemptive strike during the seven-day timeline?"

"Of course," Sheila said.

"You can't do that!" Jax exclaimed. "You can't go shooting down planes if Addie might be on them, and you can't bomb their hideout during the seven-day timeline. She'll be killed!"

Riley leaned forward and spoke directly to Sheila. "Give us a chance to extract the girl before an air strike. I managed it on the pyramid. I can do it again."

"The circumstances were different," Sheila Morgan said.

"The girl chose her side," Oliver Bors remarked. "And the consequences that go with it."

"She was running away from your clan!" Jax retorted. "You were planning to kill her *and* my liege lady to end the eighth day."

A couple members of the Table actually snickered at his outburst. "Sorry, Aubrey," said Ash Pellinore. "I can't imagine the Dulacs wanting to end the eighth day and give up their magic!" Meanwhile, Sloane looked like she'd snorted up seawater and her uncle appeared to be holding his breath.

"That's because you don't know they've been experimenting with brownie holes to replace the eighth day as a source of magic," Jax said. "Only for themselves, of course. All you guys would be demoted to Normals."

"Brownie holes?" Pellinore guffawed in disbelief.

"I saw them in use," Riley said. "And Sheila, you know that's how Evangeline escaped from their building that night." When Sheila nodded, Riley continued, "Only members of the Dulac clan have gained entry—plus Jax, because he's related to them."

"Do you want to address this, Sloane?" Bedivere asked.

Sloane's eyes flicked toward Mrs. Crandall, the truth teller, before answering. "Grandmother wanted to investigate the magic potential of brownie holes in the event a catastrophe destroyed the eighth day. With so few Emrys heirs left, there's a possibility the spell might end and cut off our source of magic."

"More than a possibility," Jax muttered, "since you had one Emrys heir prisoner and were trying to make me bring you the other."

"Grandmother was killed because of those brownie holes," Sloane said stiffly. "We've discontinued experimentation."

"Are you telling me the Dulac clan can pop out of brownie holes?" Pellinore had finally reasoned out what *experimentation with brownie holes* meant. "Anywhere? Like in my home?"

"Of course not," Oliver Bors said. "Very few people were included in the trial runs, and no one else can be given access now, because Luis Morder, who knew the necessary spell, was killed by the Llyrs. Besides, to reiterate Sloane, my mother died because something monstrous came out of the brownie holes. We're no longer using them."

Jax glanced at Mrs. Crandall. She didn't call either Sloane or Bors out in a lie. Their words were literal truth with a lot of omissions. "Even if the Dulacs have temporarily quit their plan to murder my liege lady and her sister," he said, hoping everyone at the Table would notice they hadn't actually denied his accusation, "you can't plan an assault against the Llyrs that will endanger Addie Emrys. I object . . . uh, on behalf of the Emrys seat!"

Sheila addressed Jax. "Do you know how many casualties there were in that hurricane?"

Jax gulped. "Yes, ma'am. I do."

"I sympathize with you." Even though there wasn't a hint of emotion on Sheila's face, Jax believed she meant what she said. "But how else do you propose we defeat them? We have an impressive array of talents at this Table, and our vassals have talents of their own. But my clansmen and Pellinore are the only ones with combat experience—and we won't be facing bullets. It'll be tornadoes, flash floods, and gale-force winds. Even *I* can't pilot a helicopter in a hurricane. You already know what they did to my planes with lightning."

Having experienced the storm produced by the Llyrs, Jax understood what a powerful talent they had. For the first time he considered how weak the Transitioners seemed by comparison. The Morgans' talent for operating machinery that otherwise wouldn't work on the eighth day, the Dulac talent for changing memories—how did they stack up against people who were practically weather gods? Even Riley's voice of command was not unstoppable. Jax had seen Wylit resist it and Evangeline, too, when Riley had tried to order her out of danger in the Dulac basement.

"You'll get no argument from me," Roger Sagramore said. "We should take every advantage we can. That was the point of the Eighth Day Spell in the first place."

Jax turned to Riley, expecting him to protest. But Riley looked worried, as if he was weighing Addie's life against thousands, maybe millions of others, and not liking the result. *Not you, too,* Jax pleaded silently.

Carlotta Lyonnesse patted Jax's hand. "If it's possible to spare the girl, we will. We don't want to see innocents killed. But the Normal population is composed of innocents, too, and the Kin don't share the same remorse. With the exception of your liege lady, I assume."

"Well, of course," Jax said angrily, moving his hand.

"You can't lump all Kin together with the Llyrs," Riley said, breaking his silence. "In fact, I'm concerned about the safety of Kin who aren't involved in hostilities. The Llyrs will be recruiting their own kind, and I doubt they'll stick to volunteers."

"We should detain them," said Sagramore. "Collect as many as we can and hold them for the duration."

"You mean like a World War Two internment camp?" Riley looked at the people seated around the table. "Please tell me that's not the way the Table operates now." He didn't come out and say *My father wouldn't have approved,* but his expression suggested he was thinking it.

Bedivere cleared his throat. "What if I offer to provide secure and pleasant living facilities for any Kin seeking sanctuary from the conflict? We'll take no one by force. Jax, you and your liege lady can inspect the premises." He met Jax's eyes and didn't patronize him with a pat on the hand. "I want to see the Emrys girl spared, if we can. Even if you doubt my humanistic motives, you must believe I have no desire to see the Emrys family decreased further and the eighth day endangered." He tilted his head slightly toward the other side of the table, where Sloane and Bors sat.

Bedivere doesn't trust them either. Jax extended his right hand. "Can we shake on it, sir? That you'll keep neutral

Kin safe? That you'll block any plan to eliminate the Emrys family?"

Jax heard the intake of breath around the table. It was pretty bold to use Bedivere's own talent against him, and Jax wondered if he'd gone too far. But Bedivere didn't seem angry. He clasped Jax's hand. "You have my word. I will not approve any action designed to deliberately result in the annihilation of the Emrys family, and I'll guarantee the safety of any neutral Kin in my care to the best of my ability."

It was a carefully worded statement, and Jax understood there were probably clever ways around it. He hadn't gotten everything he wanted, and Addie was still in danger. But Jax saw respect in Bedivere's eyes and felt the tingle of magical potential in his handshake. Considering this was his first time facing the Table, Jax didn't think he'd done too badly.

9

CALVIN BEDIVERE'S SUPPORT DID not sway the council, however, which voted six to four in favor of a preemptive strike during the seven-day timeline if the Llyrs' hiding place was discovered. Sheila Morgan did tell Jax they would try to "incapacitate" rather than "annihilate," although that didn't comfort him much.

After the meeting, Oliver Bors headed for the door with Roger Sagramore on his heels. Sloane followed, but made a point of passing by Riley on her way out. "Just so you know," she said, flipping her long brown hair over one shoulder, "a cheap suit and a bad haircut don't make you look any less like a punk."

"Stop checking me out, then," Riley replied.

"You wish!" Sloane hissed.

After Sloane left, Carlotta Lyonnesse approached Riley. "My dear boy, I am so very sorry about your family. Your mother and I weren't *closely* related, but I felt her loss all the same. I don't know if you remember, but my grand-daughter dated one of your cousins . . ."

"I remember," Riley said gruffly. He shifted uncomfortably from one foot to the other, clenching and unclenching his hands, while Carlotta ran through condolences for seemingly every deceased member of his family. Riley stood there and endured it.

Jax was trying to think of a way to rescue him when he heard footsteps behind him and turned to face Sheila Morgan. She had such a powerful personality, Jax had forgotten how tiny she was, just like her daughter Deidre. "You did well today," she said. "Both of you. *You* took everyone by surprise, and *he* made a good impression without overreaching himself—like Sloane did. It's a shame you came late. You missed her getting a smackdown from Pellinore."

Jax *was* sorry he'd missed that. "We came late on purpose," he explained. "Riley wanted me to apply for the Emrys seat in front of the whole council. He was afraid I'd be turned away without a full vote if we came early."

"Not a bad strategy," Sheila said. "It's enough of an upheaval for three vacant seats to be filled at one time. But to have you show up as a solid voting block—Pendragon, Kaye, and Emrys—that's thrown off the balance of the entire Table. No wonder Lyonnesse and Bedivere are making friendly overtures."

Is that what they were doing? Jax glanced around. On the other side of the room, Bedivere was engaged in conversation with Mrs. Crandall, while Pellinore watched with crossed arms and hunched eyebrows.

Dulac and Bors always voted together, Jax guessed. And from the way Sagramore had left the room in their company, he was probably their ally. Now three new votes threatened their power at the Table. *Sloane must be hopping mad!* Bedivere seemed to be neutral, along with Sheila. Pellinore was abrasive, but at least he wasn't in Sloane's back pocket.

"Can you help me out with something?" Jax asked Deidre's mother. "I'm still trying to learn who everybody is and what their talents are. How was Lyonnesse related to Riley's mom?"

"They were distant cousins. The Lyonnesse talent is linguistics—mastering any language, spoken or written. Riley's mother was from a branch-off line and had a similar talent, limited to spoken language."

"How about Sagramore?"

"Sagramore is a facilitator. He can't do anything on his own, but he can link the talents of other people to produce new and creative results. An ironic talent for such an unsociable man."

Did Sheila Morgan just make a joke? Jax hadn't thought she possessed a sense of humor. "What's the Bors talent?" he asked.

"You don't know? Aren't they *your* relatives?"

Jax tried to figure out the relationship on his fingers.

If Ursula Dulac had been his great-aunt, then her son Oliver would be some sort of cousin—maybe once or twice removed?

Sheila got tired of waiting. "The Bors talent is suppression of magic within a certain radius. The more of them working together, the larger the suppression field. That might be useful for fighting the Llyrs, although Oliver and his brothers don't have experience in anything more combative than the floor of the Stock Exchange."

"And Pellinore?"

Sheila almost smiled. "You've heard of werewolves?"

Jax gasped. "No. Way."

"I'm exaggerating, but not by much. If you ever have the chance to see him in action, you'll never forget it." Jax's eyes nearly bugged out of his head, staring at the bearded man across the room, but Sheila didn't give him much time to dwell on the idea. "Now *you* tell me something. Brownie holes. It's true? You can get into them?"

"Yes." Jax ripped his gaze away from Ash Pellinore.

"What sort of military application do they have?"

"Uh . . ." How was Jax supposed to know? "I used them to sneak around the Dulac building. And I was able to move in time a bit. Backward or forward by a couple hours."

Her eyes narrowed. "Is it true what Oliver said? They lost the only person who could grant other people access?"

"Yeah, their spell caster was the expert." *Was* the expert. Now Dorian was the expert.

Suddenly, Jax realized why Sheila was talking to him when there were other, more important people in the room. She was doing exactly what she'd said Bedivere and Lyonnesse were doing: making friendly overtures. Jax was *worth* something to her. He had inside knowledge of something she saw potential in.

That was why he dared to ask, "Can my liege lady request a favor of you?" Sheila arched a dark eyebrow, but Jax plunged on. "Bedivere said he'd take in Kin refugees, and I know of a house that's full of them—mostly children. We could use help moving them to safety before something bad happens to them."

"Why would I be interested in this?" Jax understood she wasn't being cold, just blunt. What benefit did she gain from transporting a bunch of Kin orphans?

"Because there's also a Kin woman living at that house who might help us. When I was there a few weeks ago, she went into a trance and told me the Llyrs were escaping from Oeth-Anoeth. I'm pretty sure she said this at the exact moment it was happening, all the way across the ocean." Jax smiled. "Would someone with that kind of talent interest you, ma'am?"

Now, Sheila truly smiled back, and her face didn't even crack.

10

ADDIE RISKED A GLIMPSE out the window, and the sight of the ground so far below made her feel dizzy. Her first time in an airplane had been after her rescue from the Dulac prison—and on that occasion she'd been more worried about the Transitioner planes pursuing them and the lightning Bran was using to fight them than how high off the ground she was. All her life, Addie had seen Normal airplanes hanging motionless in the sky on the eighth day, but that was different. Magic held them there. Addie knew the power of magic. What was holding this plane up while it flew? Science? Addie had no faith in the power of science.

Neither, apparently, did Bran. He'd questioned Madoc extensively about the plane and especially about the Normals who serviced it. "If the mechanics don't excel at their job *and* keep their mouths shut," Madoc had explained, "they won't receive their exorbitant salary."

Normals were motivated by money, according to Madoc,

which was why he'd spent centuries acquiring it. Addie wondered what the Normals thought of their mysterious, anonymous employer. When Madoc first started amassing his fortune in the early 1700s, communicating through the use of handwritten letters wasn't unusual. Now, Normals conducted business with phones and computers and other devices Addie had never seen in operation, but according to Kel, Madoc issued instructions to his employees the old-fashioned way and paid them well enough not to question it.

Madoc's money would finance their search for the Treasures of the Kin, but once they were found, it would be up to Addie to use their power to weave the eighth day into the Normal timeline and end the exile of her race. To do this, she would have to master a spell that had confounded her father—a spell that might not have been successfully cast since her ancestor Merlin did it centuries ago.

So, before they boarded the plane to Vermont to speak to the Corra oracle, Addie had met with Bran Llyr for her first tutoring session. The sun had just risen over the ocean when she joined him on the patio outside Madoc's living-room windows. "What can you do?" Bran had demanded of her without any kind of welcome.

Addie glanced around, unsure of what he wanted. Her eyes passed over the embers of last night's bonfire—cold, dry, scattered embers, because *last night* had really been a week ago. Seeing the remains of the fire, she made up her mind to give Bran the best she had, rather than build up to it. She snapped her fingers and, with a purple starburst of magic, produced a five-inch flame that danced on the tips of her forefinger and thumb. It wasn't the invisible magic fire her father had taught all his children as a defensive spell, the one that burned her palms and drained her of energy. This was an actual flame, although it didn't burn *her.* She smirked a bit.

Bran's expression didn't change. "So, you can light Madoc's cigarettes without a match. Is that all?"

The smirk fell off Addie's face. *Is that all?* Sure, the fire starter she'd copied this magic from had been able to do it naturally; that had been his *talent.* The point was that Addie could mimic his talent so effortlessly. "I can also write curses," she said, shaking the flame out and trying not to sound huffy. Addie had picked up all kinds of things from the refugees passing through the Carroway house. It had been against the rules for the residents to share their talents with one another. But Addie had sharp eyes, and she wasn't afraid of a spanking when caught.

"Can you defend yourself?" Bran asked, tapping his staff on the patio stones and throwing out his other hand.

Addie saw a wall of white flying toward her before she was slapped to the ground by a gust of wind. Her rear end hit the stones, followed by her elbows, and very nearly the back of her head. She propped herself up, gasping, until Bran dropped his hand and the wind ceased instantly. "Obviously not," Bran observed.

Sucking in air, Addie thought of a barrier spell she might

have used to block the wind. *Too late now.* At least she could show him she was a quick learner. She jumped up and thrust both hands out. Bran's long white hair rustled slightly in a faint breeze. It wasn't as impressive a display as she'd hoped for, but she shrugged. "It takes practice for me to get it right. But I can do wind now. Thanks."

Bran looked down on her impassively. "How does a spell caster copy the magic of others without casting spells?"

"I am casting spells," Addie corrected him. "I just learned to do it without all that silly ritual stuff—symbols and incantations. I don't need them anymore."

"You can't *change* your talent through learning," Bran said. When Addie shrugged again, he pressed her further. "You said you were taught this by someone. Who?"

"An old woman," Addie said, watching his face to see if he figured it out. "Really old. You could even call her a *crone.*"

Bran Llyr was skilled at not giving away his thoughts, but Addie saw the skin tighten around his eyes as he considered her answer. Then the quiet of their surroundings was broken by several Aeron boys running along the beach, yowling with mischief and mayhem, and Madoc emerged from the house to ready his plane for their journey, followed by Griffyn and Ysabel.

Addie's private lesson came to a premature end.

The airplane dipped. Addie felt the sensation of falling in her stomach and looked at Kel, but he seemed perfectly calm. However, Griffyn, seated with Ysabel a row ahead, threw a newspaper he'd been reading to the floor. "Tell your father to stop that!" he growled at Kel.

"He has to descend," Kel replied. "We're almost at our destination."

That made Addie squirm in her seat more than the drop in altitude. The Carroways were going to be so *angry* at her for bringing these people to their house. She wished Griffyn and Ysabel had stayed behind. If it was just she and Bran, she'd have a better chance of convincing her foster parents that what she was doing was right for her people. No Transitioners knew better than Emma and Dale Carroway how much the Kin had suffered from their banishment to the eighth day. They'd devoted their whole lives to serving members of the unfairly imprisoned Kin race, even though it meant avoiding other Transitioners and keeping themselves in a self-imposed isolation.

Madoc landed the plane on a street in the middle of town, bringing it to a stop between a candy store and the library. Although Addie had skateboarded down this street dozens of times, she had never set foot inside either the store or the library. Normal establishments were closed to her.

Addie chewed on a fingernail. *Emma will know we're here.* Her foster mother was a sensitive who detected emotions. Emma would immediately sense strangers in her town, but she'd also recognize Addie. *Can she feel me wishing her to be calm . . . to trust me?*

Kel opened the outer door and lowered the stairs that

unfolded from the body of the plane. "Make Adelina go first," Madoc called from the cockpit. "Her presence might prevent Transitioners from attacking us, and we'll need her to find the house."

Dale Carroway's talent was obscuring his location from others. But he couldn't hide himself or his house from Addie. She'd known him too long and lived in his house half her life.

As she walked down the aisle, Addie picked up Griffyn's newspaper from the floor and tossed it into an empty seat. The front page headline caught her eye. "Death Toll from Freak Hurricane Tops 500 in 3 States. Beach Towns Devastated. Staten Island under Water." Belatedly the words sank in, and she stopped in her tracks. Death toll? Freak hurricane? Did they mean the storm the Llyrs had created?

Bran pushed her forward, and Kel took her arm to help her onto the stairs to disembark from the plane. Addie steadied herself, feeling off balance. She hadn't realized the storm would do that kind of damage. Somehow, Addie had imagined it singling out the Dulac building—hovering over it and striking it with lightning, like in the cartoons the orphans watched on the Carroways' VHS cassette player.

"You'll let me talk to them, right?" she asked, turning around. Bran frowned, not understanding her, and she tried again. Her mouth had gone dry. "At the Carroway house. You'll let me talk to my foster parents and convince them not to interfere. You promised."

"I will not bargain with Transitioners. We've come to get

our oracle. If *you* convince the Transitioners to stand aside, so much the better." Bran pushed Addie forward again.

She led the way down a street she knew like the back of her hand. Griffyn peered through store windows, and Ysabel disappeared down an alley, heading off on her own. The Mathonwys brought up the rear, Madoc smoking a cigarette—which reminded Addie of the flame she'd summoned with her silly finger snap.

Did I really think I'd impress Bran Llyr with that trick? A man who raised a hurricane the first time he was free to use his talent to its full extent?

I've made a mistake.

When they reached her home street, she spoke over her shoulder nervously. "I'm leading you to house number seventeen. You won't be able to see it. But trust me; it's there."

"What's she talking about?" grumbled Griffyn. "I see it just fine."

Addie snapped her head around. "You do?"

"I see it," Kel confirmed. "They must not be here."

He was right. If Dale was at home, the white Victorian house would be invisible. Had they abandoned it? Moved somewhere else with all the homeless refugees in tow? Had something *happened* to them?

Then the front door opened, and Dale and Emma Carroway stepped onto the wraparound porch. Emma met Addie's eyes immediately and mouthed her name—*Addie!*—looking stricken and worried and happy to see her all at once.

Dale marched down the porch steps. "Stop! None of you but Addie is welcome here."

Bran and Griffyn didn't break stride, and Addie ran ahead, trying to stay in front of the group. "We aren't here to hurt anyone!" she shouted. "We just want to talk to Aine Corra!"

Dale shook his head. "They said you might bring these people here, Addie—but I thought we raised you smarter than this."

Who said she'd be coming? Who could possibly know she was with the Llyrs—except the Dulacs? Addie looked around, wondering if there was an army of Dulacs and their vassals hidden in the neighboring houses.

"Corra!" Bran shouted at the house. "Come out of there! We have business with you!"

"You have no business with anyone in my house." Dale was still walking toward them. It reminded Addie of how Dr. Morder had walked up to Bran after Addie was rescued—as if he expected to converse with the Llyr lord equal to equal. He'd paid for that error with his life.

Dr. Morder was the main person to credit for Addie's escape from the Dulacs. While she was a prisoner, Morder, a half-Kin, half-Transitioner spell caster and Dulac vassal, had told her that he wanted to join the Kin and was willing to betray his liege to do so. Under the circumstances, Addie had been reluctant to trust him, and Morder had tried to prove himself by using his magic to contact the only person who'd escaped the ambushed Hummer—Kel—and apprise him of Addie's whereabouts.

For this service, Dr. Morder had expected gratitude. Instead Bran had struck him down without a word of warning or a moment's hesitation. And Morder had been half-Kin. What would Bran do to an angry Transitioner who confronted him?

Addie held out a hand to warn her foster father not to come any closer. "Dale, please send Aine out to speak to us, if she's here. If not, we need to know where she's gone."

"They've fooled you," Dale replied. He looked over her head at Bran. "Are you proud? That you've twisted a little girl's head around so she doesn't know right from wrong?"

"Let me shut his mouth," Griffyn hissed, reaching toward one of his throwing knives.

Addie waved an arm without thinking, and a gust of wind knocked Griffyn sideways. Griffyn stared at her in shock and muttered under his breath to raise a counterattack. Addie saw the white magic gathering around him.

Just then, a group of children appeared from behind the house, herded by Ysabel. Many were crying. The older ones carried the younger ones, and Aine followed, holding her infant son in one arm and her toddler daughter, Brigit, in the other. Addie now understood what Dale had been up to. He'd known Addie was with the Llyrs and hadn't bothered trying to hide the house. Instead, he'd stalled them while Aine and the refugee children fled out the back door and escaped.

At least until Ysabel caught them.

Griffyn strode forward and wrenched Brigit away from Aine. He dumped the toddler unceremoniously on her diapered backside among the other children. Aine managed to pass her baby to Dale before he could receive the same treatment. Then Griffyn dragged her over to face his father.

Aine looked dazed, as if she barely understood where she was or what was happening. It was a confusion Addie had seen her experience many times and one of the reasons Addie had concluded she was a Corra. The oracle talent of the Corras was uncannily accurate and completely involuntary.

Bran looked down at Aine. The top of her head barely came to his shoulder. "We have come for an oracle," he said. "Where are the Treasures of the Kin?"

Aine shook her head. Her eyelids fluttered; her lips trembled. "I will not aid you."

To Addie's horror, Dale handed Aine's baby to Emma and stepped forward to intervene. *No!* Addie shook her head at him urgently.

Griffyn turned Aine's hand over and slapped a coin into it. "Now you *must* prophesy for us," he said. "I've crossed your palm with silver."

The touch of the silver coin compelled her talent even more than Bran's request and the intensity of the situation itself, but Aine fought it. Her body shook, and her eyes rolled up until they showed mostly white. Nevertheless, her trembling lips curled in a smile. "I'll gladly foretell the fate of Griffyn Llyr, who will die by the hand of an innocent."

Griffyn's face blanched at her words. Then he cursed vilely in Welsh, threw up a hand, palm out, and struck Aine with a bolt of electricity.

11

ADDIE SCREAMED. THE CHILDREN echoed her.

Dale ran toward Aine as she collapsed, but Bran swung his staff to block him, striking him in the head. Dale staggered and fell. The children sobbed and clung to Emma, who moaned and pressed their faces against her dress. One of the older kids, a boy named Gawan, picked up Brigit to keep the toddler from seeing what had happened.

Addie threw herself to the ground beside Dale's crumpled body and cradled his head. Blood oozed from his scalp, but he was breathing. It only took a glance to see that Aine was not, although Bran knelt beside her to check anyway. Then he looked up at Griffyn and said something in Welsh. Addie's command of Welsh was poor, but she thought Bran was calling his son a cretin.

A monstrous, murdering cretin! Addie thought, tears running down her cheeks. But that didn't change the fact that *she'd* brought him here. She'd led these violent people to her home and put everyone who lived here at risk—all to impress Bran Llyr. *It's my fault he killed her!*

"The woman prophesied my death!" Griffyn said to his father indignantly, as if his act had been justified.

"Did you think this would undo it?" Bran growled. Oracles spoke of what would be; the speaking itself did not *make* it be. Killing Aine wouldn't stop the future she foretold. Impatiently, Bran beckoned for Ysabel.

Even Ysabel, who was normally Griffyn's biggest fan, shot him an angry glance as she approached Aine's body. A live oracle would've been useful to them in the future. However, with an Arawen present, death wouldn't stop them from getting the prophecy they needed right now. Ysabel squatted and placed a hand on Aine's forehead.

Addie shuddered at the foul, black cloud of Arawen magic at work, but forced herself to watch as Ysabel stiffened and voiced words pulled from the dead woman's mind.

"Four treasures from the land of frost:
One corrupt and long ago lost,
Another repaired by girl's command,
Two, spoils of war,
Claimed by the voice and the hand."

Ysabel took a long breath and withdrew her hand. When she stood up, Griffyn growled at her, "Forget the Treasures!

What the woman said to me—that was a lie, wasn't it?"
Ysabel didn't answer.

"Are we taking the children?" snapped Madoc. "Even the small ones?" He was either unconcerned with Griffyn's future demise or trying to divert attention from it.

"You can't take the children," Emma protested, her voice shaking. "I won't allow it."

Addie frantically signaled her to not argue with them, terrified that one of them would strike her down next, but Bran ignored Emma completely. "The infant isn't old enough to be weaned. Leave it. The others are our future allies. If that little girl is a Corra like her mother, she will be a great advantage to us someday. Put the Transitioners in the house and find a place to lock them in."

Lock them in. Addie sagged with relief. He wasn't going to kill them. It didn't erase her responsibility for Aine's death, but at least her foster parents would be spared. Griffyn hefted Dale's limp body over his shoulder. Ysabel pulled Emma away from the children and toward the house. Emma clutched Aine's baby to her chest and looked back at Addie in despair. Addie wanted to sink into the ground with guilt and regret.

"Help me get the children back to the plane," Kel whispered in Addie's ear, pulling her gently but firmly away from Aine's body. Addie thought he was trying to distract her from what had happened. It wouldn't work, but perhaps she could prevent anyone else from being hurt.

Wiping tears from her face, Addie went with Kel to corral the children. She tried to take Brigit from Gawan, but he recoiled from her. "Traitor!" he hissed.

I'm not, Addie wanted to protest. *I'm trying to do right by us. I want candy stores and libraries for you and every other Kin kid. I want us to have a future in the real world. We didn't do anything wrong. It's not right for us to be imprisoned in this eighth day like criminals.* But she didn't say any of that. It suddenly sounded very naive.

"Do what you're told before worse happens," Kel told Gawan. Taking small children by the hands, Kel turned away from the house—and froze.

A large black bird swooped down and landed in the street in front of the children.

Then another. And a third.

A dark-haired girl walked up the street toward them. Wherever her bare feet touched, worms and insects bubbled up from the pavement. She wore a shapeless white dress. No, Addie realized—not a dress, an oversized white T-shirt with faded letters printed across the front. She wore shorts too, barely visible below the hem of her shirt. Her arms were bare, her left wrist unmarked. She wasn't Kin, and she wasn't a Transitioner. This was a Normal girl, not much older than Addie, whose body was hosting something that wasn't normal at all.

The Morrigan.

Kel pushed all the children in his reach to their knees.

"Close your eyes. Don't look at her," he whispered. Drawing the attention of the Morrigan was dangerous. She was known to choose sides, select victors . . . and casualties. Addie sank to her knees, but kept her eyes open.

Madoc kneeled and stared at the ground. Bran bent on one knee as well, holding his staff in front of him. "Great Morrigu," Bran greeted her with an old Welsh version of her name. "We are honored to serve you."

The girl's face was blank, her eyes wide but unseeing. From behind ordinary brown pupils, something dark and dangerous peered out. "Do you serve me?"

"I do," Bran swore. "When I saw you at Oeth-Anoeth, I knew the time had come to redeem pledges my ancestors made to you centuries ago. By your grace, we escaped that prison."

"The prophetess has given you your oracle," the Morrigan said.

"Yes. But an Emrys tried this once already, and even with two Treasures recovered, his venture failed." For all he spoke on bended knee, Bran came perilously close to complaining.

"*He* failed," the Morrigan replied. "It is up to the progeny to fulfill the failed destiny of the parent, and to that end, a gift has been bestowed on her that will aid you." The girl's eyes—unfocused and unseeing but still chillingly inhabited—glided past Bran to Addie.

Addie recognized that gaze. Not the girl; Addie had never seen the girl before. She recognized the entity *inside*, the same one who'd looked out at her through a set of much older eyes a year ago.

The Morrigan was three deities in one: the Old Crone, who touched key figures with the hand of destiny; the Washer Woman, who washed the clothes of those who fell in battle; and the Girl of Crows, who gathered combatants and drove them toward their doom. Addie had met the first incarnation already, and now she found herself transfixed by this one, who always appeared in a young body even though the being inside was as old as time itself.

You were chosen, the Morrigan conveyed to Addie in her gaze.

Addie trembled. *I know.*

And Bran knew, too. Addie saw it in his unguarded expression. He might have suspected before—Addie had certainly given him a good enough hint—but now the source of her altered talent was confirmed. Addie Emrys could master spells and mimic other people's talents with almost no effort. This was the gift meant to aid them in their cause.

"The Stone of Fal and the Sword of Nuadu are in the hands of our enemies and must be recovered," Bran said, addressing the Morrigan. "But the Spear of Lugh"—he lifted his staff—"this is all that remains of the Spear. It was broken long before it was passed to me."

"I knew it," Kel whispered to Addie. "I knew he had the Spear."

"Not broken," the Morrigan said. "The Spear was disguised

so your ancestors could smuggle it into Oeth-Anoeth. Bring me the knife you passed to your son when you received the staff."

Griffyn and Ysabel had stopped in the doorway of the house after locking up the Carroways. Fingering a knife sheathed near his right hand and looking as if he'd rather do anything else, Griffyn descended from the porch. He knelt and handed the knife to his father with his face turned away from the Morrigan.

"The knife and staff have passed from Llyr father to Llyr son for ten generations," Bran said. "We always believed they were made from the Spear, but no magic could reunite them."

"No magic of *yours* can reunite them." The Morrigan reached for the items.

To Addie's astonishment, Bran withheld them. "Forgive me, Great Morrigu, but once in the hands of the proper Llyr heirs, no one else has ever been able to hold either the knife or the staff without harm. And you are using the body of a Normal girl."

"This girl is no longer merely human." The Morrigan took the staff in one hand, the knife in the other, and Addie squeezed her eyes shut an instant before a blast of brilliant magic flared against her face. Her ears rang, and she swayed on her knees. When she opened her eyes, the Morrigan was handing back the whole Spear, which Bran accepted reverently.

"The Spear embodies your intention and purpose," the

Morrigan said. "You will never be deterred from your path while you hold it. Now, find the Stone and the Sword." The crows surged up from the ground in a flurry of wings and beaks, causing the children to shriek and flinch. The Morrigan vanished like a flame blowing out, leaving worms and beetles wriggling on the pavement where she'd been standing.

Bran whirled, holding aloft his restored Spear, and shouted triumphantly at the sky. A bolt of lightning—not from Bran's hand but from the heavens—struck the side of the Carroway house with a mighty crack. The wood siding ignited, and Ysabel launched herself from the porch just in time.

"No!" screamed Addie, staggering to her feet. "You promised!"

But he hadn't promised. Deep down, Addie knew he'd never promised not to harm the Carroways. He'd flattered her and praised her, and she wanted to believe they would work together as mentor and student. She'd been as stupid as Dr. Morder had been, expecting him to reward her.

Bran admired the flames, then hoisted the Spear again and repeated his incantation twice. Two more lightning bolts fell in quick succession, striking the houses to the right and to the left.

"Stop it!" Addie shouted. "Don't do this! Stop!"

Three more bolts of lightning. Three more houses full of Normal people Addie had never met, people who would die when their homes burned down on a day they could not escape. Bran looked at Addie, expectantly. For every outcry of defiance, he was going to set another house afire.

Kel grabbed her around the waist, pulling her backward. "Help me get the kids to the plane. Now, Addie!" The children were crying, even Gawan, and Kel's eyes darted from child to child like he was wondering who Bran and Griffyn might kill next.

They can't kill me, Addie thought. *The one person they dare not kill is* me.

She pushed Kel away. There was nothing she could do to save the Normals, but she refused to abandon Emma and Dale. She'd already lost her real mom and dad; she would not allow her foster parents to die, too. She was going to run into the Carroway house and . . .

Griffyn cuffed the side of her head with his fist, making the world spin. "Stupid girl," he said, throwing her over his shoulder and carrying her back to the plane.

Addie didn't make it easy for him. She kicked and pounded him with her fists. She bit him.

But her home still burned with people she loved inside it.

12

ON GRUNSDAY MORNING, RILEY, Jax, and A.J. met Deidre at a private airfield in central Pennsylvania. Jax was already familiar with Deidre's car, a blue Thunderbird convertible. So he wasn't surprised that her air transport was something equally cool: a four-prop plane from the 1960s. The interior had been gutted and replaced with modern leather seats and tables. There was a tiny kitchenette and a fold-down bed. Deidre could live in it.

"Were you mugged by a barber?" Deidre asked Riley, staring at his hair when he climbed aboard with Jax and A.J. Then she looked behind him. "Where's Evangeline?"

"Not coming," Riley said shortly. He didn't explain further, so Deidre raised her eyebrows in speculation and went to ready the plane for takeoff.

They'd departed the mountain cabin on Wednesday evening in A.J.'s truck, leaving the Land Rover—and Evangeline—behind. On the day of the Impossible Storm,

Evangeline had been exhausted from scrying and sick with a migraine after being attacked through the spell. So, the idea had been for Mrs. Crandall to meet her when she reappeared in the Land Rover at 12:01 and whisk her off to bed. By this morning, however, Evangeline had probably recovered enough to ask where Riley and Jax were, and Jax didn't envy Mrs. Crandall the job of explaining.

Addie knew where the Carroway house was, and Addie might be working with the enemy. That was Riley's thinking. He'd called the Carroways ahead of time, warned them that they could be in danger, and told them to have all their foster Kin children ready for transport when Deidre's plane arrived on Grunsday. Mr. Carroway hadn't wanted to believe Addie might betray them, but in the end he'd agreed to an evacuation.

Riley's original plan had been to leave in the early hours of the eighth day, but Deidre—newly returned from the ongoing search for the Kin hideout—had called him saying she needed a few hours to sleep and to service her plane. Riley had been impatient at the delay, which he thought increased the danger, and had almost changed his mind about bringing Jax with them. But it was Jax who'd made this arrangement with Sheila Morgan: safe transport of the orphan kids for an introduction to the woman with visions. He had to see it through. He was representing Evangeline's interests and paving the way for a possible Emrys-Morgan alliance. The firmer the bond he could establish with Sheila Morgan on behalf of a Kin clan, maybe the less willing she'd be to see Kin wiped out in an unfair, one-sided assault.

"At least Jax will run if I order him to," Riley had muttered to A.J.

Jax knew it perturbed Riley that Evangeline was capable of fighting off his commands, and he also knew Evangeline was going to be ticked off when she found out they'd left her behind.

"C'mon, cutie." Deidre patted the copilot's seat. "You ride up here with me."

Jax grinned. He'd face Evangeline later.

Somewhere over upstate New York, Stink popped out of the ceiling and landed on Jax's shoulder. Deidre burst out with a creative string of swear words, but her hands remained steady, and the plane never wavered.

A.J. groaned. "Is that thing going to follow you everywhere?"

"What's it doing on my plane?" Deidre exclaimed.

Riley laughed. "That's Jax's pet, Stink."

Deidre threw a look over her shoulder at Riley. "Tell it to stay out of my food stores and not to poop on my new carpet or anywhere else."

Riley looked sternly at Stink. "You heard her."

"All right. 'Fess up, Riley," said Jax. "What's with you and the brownies?"

Riley shrugged innocently, but Deidre grinned. "Don't you know? About the Pendragon talent? Voice of Command and King of Brownies?"

"Ha, ha. Very funny." Riley turned up the sleeves on his jean jacket with injured dignity. "The thing with the brownies is *not* part of the Pendragon talent."

"Oh sure," said Deidre.

"Alanna used to make them fetch and carry for her, remember?" A.J. asked Deidre, referring to Riley's sister.

"Oh, I remember. Personally, I wouldn't want the adoration of glorified rats, but Alanna seemed to enjoy it." Deidre glanced sideways. "No offense, Stink."

Riley ignored them both and explained to Jax, "As near as we can figure, they obey us because sometime in the past, a Pendragon did the brownies a really huge favor. Maybe even the Big Guy himself." He meant King Arthur. Then he added quietly, "I'd forgotten how much Alanna liked brownies."

"Maybe because you never talk about her," A.J. pointed out.

"Or any of your family," Deidre murmured.

Riley grunted something that might have been agreement or just *mind your own business*. Jax understood why Riley didn't want to talk about his family. But Deidre and

A.J. were right. It was like losing people all over again if you shut them out of your memory.

Stink chattered loudly and leaped off Jax's shoulder to the control panel where he pressed his flat nose against the window. "Hey, you!" Deidre protested. "Off!"

"Come here." Jax leaned forward to grab his pet, but then he spotted what Stink was looking at. "Deidre, do you see that smoke?"

"I see a *plane*." She was staring at a speck silhouetted against the clouds in the distance. Deidre slammed her hand flat over the radio, not bothering to flip any switches or pick up the mike, just calling on her talent to make it work. "Mother, come in! We've got a plane out here. Too far away for me to make out the model, but there are houses on fire at our destination. It's got to be them. Over."

"Roger that," replied Sheila Morgan's voice. "Is your plane armed? Over."

"Negative. I only have my personal weapons. I was expecting to transport children. Over."

"Pursue them. But keep your distance. Over."

Riley shot out of his seat and grabbed the back of Deidre's seat. "Not with Jax on board you don't! After what they did to your other planes?"

Jax swallowed hard. "Deidre." He pointed a shaky finger at the smoke coming from the ground. "People are in danger down there! We have to do something."

Deidre cursed, then said, "Negative on the pursuit, Mother. I've got a child aboard and a rescue in progress." She rattled off a string of coordinates estimating the flight path of the enemy plane and yanked her hand off the radio while her mother was still trying to give her orders.

Deidre landed as close as she could to the burning houses, taking out a row of hedges and someone's garden. Riley and A.J. unlocked the plane's hatch door, swung it open, and leaped out. Jax followed, with Stink clinging to his shoulder. He'd seen from the air that the Carroway house was one of the buildings on fire, as if there'd been any doubt.

"A.J.!" Deidre yelled from behind them. "This way!" A.J. looked back, and so did Jax. Deidre was pointing in another direction. "I need muscle! Stat!"

"Go!" shouted Riley. A.J. turned and headed back while Riley and Jax kept running toward the billowing smoke.

The last time Jax had been here, the Carroway house had been invisible. But there was no missing it now. Flames climbed the right side of the house, consuming one section of the wraparound porch and spreading toward the front. The houses on either side of the Carroways were also on fire, as well as three across the street. Six houses total.

Riley, several yards ahead of Jax, slowed and bent briefly over someone lying in the street. But he paused only a second before straightening and running up the front steps. "I'll see if anyone's in here," he shouted over his shoulder. *"Stay outside, Jax!"* Riley pulled his shirt up over the lower half of his face and disappeared.

He'd used the voice of command, darn him. Trust Riley to run into a burning building but order Jax to stay out of it! Jax let fly with the string of curses he'd just learned from Deidre and stumbled to a halt beside the woman on the ground. Immediately, he saw why Riley hadn't stopped to help her and recoiled. *Oh no, no, no . . .* He turned away and bent over, hands on knees, trying not to puke. Jax hadn't even known this woman's name, but he remembered the way she'd helped Evangeline, and the message she'd given to Jax in a trance. She'd been a good person.

He turned in a circle helplessly. Smoke poured from the Carroway house, but Riley's command prevented him from going in. *What can I do? Where are A.J. and Deidre?*

Stink squealed from a perch on the garden-hose reel of the house next door. "If that's all we got," Jax said, running across the yard. He twisted the faucet open as far as it would go, then unwound the hose. Stink scrambled back to his shoulder, and Jax turned on the hose full blast. He pointed it at the Carroway house, then the neighboring house, alternating pelting at the flames with a stream that was about as useful as a water pistol. The fire had spread to the Carroways' kitchen, and the house next door was going to lose its screened-in porch. Jax couldn't even reach the other houses with this hose. "Riley!" he yelled. Why wasn't he coming out?

A car hurtled into view, barreling out of a side street and skidding sideways before screeching to a halt. The driver's door flew open, and Jax recognized the man who leaped out as Mr. Carroway's son. "Are my parents in there?" he shouted.

"I don't know!" Jax sprayed the house with his hose.

Carroway Jr. dashed up the porch steps and encountered Riley coming out with Mrs. Carroway in his arms. Riley called out directions to the newcomer then staggered down the steps to the ground. Jax dropped the hose and helped Riley lower the old woman to the grass. She was choking and struggling for air.

"Those barbarians stuffed them into a bathroom with no window and barricaded the door." Riley's voice was hoarse. "Jax, you gotta help." He unzipped his jean jacket, fumbling out a bundle of cloth—no, *a baby*—wrapped in a wet towel. "Is he breathing?"

"Crap!" gasped Jax. *Is he breathing? He's blue!* Jax had never held a baby in his life, but he snatched the infant out of Riley's hands. Laying the little body flat on the ground, he opened the baby's clothes and felt along his breastbone. *Two fingers, quick compressions, thirty of them.* He tipped the baby's chin up and enclosed the tiny nose and mouth with his own lips. *Two breaths, one second each. Back to compressions.*

He was on his second round of chest compressions before he understood *why* he knew how to do this. In phys ed last year, while running laps as slowly as his gym teacher would allow, Jax had amused himself by surveying the posters hanging on the gymnasium walls. *CPR. Heimlich. First Aid.* He hadn't realized he'd absorbed the information until now.

Carroway Jr. returned, carrying his father. Jax saw blood on the old man's face, but he was coughing and therefore breathing. Jax kept his attention on the person who was not.

Thirty compressions. Two breaths.

The baby twitched. His chest expanded on its own, and he began to cry.

"Attaboy, Jax!" Riley clapped him on the shoulder. "I knew you'd know what to do."

Jax gulped. "*I* didn't know I knew." Mrs. Carroway held out her arms, and Jax lifted the baby awkwardly. Now that he was crying and wiggling, Jax was afraid to pick him up.

Carroway Jr. pulled off his shirt and made his father press it against his head wound. "I'm going back in, to check upstairs," he said, standing. Riley stood, too.

"No, don't," Mrs. Carroway said, reaching out toward her son. "The children are gone."

A fire-truck horn blared then, low and loud, and a pumper tanker sped up the street. It was brand new, shiny, and probably full of so many computerized systems and gauges that it shouldn't have worked at all on the eighth day. But Deidre stood in the cab, her hands on the dashboard, willing it with her talent to do its job. A.J. steered and blew the horn, even though there was no one to get out of the way and no one to warn.

Jax didn't blame A.J. He would've blown the horn, too.

To put out all six fires they had to drain the tank and hook up to the hydrants. Riley, A.J., and Carroway Jr. handled the hoses, while Jax operated the switches on top of the fire engine—flipping the correct ones with talent and adrenaline instead of conscious decision. Deidre treated the old couple and the baby with oxygen, bandaged Mr. Carroway's head, and occasionally coaxed an electronic switch into working. Stink ran around underfoot and managed not to get trampled.

As soon as he found a spare second, Jax took a blanket out of the medical supplies and covered the dead Kin woman's body. He really didn't want to approach her again, but the Carroways were weak and injured, everybody else was busy, and he owed her that bit of dignity. Even though it made him cry a little when he did it.

When the fires were out, they broke into the houses that had been in danger. "Is this what you call adding insult to injury?" Jax asked, as Riley kicked in a front door.

"Can't be helped," Riley said. "Check every room. Don't leave anything smoldering that could reignite after we leave. Open the windows to make sure the smoke clears."

"The people will be okay, right?" Jax asked.

"They weren't here when their houses were filled with smoke, and by the time they reappear, the smoke should be gone. Hopefully, everyone is okay." But all six houses had inexplicable fire damage—blackened siding, burned roofs, warped doors, verandas reduced to kindling, and screened-in porches gutted. Riley didn't say it, but Jax knew that if any of these homeowners had been out of bed on Wednesday at midnight, watching late-night TV in their sunroom or admiring the stars from the veranda, they were likely dead despite Riley and A.J.'s best efforts.

Jax took a deep breath. "Mrs. Carroway said Addie was here with them."

Riley had started up the stairs to check the second floor, but he paused.

"She *said* it wasn't Addie's fault," Jax went on. "Seems to me like everybody wants to excuse Addie. But when bad things happen, she's always in the thick of it." The security people killed at the Dulac building. The Morgans' planes. The attack on Evangeline through the scrying spell. And now this. Jax looked at Riley, hoping he had some reassurance to offer.

Instead, all Jax learned was that Riley couldn't duck his head and hide his feelings behind a curtain of long hair anymore. His opinion of Addie Emrys was very plain on his face.

13

JAX GOT ANOTHER RARE compliment from Riley after they left Deidre's plane that afternoon. "Good job today, squirt. Infant CPR, working those pump switches—that's some talent you've got."

"He'll be doing brain transplants next," said A.J.

"You can be my first case, soon as we find a donor." Jax yawned and fell immediately asleep in the back of A.J.'s truck. He was aware of Riley and A.J. talking in the front seat and Stink curled up under his arm. He dozed through their conversation for most of the ride but woke instantly when he heard A.J. say, "Uh-oh. Look who's coming."

Jax sat up, rubbing his eyes. They were about three miles from the cabin. Coming toward them was a familiar black Land Rover, the driver identifiable by her silver-blond hair.

Riley had decided that Evangeline should learn to drive, but recent events had kept them busy enough every

Grunsday that he'd only found time to give her one lesson. Today, however, Evangeline was apparently getting one from Mr. Crandall. As Jax watched, it seemed like Evangeline suddenly lost control of the SUV, which crossed the center line. A.J. hit the brakes. When Evangeline wrenched the vehicle sideways, threw open the door, and jumped out into the road, Jax realized she'd blocked them on purpose. She marched toward them, arms stiff at her sides, hands clenched into fists.

"Somebody's in trouble." A.J. sank down in his seat. "But I don't think it's me."

Stink didn't want to be involved either—or maybe he was honoring Riley's request to stay away from Jax's liege lady. He popped through the side of the truck, disappearing to wherever he went when he wasn't with Jax.

Riley heaved a sigh, opened the passenger door, and stepped out. Jax considered staying with A.J., but that was cowardly. He pushed Riley's vacant seat forward and climbed out.

"You left me!" Evangeline exclaimed.

Riley nodded. "I thought that was best."

To Jax's shock, she unsheathed the honor blade at her waist and offered it to Riley. "If you're going to go back to treating me like a prisoner, I'll return this right now."

It was the Pendragon dagger Riley had used since childhood. He'd sent it to Evangeline when she was in danger and then offered it to her permanently as a symbol of alliance between them. Riley made no move to take it back. "I thought you trusted me to make decisions on the seven days I can't consult you," he said.

"That doesn't include sticking me someplace and leaving me like baggage!"

"What happened?" Mr. Crandall demanded, walking up behind Evangeline. "You two smell like smoke."

Riley told them the whole story. Evangeline cringed, and Mr. Crandall shook his head angrily. "Do the Carroways need a safe place to stay?" he asked.

"They went to their son's home," Riley said. "And took the baby with them."

Evangeline lowered the dagger, but didn't put it away. "Was Addie with the Llyrs?"

Riley nodded. "If we'd arrived any earlier, we would have run into them there. If you'd been with us, they could have captured you."

She stiffened. "Or maybe I could have rescued my sister."

"No." Riley didn't even consider it. "They went to Vermont for an oracle from that Kin woman and killed her in a fit of temper. And they still got what they wanted after she was dead, because they have an Arawen with them. They're *barbaric*, Evangeline. Incredibly powerful and without any morals. I shouldn't have brought Jax."

"Hey!" Jax protested.

Riley looked at him. "You were great. You know you

were. But I'm responsible for you, and it was a bigger risk than I realized. I'm not afraid to die," he said, turning back to Evangeline. "But I don't want to die stupidly. We can't confront these people without an army backing us up."

Evangeline had gone from flushed to pale. "I'd prefer you avoid dying."

"Well, yeah, me too." Riley looked at his old dagger in her hand. "Can we go to the house and talk about this?"

She turned on her heel and stalked back to the Land Rover. Mr. Crandall started to follow, but Evangeline slammed the driver's door closed, put the car in reverse, and made the worst three-point-turn Jax had ever seen. Tires squealed as the SUV lurched down the road.

"Guess I'm riding with you." When Mr. Crandall saw Riley staring unhappily after Evangeline, he gripped his liege lord by the back of his neck and shook him fondly. "Give her time to cool off, son. She's a smart girl. She'll find a way to back down while still claiming she was right. Trust me on this."

When they got back to the cabin, the Land Rover was parked crookedly beside the house, and Mrs. Crandall met them at the door. "She's in the kitchen," Mrs. Crandall said. "Blade on the table." Riley nodded grimly.

Evangeline was sitting at the table with the Pendragon blade in front of her—which Jax guessed meant that she was still ticked. She was threatening to end her alliance with Riley, but would she really? *I hope she's bluffing, because what am I supposed to do if she walks out?* Jax thought.

Riley took a chair across from her, looking miserable. He laid Excalibur beside his old blade. Jax remembered a previous meeting like this one and brought his own dagger out to join the others. This was a formal meeting between the Pendragon and Emrys clans. Alliances and loyalties were literally on the table and under review. Jax sat beside Evangeline. Riley was . . . well, Riley was like a brother to him. But Evangeline was Jax's liege.

"I know you did what you thought was right," Evangeline said, opening the conversation. "But that's *my sister* in the hands of barbarians with no morals. If it was your sister, how would you feel if I left you behind?"

"I'd be furious," Riley admitted.

"If I'm going to trust you making decisions for me, seven days out of eight, I need to have faith that if there's any chance in the future of getting to my sister—seeing her, contacting her, rescuing her, *anything*—you'll include me."

"If the risk is too great . . ."

"Risk?" Evangeline interrupted him. "You mean like when you delivered yourself bound and gagged to the pyramid so Wylit could sacrifice you? Risk like that? How about when you ran full tilt at a wyvern to rescue Billy? That wasn't a risk?"

Riley heaved a sigh. "Okay, I see your point. I'm sorry."

Evangeline lowered her confrontational glare. "I also hear I've joined a Transitioner council in the past week and agreed to provide them with information on my father's plot."

"That was me," Jax spoke up. "I promised that. I'm sorry if I was wrong."

"I can't defend or excuse what he did. I'll tell you whatever I can." She looked at Riley. "But your family participated in the attack on my home, didn't they? You must already know most of it."

Jax gasped out loud and looked back and forth between the two of them. Riley had told him that Evangeline's father was "stopped" before he could succeed in breaking the Eighth Day Spell, and Jax had rightly interpreted "stopped" to mean "killed." But he hadn't known the Pendragons were the ones to do it. Riley looked even more miserable, if possible. "There never seemed to be a good time to bring that up," he said. "I didn't know if you knew or not."

"I never got a good look at the Transitioners. My mother told me to take Addie and Elliot and run, and that's what I did," Evangeline said. "But when we were on the pyramid, Wylit made a comment about your father as if they'd met and fought one another. I guessed he probably meant that day."

"Wylit lost track of the years," Riley said. "It was my

grandfather he met, not my father. And for the record, my grandfather wanted to take everyone alive."

Evangeline stared at the table. "My father would never have surrendered."

Nobody spoke for a moment, and Jax squirmed uncomfortably. There wasn't anything they *could* say. Riley couldn't apologize for things that had happened before he was born, any more than Evangeline could apologize for her father being a traitor.

"What do you want to know?" Evangeline asked finally.

"Who the conspirators were," Riley said. "You told me Dr. Morder said he was working with people who were in on your father's plan. Can you give me names? We know some."

Evangeline listed the names of Kin families that had been working with her father. Riley recognized many of them. "We know about the Aerons," he said. "I don't know why they weren't locked up in Oeth-Anoeth with the Llyrs fifteen hundred years ago."

"They switched sides," Evangeline said dryly. "That's what my father told me. The Aerons were spared because they helped Merlin at the end."

Riley grunted and made a face, as if he thought Merlin's judgment had been lacking. "What about Mathonwy? I'm not familiar with that name."

"He wasn't very important. I remember my father

saying he was included only because he had money."

Riley sat up. "Money?"

"Yes, a lot of Normal money. That's the Mathonwy talent—prosperity. Is it important?"

"Somebody bankrolled the military strike on Oeth-Anoeth. The Llyrs are traveling in a plane, and the Dulacs took Addie from a Hummer. This might be the connection we were missing."

"Is that the treasure mentioned in the prophecy—money?" Jax asked. Mrs. Carroway had heard the prophecy the Llyrs got from the dead woman, but she'd been so upset she didn't remember much of it.

"No," said Evangeline. "That must refer to the Treasures of the *Tuatha Dé Danann*." When Jax looked blank, she explained, "It means 'the tribe of gods' or 'the Kin' in the old language. The four Treasures were the Cauldron, the Spear, the Sword, and the Stone."

Jax's eyebrows shot up. "The sword in the stone? When Arthur pulled Excalibur out of a stone and was named rightful king of Britain?"

Riley rolled his eyes. "No, Jax. That's a Disney movie." Jax made a face back at him. How was he supposed to tell which legends were real and which ones weren't?

"The four Treasures are magic artifacts," Evangeline explained, "brought from four Kin cities in our ancient home in the North Sea. The Cauldron of Dagda was destroyed long ago, but my father obtained the Sword of

Nuadu and the Stone of Fal." She looked at Riley. "I suppose you know what became of them . . . afterward."

"I do. They're safe." Riley didn't offer any more information than that.

"So," said Jax, "your father was going to use these items to break the Eighth Day Spell? Like Wylit tried to do with Excalibur and that mummy?" Wylit had gathered ancient relics to reinforce his spell, including King Arthur's honor blade and the mummified body of Niviane Dulac.

"My father didn't want to *break* the spell. Trying and failing to destroy it could kill the caster. That's how my brother died." Evangeline paused, then blinked and cleared her throat before going on. "My father was working on a *counterspell*. Something to reverse the effects of the Eighth Day Spell the way an antidote counteracts a poison."

"O-kay," Jax said cautiously. "Is that a big difference?"

"A counterspell might not work, but it won't backfire and kill everyone involved. It'll just fail. Do either of you know how the Eighth Day Spell was originally constructed?"

"I only vaguely know," Riley admitted. "Niviane conceived it. Merlin cast it. Arthur commanded it to stick. That's what I was taught."

"Niviane Dulac imagined a reality where the Kin were confined in a separate timeline," said Evangeline. "She planted that memory in the minds of everyone participating, causing them to *believe* it was true. Merlin Emrys cast a Spell of Making, which creates reality from belief. Arthur Pendragon commanded the universe to obey, and all of his vassals, allies, and peers threw the power of their talents behind his command."

"Wow," said Jax, picturing it.

"My father wanted to cast a counterspell that would stitch the eighth day back into the other seven, negating the original spell and releasing the Kin," Evangeline went on. "He was trying to learn the Spell of Making, which only a few spell casters have ever mastered, and he wanted the Treasures to magnify his power."

"How did brownies get stuck in the eighth day with the Kin?" Jax asked suddenly. Evangeline looked at him in surprise. "They are, aren't they? I've never seen one outside the eighth day except when the Dulacs had them trapped in a warded cage."

"Magical animals like brownies, kobolds, wyverns, and unicorns ended up enclosed in the separate timeline. I don't know if it was accidental, or if Niviane did it intentionally. Maybe she meant to stick all nuisances and pests with the Kin."

"Unicorns," repeated Jax. "Really." *Is she kidding?*

"The big magical animals died out pretty quickly," she said in complete seriousness.

"I'm not sure brownies *are* trapped," Riley put in. "You don't normally see them outside the eighth day, but my sister thought they could go anywhere they wanted. Being outside the eighth day causes them discomfort, though, or messes with their magic. If they were being held captive in the seven-day timeline, they were probably in a lot of distress. No wonder they dumped a wyvern on the Dulacs."

"I have *never* heard of that happening before. I had no idea something could be brought from that far in the past." Evangeline pushed her chair back from the table as if ready to conclude this meeting. "I wouldn't wish a wyvern on anyone," she said, "but I have to admit I wouldn't mind seeing Sloane Dulac infested with kobolds."

Riley snorted. "Me either."

Jax didn't know what a kobold was, but Evangeline's attempt to end the discussion with a joke, even one directed at Sloane, seemed forced.

Riley waved a hand at the honor blades on the table. "Are we good?"

She nodded stiffly. They stood up and reached for their respective daggers. Jax watched them while pretending not to. Evangeline didn't look directly at Riley, and Riley made sure not to touch her hand when picking up Excalibur.

It didn't seem to Jax that they were "good" at all.

14

SOMEONE KNOCKED ON THE bedroom door while Jax was changing clothes. He pulled a T-shirt over his head before answering, knowing it had to be Evangeline. Riley or A.J. would've come in, since all three of them were sharing this cabin room, and Mr. or Mrs. Crandall would've called to him from outside.

"Hey," he said when he opened the door. "Still mad at me?"

"I wasn't mad at *you*." Evangeline gave him a hug. "I hear you saved lives today."

"No big deal. It's what we do, right?" But he couldn't suppress his grin.

"It *is* a big deal." She let go of him. "Do you have my sister's letter? Mrs. Crandall thought you did, but when I looked for it earlier . . ." Evangeline made a face at the room.

Jax looked around. With the three of them jammed in here, it was kind of a mess.

Okay, mess was an understatement. *Disaster zone* might've been better.

"I don't have it, but I think I know where it is." He located Riley's duffel bag and started rummaging through it. Luckily, Riley was such a slob, he hadn't unpacked the bag since last week. The letter was still at the bottom. "Here," Jax said, handing it over.

Evangeline's eyes were on the duffel bag. "I see," she said coldly. "Riley had it."

"I'm sure he just hasn't had a chance to give it back to you."

She lowered her voice. "I need you to do something else for me—and tell no one. Get me saffron before next week."

Jax hesitated. "Are you sure it's safe to try again?"

"I won't be caught off guard now that I know they can strike at me through the spell." When Jax didn't immediately agree to her request, Evangeline said stiffly, "As your liege, I'm requiring this."

That hurt. She hadn't ever given him an order before. "I'll do it. But why don't you want me to tell anyone?"

"There's no saffron in this house, and Mrs. Crandall refused to get any for me. She said Riley decided there would be no more scrying. He doesn't have the right to make that decision, Jax, and I won't stand for it."

Jax sighed. Maybe Riley *hadn't* just forgotten to give Addie's letter back. This friction between his liege lady and his guardian was making him more and more uncomfortable. "He's trying to keep you safe, you know."

"I realize that, but our goals aren't aligned right now. I would do anything to rescue my sister. *Anything.* He doesn't get to choose for me. I'm his ally, not one of his vassals. He's so used to ordering people around, he tends to forget that."

"I thought you were also his girlfriend. Right?" It was none of Jax's business, but he could hardly help but notice . . .

She looked at Jax sadly. "I guess so. For now. Until he ages past me and decides he'd rather be with a Transitioner."

Jax gaped at her. Yes, Evangeline lived on a different timeline from the rest of them, growing only one year older for every seven of theirs, but did she really think Riley would let that stop them from being together? He hadn't said anything, but Jax was pretty sure he knew what Riley was planning to do about that problem.

Evangeline wiped the sadness off her face and attempted a weak smile. "Anyway, it still doesn't give him the right to tell me what to do." She poked Jax in the chest with her index finger. "Best you learn that now, Jax!"

He held up both hands innocently. Right. No bossing around a girlfriend. If he ever got one. "I'll score some saffron for you," he promised. "And I'll help you do the scrying, too. Figuring out Addie's location before Sheila Morgan finds the enemy hideout is still our best chance at getting your sister out of the way of a preemptive strike."

Evangeline froze. "*What* preemptive strike?"

Jax's mouth went dry. *Oh, heck. Nobody told her.* "If Sheila's people find out where the Llyrs are hiding, she . . . uh . . . plans to attack them during the seven-day time-line. To incapacitate them, not annihilate . . ." Jax knew that distinction was pointless. He hadn't felt any comfort when Sheila had said it to *him.* And watching Evangeline tremble at the news made him feel even worse.

"Riley told me nothing about this," Evangeline finally said.

"Well, he voted against it, but—"

"*Voted* against it," she repeated. "How good of him." White lipped, with her hand clenched around Addie's let-ter, Evangeline turned on her heel and stalked toward the stairs, no doubt planning to confront Riley on yet another breach of trust.

"He probably didn't want you to worry!" Jax called after her, knowing it was a lame excuse. She didn't answer or look back, and Jax closed his bedroom door and banged his head against it repeatedly. *Stupid, stupid, stupid. I just made everything worse!*

But realistically, what was Riley supposed to do? Yeah, he should've told Evangeline, but he didn't have the power to defy the Morgans and the Dulacs and everyone else who'd voted for this at the Table. Riley's resources consisted of three vassals—four, when you counted Billy—and not much else. Even if Evangeline and Jax secretly scried for Addie against Riley's wishes and uncovered a clue to her whereabouts, they had no way to communicate with her, no way to reach her . . .

And suddenly, it hit him.

There *was* a way to reach her.

Jax shot off an email seconds after midnight, as soon as his computer started working again. A few hours later, he had an answer. Jax figured that when a kid was grounded for thirty years, he had a lot of time to hang out on the computer checking email. And if he was secretly experimenting with brownie tunnels, like Dorian was, he had extra time.

Jax asked his cousin to join him in a video chat very early Thursday morning, before the other residents of the cabin were up and about. Dorian looked different from the last time Jax had seen him. He wasn't wearing his school uniform, and his thick hair, the same dark brown as Jax's, was sticking up at the front of his head. "Hey, Jax," Dorian said with a grin.

"Hey, Dorian. How's Lesley?"

His cousin's smile wavered. "Not that great, really. She still has nightmares. And she's cranky. Moody. Won't talk to me. Slams the door in my face when I ask what's wrong."

Jax felt a surge of protectiveness. "Is your dad starting up with her again?" Dorian's sister was the only one of Jax's long-lost relatives he'd liked at first. He'd warmed up to Dorian eventually, but Lesley was different. She'd never transitioned, wasn't marked with her family tattoo, and had no magical talent. Uncle Finn had been trying to "cure" her—first with brownie tunnels and then with blood magic—but his experiments had been nothing but torture for her.

Dorian shook his head. "Dad's way too busy helping Sloane with clan business to bother Lesley. I dunno. Maybe it's just normal for girls."

Jax thought about Tegan, who practically defined *cranky* and *moody*. "Yeah, maybe. So, what'd you find in Dr. Morder's notes? Have you learned how to work the brownie tunnels?"

"Well, I've learned a few things. Turns out, Dr. Morder didn't invent the spell that allows humans access. He told us he did, but really he found it in some ancient writings. I've got the original source here, but I can only read the part he translated." Dorian bent over and started moving stuff around on his desk.

Jax leaned closer to the screen. Was that— Yes! Dorian was using hair gel. His hair was spiked on purpose. *Aunt Marian must be having a cow.*

"See?" Dorian held up a book written in some

incomprehensible language. Then he frowned. "What are you grinning about?"

"Nothing," Jax said quickly. "Have you learned anything from his notes?"

"Morder was trying to figure out the rules of object permanence outside of time. You know how from inside the tunnels you can see furniture and buildings, but not people? Well, you also can't see objects that move around a lot, like cars or iPads or shoes. Movable objects *do* become visible if they stay in one spot long enough, though. *How long* varies; it can be a couple days or up to a week. I've been experimenting with different objects in my bedroom. The problem is preventing Mom from moving them when she dusts . . ."

"Fascinating," said Jax, although he had no interest in *object permanence*. "Did you find out anything about using the tunnels to jump to a new location, the way brownies do?"

"Sure, but some of it I already knew." There was a hint of showing off in Dorian's voice. "Tunnels are like runways for brownies, used for takeoff and landing. That's a simile. Jumping for brownies is like flying for planes."

"I got it, Dorian."

"There are more tunnels in our building than there should be, thanks to your dad having a pet brownie when he lived here. It was in and out of everybody's garbage, which explains most of the upstairs tunnels. The tunnel in the basement leading from the lab to Central Park was made by the brownies Morder experimented on. Every time he released some, they used that tunnel to escape. But Morder couldn't figure out why that tunnel was so much longer than the others—why the brownies took so long to jump."

"Well, I know that." Jax could show off, too. "It's because their magic was messed up from being held in the seven-day timeline. It must've been harder for them to jump, and they needed a longer runway."

"Ya think?" Dorian made a note in Morder's notebook. "Awesome."

"But Dorian . . ." Jax wasn't getting the information he wanted. "*How* do you jump from place to place?"

"Concentration," Dorian said, looking up. "Focus on where you want to go, like we did when we were moving through time. Except, I guess our brains aren't wired like brownies' brains, because I don't usually land where I'm aiming."

"Oh." That was bad news.

"The first time I tried it, I wanted to reach the room where my dad was holding Addie, but I landed in Riley's cell—maybe because Addie's was warded. The other day, I was aiming for Central Park, but I ended up outside my favorite restaurant in Chinatown."

"So, it's random."

"Well, I *was* hungry."

"Anything else I need to know?"

"Yeah. The brownie holes are made when brownies jump in or out of real time. We can use them, but we can't make our own. The time I was trying to reach Addie, the tunnel spit me out in Riley's cell and closed up behind me. I got stuck there. So if you're planning to try this, you've got to be careful or you might end up stranded wherever you land."

"Unless I take a brownie with me."

Dorian's eyes narrowed. "What are you planning, Jax?"

"I'll tell you if it works."

"What if it doesn't work?" Dorian pointed a finger at him in warning. "Don't make me have to come rescue you, cuz."

Jax grinned. "Bye, Dorian." He logged off and sat back in his chair, thinking.

Brownies.

Glorified rats, Deidre had called them. Transitioners and Kin alike viewed them as pests and nuisances but didn't normally think of brownie holes as a security risk or an entryway for intruders.

However, Dr. Morder's experiments for the Dulac clan had granted certain families access to the tunnels, like the Dulacs and the Ambroses. Jax's talent had branched off from the Ambrose family, but he was closely enough related that he shared their access to the brownie holes. And because Dr. Morder had been planning to smuggle Addie out of the Dulac building by way of those tunnels, *she could use them, too.*

If Stink could help Jax track Addie down, he should be able to snatch her right out of Llyr hands.

15

JAX TOLD NO ONE his idea.

First of all, Riley would *hate* it because he couldn't come along—or go in Jax's place. Riley wasn't able to enter the brownie tunnels, but he was perfectly capable of commanding Jax not to because it was dangerous.

As for Evangeline—Jax was torn. Obviously, she was the best person to convince her sister to climb into a magical tunnel. But as far as Jax knew, something like this had never been done before. Evangeline had used the tunnels to get in and out of the Dulac building, but she didn't know humans could jump like brownies to a different location. Jax had never done it, and Dorian, who had, admitted he rarely landed where he meant to. Jax wasn't sure he could get to Addie even with Stink's help, let alone take Evangeline with him. Plus, he'd be jumping into the enemy's stronghold. He didn't want to accidentally hand Evangeline over to the Llyrs!

He had to try this alone. If he ended up having to come back for Evangeline's assistance after he'd scoped out the situation, so be it. But first he had to *find* Addie.

That was when he realized how short-sighted he'd been. Stink was going to need something belonging to Addie to find her. He'd tracked down Jax with socks. Addie's letter would probably serve the same purpose, but Evangeline must have kept it on her person, because Jax couldn't find it. He searched her room, which was nothing more than a large closet under the stairs. It felt weird, checking her sleeping bag and under her pillow while she was sleeping there—or rather, while she *had been* sleeping there and *would be* again. Jax had never figured out a verb tense for expressing Evangeline's state of existence between Grunsdays.

"Looking for something?"

Jax jumped when he heard Riley's voice, banging his head on the low, slanted ceiling. Sheepishly, he backed out of the closet. "Yeah, I was looking for . . ." Dang it. Evangeline didn't *have* anything. The girl literally had no possessions.

Luckily, Riley didn't wait for him to finish the sentence. He held up his cell phone with one hand clasped over the microphone. "Call for you. Calvin Bedivere."

For me? Jax mouthed, pointing at his own chest. Riley nodded and handed him the phone, then stood with his tattooed arms crossed, obviously planning to listen in. "Uh, hello, Mr. Bedivere?" Jax said hesitantly.

"Hello, Aubrey," the man on the other end of the phone said. "I understand that the children we were expecting to house have regrettably fallen into the hands of the enemy."

"Yeah," Jax said mournfully. "We were too late."

"Very unfortunate, but it proves Riley Pendragon was right. The Llyrs are recruiting their own kind, and it would behoove us to provide sanctuary for as many neutral Kin as we can convince to trust us. Certain properties have been prepared—mostly vacation condos that were vacant and suitable for this purpose. I promised that you and your liege lady could inspect the premises, and I *would* like to meet her in person. She may have thoughts on how best to approach Kin who desire a safe house but are wary of Transitioners."

Jax put his hand over the microphone and whispered to Riley. "Is it safe for Evangeline to meet him?" Riley nodded. Jax removed his hand. "That's a good idea, Mr. Bedivere. But my liege lady will come with Riley. I'd just be in the way." Riley narrowed his eyes at Jax.

"Very well. Shall we say ten a.m. on the next eighth day?"

"Sounds good." Jax ended the call and handed the phone back.

"I know what you're up to," Riley said.

"Uh, you do?" Jax doubted it. Riley would look a lot angrier if he did.

"Me going alone with Evangeline isn't going to patch things up between us."

As Jax had feared, his spilling the beans about the Table vote had precipitated another argument between Riley and Evangeline. This one had been private—no blades on the table or anything—but apparently emotional. Jax had spotted Evangeline afterward with reddened eyes and a splotchy complexion, like she'd been crying. And Riley had taken off noisily on his motorcycle to blow off steam or sulk or whatever guys did after fighting with their girl-friends. Sending them together to Bedivere's might not be a bad idea. "Why not?" Jax urged. "You could take her on your motorcycle, maybe bring a picnic basket and make a date out of it." *Apologize for keeping secrets from her—and tell her about your plan for staying together, you big dummy.*

Riley stalked away, muttering, "It'd be pitiful if I had to take advice from an eighth grader." But he didn't say he wasn't going to try it, which was all Jax needed to know. Sure, he really hoped Riley and Evangeline made up. But more importantly right now, Jax wanted them out of his way on Grunsday.

Over the course of the next few days, Riley and Jax received updates sent by Sheila Morgan to all the Table members regarding the search for the Llyr hideout. Deidre didn't think the enemy plane had spotted hers, so there was no reason to believe the flight path she'd seen them on had been a diversion. The plane had been too far away to identify their heading with precision, but the Morgans were concentrating their search in northern Vermont, New Hampshire, Maine, and Canada, especially in remote mountainous and wooded areas where a group of Kin could escape detection.

Other Transitioners had thrown their resources into the effort, too, and Jax had a bad feeling that time was running out. If the Morgans found that plane—or any of the others involved in the Oeth-Anoeth prison break—they'd bomb the site. Addie would be killed, and there was nothing Jax or Riley could do to stop it from happening.

Meanwhile, Jax acquired the saffron Evangeline wanted and wondered what he would do if Stink didn't show up next Grunsday. He didn't have a way to summon the brownie. He wasn't even sure he could convey his wishes to Stink, or if Stink would comply. The brownie clearly felt an affinity to Jax, but Riley was the only one he obeyed. How smart was he? Like, service-dog smart? Or signing-chimpanzee smart?

Jax was also worried about the children stolen from the Carroway house. If he successfully located Addie, he could smuggle her away from the Llyrs via the brownie tunnels, but he wouldn't be able to take any of the other children. That bothered him a lot, but maybe if he could save Addie, she would have information for Transitioner forces that would help them capture the Llyrs without unnecessary deaths.

It seemed like a long shot, but it was the best hope those kids had.

An unexpected gift arrived on Wednesday afternoon, when Riley's phone started buzzing on the dresser while Riley was in the shower. Jax checked the text in case it was urgent.

Billy: FOUND THEM!!!!! CALL ME

Jax gasped. *No way* could Billy Ramirez, working on the internet, have located the Llyrs. But Billy wouldn't waste the caps-lock key on nothing. Jax went into the hallway to make sure Riley was still in the shower, then took the phone downstairs and out the front door, punching in Billy's contact number.

"Hey, dude. It's Jax. Riley can't talk right now, so he asked me to call you back. What's up? You didn't really find these guys, did you?"

"I *so* did. I have stuff to send Riley. Does he still not have email?"

"Yeah, he's like from the Dark Ages," Jax said. "Send it to me."

"Done!" Billy proclaimed. "Jax, I got 'em. I know I got 'em."

"By looking up elves and vampires?"

"By looking up the paranormal, the supernatural, and the weird. After what happened in Vermont, Riley told me to focus on the northeast U.S. and Canada, and based on something Evangeline said, he mentioned that these Kin might have a lot of money. Those two things ended up being the final clues I needed to track them down."

"How?"

"Jax, you won't believe how many paranormal websites I've searched in the past three weeks. I mean, I love this stuff, but my brain was turning to mush. Then," Billy exclaimed, his voice rising in enthusiasm, "after Riley narrowed the search, I stumbled across a blog site called *Richie's Haunted New England*—"

"Billy. Really?"

"Don't knock it till you've looked at it! Anyway, there's a string of private islands off the coast of Maine owned by millionaires. One of them happens to have a single mansion, its own airfield, and a reputation for being haunted. The plane looks just like the one Riley described, and it's serviced by people who operate only from written instructions. One of the housekeepers was interviewed on the blog. No one ever sees the plane take off or land, even though the fuel gets used up. The housekeeper takes a ferry to the island every Thursday and cleans the house and delivers food, even though nobody lives there. Somebody eats the food, though."

Jax nodded, holding the phone to his ear. "Interesting . . ."

"More than *interesting*, Jax." Billy sounded very sure of himself. "The island is owned by a company with a lot of properties—a company that's been around a long time, under a lot of different names, going back practically to the Mayflower. They own suppliers of military equipment! Guns, helicopters, planes!"

Now Jax's heart was racing. *Unbelievable*. Billy had done what the Morgans hadn't been able to do—on his computer—through pure geekiness, perseverance, and a willingness to read through a lot of weird crap. "You sent me an email with what you've got?"

"Pictures of the island, links to the paranormal website, stuff I dug up on the company . . . You'll give it to Riley?"

"Right away."

"Tell him to call me back."

Jax hesitated. Billy wanted Riley's praise, of course. But what would Riley do with the information? Fulfill his duty as a member of the Table and hand it off to the Morgans? Or withhold the information until he came up with a plan to "extract" Addie on his own?

Jax had no doubt that Sheila could send a military team to that island before the end of Wednesday to do whatever she thought most prudent—no matter if Addie and other innocent Kin children were killed in the process. He was less sure how Riley would manage to get himself to an island in Maine without the help of Deidre's numerous and convenient modes of transport, let alone what kind of action he'd take to pluck Addie and the orphans out of the Llyrs' hands. Time was of the essence. The Morgans had concentrated their search in remote areas first, assuming that the Llyrs would be *hiding*—not living blatantly in a mansion on a private island. Eventually, though, the Morgans would find this island even without Billy's tip. The time advantage Jax had was short.

Riley knew his limitations. *I don't want to die stupidly,* he'd said. *We can't confront these people without an army backing us up.* But if the Morgans killed Addie on information Riley gave them, Evangeline would never forgive him.

"I'll tell him, Billy," Jax said finally, "but he's going to want to jump on this right away. If you don't hear from him, it's because he's figuring out a plan. I'll keep you informed, but I might not be able to get back to you till Thursday."

"Dang. I hate being a Normal," said Billy. "Tell Riley to be careful. You too, dude."

"I will." Jax ended the call and deleted the text. He got into the settings and blocked Billy's number in case he tried to call back. Then he put the phone back on Riley's dresser where he'd found it.

I'm taking the decision away from you, bro. You can thank me later.

16

ON GRUNSDAY MORNING, JAX waylaid Evangeline as soon as she woke up. She came out of her closet-bedroom yawning and rubbing her eyes, wearing shorts and an old T-shirt of Riley's. Seeing her dressed like that, with the too-large shirt hanging almost to her knees, reminded Jax of something he couldn't put his finger on.

"What's happened?" she asked when she spotted Jax waiting for her. "Did Sheila Morgan find them? Did she—"

"No!" Jax quickly reassured her, the fragment of memory gone. "The Morgans haven't found the Llyrs." That was literal truth. The Morgans hadn't found them. Billy had. Jax couldn't lie to his liege, but he could leave out a detail here and there. "I just wanted to let you know there's been no bombings or anything and give you a heads-up about your day." He explained about the meeting she and Riley had with Bedivere. Then he handed her a packet of saffron. Evangeline reached under the hem of her shirt and slipped the container into her shorts pocket. Jax heard the crinkle of paper from something already in there. Addie's letter. Which explained why he hadn't found it while she was absent.

"I was thinking," he said. "Maybe you should split up the last pages of that letter. Give one to me rather than keep it all in one place."

Evangeline frowned. "Why? Was *he* looking for it?"

"No," Jax said quickly, not wanting to get Riley in even more trouble. "*I* was. It's all you have of Addie. We don't want anything bad to happen to it."

She eyed him skeptically. "I know what you're doing, Jax. You want to try the scrying spell on your own."

Jax sighed. Nobody seemed to take him at his word these days, but at least they weren't guessing his real purpose. "I won't waste it. I promise."

"It's not that. But I know how to be on guard against another attack, and you—"

"I can be on guard, too. You said my sensitivity for information would make me good at this, and if there's any sign of danger, I'll break the connection." Still, she hesitated, so he added, "I can try while you and Riley are out this morning. We'll tag-team her and wear her out."

With a sigh, Evangeline removed the letter from her pocket. "There's only one page left. Good thing Addie's such a complainer, or we'd have run out before now." Then she frowned. "This meeting with Bedivere and Riley. Why aren't you coming?"

Jax stuck to the story Riley believed. "Well, after last week's . . . *disagreement*, I thought you two might like some alone time. To, uh, *make up*, if you know what I mean."

"Oh, Jax!" Evangeline smacked his arm with Addie's letter. But she also blushed and didn't try to convince him to come with them. Just like Riley hadn't.

Instead, she gave him half the remaining page of the letter and cautioned him to be careful—twice. Jax promised he would and folded the half sheet into his pocket.

When Stink hadn't shown up by the time Riley and Evangeline left for their meeting, Jax started getting worried. He considered jumping on his own, but if Dorian couldn't reliably land in the park across the street, how was Jax supposed to make it all the way to New England?

Then he heard a commotion in the kitchen—the sound of a metal bowl hitting the floor and Mrs. Crandall shouting. Jax heaved a sigh of relief and ran toward the noise. Stink scampered out of the kitchen just a few steps ahead of Mrs. Crandall's broom. "Jax! Your brownie chewed a hole through the window screen!"

Jax smacked himself in the head for being so stupid. Stink couldn't jump into the cabin via brownie tunnels. The house was warded against magical intruders, just like

Addie's cell in the Dulac basement had been.

Stink sprang from the floor, caught the front of Jax's shirt, and climbed to his shoulder. "I'll get him out of here," Jax said. "Maybe we'll go for a bike ride."

Mrs. Crandall made it clear she didn't care where he went, as long as he took Stink. With the brownie clinging to his shoulder, Jax pedaled out to the grounds of the neighboring ski resort, which was closed for the summer. He maneuvered around the barricades that blocked off the parking lot and coasted to the edge of ski trails that were knee deep in unmowed grass. A metal rack for stowing snowboards and skis made a handy place to lock up his bike. He pulled out the papers tucked into the back pocket of his jeans.

One was Addie's letter. The others he'd printed from Google Earth last night. He unfolded several aerial photographs of an island off the coast of Maine and spread them on the ground. There was a close-up view of the house on the island, its outbuildings, and the runway. Jax had been skeptical about Billy's find until he saw the airplane hangar with its white wooden siding. Painted white boards. That was the image Addie had used to block the scrying spell, right before Jax and Evangeline had been zapped with an electrical charge.

He'd also printed a zoomed-out view that showed the position of the island in relation to the mainland. He'd circled their present location in red marker and drawn a line out to the island. "Let's see how smart you are, Stink. We're *here*." Jax pointed. "And I need to go *there*. To this island and this house." He held up Addie's letter. "To find this girl."

Stink sat on his haunches and looked back and forth between Jax and the maps. He lifted up his smushed-in little face and rubbed it against Addie's letter like a cat. Then he bounded into the tall grass, gave a hop, and vanished.

"No, wait!" Jax stood up. "Not without me!"

Seconds later, Stink reappeared and scampered on all fours back to Jax. He'd just made a brand new hole at Jax's request.

Jax gathered up the printed photos and got down on hands and knees to enter the tunnel, which was little more than a pocket of magical *substance*. He could feel it pressing against him, crinkly, but soft and elastic. The world around him was visible through the translucent walls: the empty parking lot, the chair lifts, and the dormant snow-making equipment. When he looked for his bike, it wasn't there. As Dorian had said, the tunnel existed outside of time, and small changes in the environment didn't register right away.

Stink ran ahead, and the tunnel expanded. Jax followed, crawling on his hands and knees. The fabric of the tunnel stretched to make room for his body, and after a few yards, Jax paused. The tunnels in the Dulac building had been tall enough for an adult man even though they were created by creatures the size of Stink. Why? No sooner had he thought of the question than the answer came to him. *Because, before I ever entered them, Dr. Morder and Uncle Finn had already been through them.*

Jax stood up. The tunnel expanded to accommodate him, ending at a height and width just his size. *Ha! Right again!* Stink continued, creating several yards of tunnel in front of Jax. Then he doubled back and scrambled up to Jax's shoulder. Jax kept walking and stared at the photos in his hand. "I want to get to this island," he said, concentrating the way Dorian had told him to. "And this house. I want this tunnel to take me to—"

The world lurched and spun. His stomach clenched, the way it did on a roller coaster at the moment of weightlessness. But the moment went on and on, as if Jax were really falling. He staggered and fell up against . . .

. . . a metal trash can.

"Really, Stink? Don't you ever think about anything but food?" Jax looked around. He was standing between a white stucco wall and two trash cans—about fifty yards from a beach. The ocean was weirdly calm and silent, without the normal swooshing and crashing of waves or the call of seagulls. A wooden walkway led toward a dock in one direction and an airplane hangar and a runway in the other.

Jax glanced at the photos in his hand, stunned. He'd jumped from the mountains of Pennsylvania to an island off the coast of Maine in a couple seconds! But if this was *the* island, there would be dangerous Kin here. He ducked behind the trash cans. Juggling the papers in his hand, he held up Addie's letter. "We're looking for this girl, remember," he whispered to Stink.

Stink scampered along the wall toward a door and sat back on his haunches.

Open the door and walk right in? That didn't sound like a good plan. But Stink couldn't burrow in if the house was warded, and it must be. That was why Evangeline had failed so many times at scrying for Addie. The times they *had* glimpsed her location—Jax glanced down the path at the white-paneled hangar—she'd been outside the house.

He had to trust Stink. Jax stuffed all the papers into his back pocket, hurried along the unsheltered wall, and opened the door. Inside, he found a room filled with mops and brooms, a vacuum, and shelves of cleaning supplies. This was the housekeeper's entrance. Jax looked at Stink. Smartest. Pet. Ever.

But Stink remained on the stoop, pacing back and forth in agitation, chittering softly. "What's wrong?" Jax whispered. He glanced outside, but saw nothing to cause alarm. "We've gotten this far. Come on!"

At Jax's invitation, the brownie suddenly ceased his complaining and bounded over the threshold. With scarcely a pause, Stink began to burrow through the shelves and bottles of Windex as if they weren't there, and

Jax followed, marveling at the power this brownie tunnel access had given him. He had jumped across the country in the blink of an eye to a magically warded building, entered normally with the turn of a knob, and was now taking a path through the house that would leave him invisible to the residents. *Sheila Morgan was right,* Jax thought. *This has military potential.*

After passing through several walls and part of a kitchen, Jax glimpsed a huge living space with stone-tiled floors and white leather furniture. A wall of glass doors faced the placid sea. If there were Llyrs or other enemy Kin present, they were as invisible to him as he was to them. Brownie tunnels were undetectable to human eyes from the outside, and from the inside, people fell into the same category as Dorian's "movable objects." They didn't register. According to Billy, a cleaning service tidied this house every Thursday, so Jax was probably seeing this room the way the maids left it every week, not the way it looked today.

The only person Jax had ever seen outside a brownie tunnel while he was inside one was the Morrigan. Since she wasn't really a person as much as a force of nature—and presumably outside of time herself—it made a bizarre kind of sense.

An L-shaped staircase led to a second story, but Stink didn't take the stairs. He angled his burrowing upward, and the spongy substance of the tunnel left the floor of the house. Now Jax had trouble keeping up. There wasn't much purchase for his sneakers and nothing to hang on to. He scrabbled and struggled, and it was a relief when the tunnel leveled out inside a bedroom on the second floor.

Stink was gone by the time he got there. Jax looked around, but this room was as clean and tidy as a photograph in a magazine. Stink's head popped into sight at Jax's knee level. The brownie made his strange chittering noise, then backed out again. Jax took that to mean it was safe to exit, so he squatted down and pushed out of the hole.

In real time, the sheets on the bed were balled into a knot. There were sneakers on the floor. A small trash can was surrounded by crumpled, used tissues that had failed to make it inside—*eww*—and a canvas bag of clothes lay nearby. Stink hopped onto a bedside table and stood on his hind legs, puffing out his chest proudly. Jax grinned. This was Addie's room. He *knew* it.

A hairbrush on the table was full of silvery-blond hair that would be useful for future scrying if he didn't actually encounter Addie in person today. He pulled a few strands from the brush and tucked them into the little square pocket that was located inside the front pocket of every pair of jeans he'd ever owned. *Always wondered when I'd have a use for that!*

He looked around the room curiously. There was a ratty, stuffed bunny half hidden under a bed pillow. That surprised him. He hadn't known thirteen-year-old girls slept with stuffed animals, and it didn't fit his image of Evangeline's rebellious sister. He picked up the canvas bag on the floor. Besides the clothes, there were two paperbacks inside—Anne Frank's diary and *The Mists of Avalon*—and one old, illustrated hardback of *The Land of Oz.*

While he was searching the bag for anything else of interest, Stink leaped off the table without warning, streaked across the room, and jumped through the brownie hole. "What the—" Jax watched him go, then turned around.

The bedroom door opened. A girl took one step into the room and froze, her eyes growing wide. Jax found himself—*finally!*—face to face with Adelina Emrys.

And here he was, caught with an arm up to his elbow in her private possessions.

Crap.

17

WHEN ADDIE FELT THE lurch that signaled her jump over
seven days, she hugged Bunny tighter and curled into a ball
in the bed. She wanted to hide from the new day, or disappear, or better yet, never have been born with the burden of
being an Emrys.

Addie had done bad things in the past, but this time other
people had paid the consequences. She pressed her face into
the stuffed rabbit. Bunny still smelled of home.

"It was not your home," Bran had said to her last night.
"They were not your parents."

But the Carroways had been her parents for almost half
her life.

*Dale and Emma are dead because of me. And Aine.
Normal neighbors I never met. Aine's baby.*

They'd had to restrain Addie on the plane ride back from
Vermont. Madoc and Griffyn had duct-taped her wrists and
ankles to the seat and taped her mouth shut. Her treatment

had frightened the other children into silence—or at least into confining themselves to muffled whimpers. When the plane landed, the kids had been unloaded and passed into the hands of the Aeron clan. Addie, still bound to her chair, watched through the plane window as the Aerons celebrated their arrival—lifting the children into the air, putting them on their shoulders, and carting them off to Madoc's boat to be transported to another Mathonwy property. The Aerons were always eager to add to their clan, probably because they got themselves killed so often. And Bran Llyr, for all his talk of "future vassals," didn't seem to have much interest in taking charge of the children himself.

After supervising the boat launch, Madoc reboarded the plane, taxied it into the hangar, and left without speaking to Addie. She was beginning to think they were going to leave her tied to the plane seat for the rest of the day, when Bran finally reappeared. Addie refused to show any fear as he walked up the aisle. What could he do to her that was worse than what he'd already done? She glared at him defiantly when he stood over her, the restored Spear in his hand.

"A strong spirit is a good thing," Bran said. "Spirit is what enabled our people to survive Oeth-Anoeth."

With Addie bound and gagged as a captive audience, Bran launched into a lengthy description of life in the ancient Welsh fortress. They'd been cut off from the world, knowing only what their captors allowed them to know about modern civilization. Children were carefully matched at birth to preserve bloodlines, but after ten generations, most of the families had died out anyway. Only the lines of Llyr and Arawen had survived, and when Griffyn and Ysabel married, their children would've been the last.

"I admire spirit, Adelina. And stubbornness. And a will to survive," Bran said. "I do not object to these qualities in you. It's your loyalty that's in question."

At that, Addie squirmed furiously in her seat, trying to tell him off with her lips taped shut. Bran ripped the tape from her face. "You would've *had* my loyalty if you'd left my parents and my home alone!" she yelled at him, blinking away tears of pain.

That was when Bran pointed out that it wasn't her home and the Carroways weren't her parents. "They were Transitioners who suppressed your magical strength just as Oeth-Anoeth suppressed ours," Bran said. "They drained the spirit of every Kin they took into their house, calling them *refugees*, convincing them to hide and pretend not to exist. Those children would have been robbed of their potential and forced to live as shadows of their true selves."

Bran pivoted the Spear and slashed the head across the tape binding Addie's right ankle to the chair. It sliced through without cutting her flesh, but a white burst of magic as painful as fire ripped up her leg. Addie ground her teeth together. As Bran had told the Morrigan, only the rightful owner could handle this Kin artifact. Anyone else who came in contact with it was punished.

"We are in a battle for survival," Bran said. "The survival of our *race*, Adelina. Those Transitioners you mourn may have told you it was a war between good and evil, but it was always about power. Theirs. Ours. They won the last round and drove us to the brink of extinction." He eased the tip of the Spear through the tape on her other leg, taking his time.

Addie cringed away from the Spear, but pain lanced through her leg. "If that was what they wanted," she gasped, "why didn't the Carroways just kill me and the other refugees?"

"Because downtrodden slaves are useful," Bran replied. "An oracle is useful. A strong spell caster is useful. Weren't you eager to please the Transitioners who took you in after your true home was burned and your real parents slaughtered?" He directed the head of the Spear at her left wrist. Addie flinched but couldn't escape.

The pain wrenched a scream from her. There was no blood spilled, no mark on her skin, but the magic burned through her flesh. By the time her hand was free, she was drenched in sweat and trembling. She panted, eyeing the Spear and knowing he was going to use it one more time. "Why did Merlin cast the spell then?" She was going to get the punishment anyway; she might as well ask. "If it was always us against them, why did he side with *them*?"

"The house of Emrys and the house of Llyr were rivals," Bran said. "Merlin Emrys wanted to strengthen his own clan and allied himself with our enemies. His plan did not go as he wanted, and he was trapped, too. Don't believe the legends that say he *sacrificed himself.*"

That wasn't the way Addie had heard the story from the Carroways, and although she'd been really young at the time, she remembered her parents explaining it a different way. Before she could decide whether or not to take any stock in *his* version, Bran cut her other arm loose.

Addie could've sworn the Spear enjoyed it. The pain was familiar now, but intense, and she thought she blacked out for a moment. The next thing she knew for sure, she was curled up in the plane seat, whimpering and waiting for the agony to subside.

"I hope that you, the very last of the Emrys bloodline, will choose your own race over the one that enslaved us," Bran said. "We rescued those children from servitude today. They are the hope of our future."

Except for the baby, who was too much trouble to bring with them.

Addie uncurled her body enough to peer up at Bran. He didn't see his mistake. It didn't occur to him that leaving that baby to die in the fire made everything he said a lie.

He didn't care about saving helpless members of his race from extinction. He'd passed the "rescued" children into the hands of a clan who had no respect for life.

This was about a long-time grudge and revenge and power. *His* power.

Bran walked away without looking back. As far as Addie

could tell when she finally found the strength to stand, nobody was waiting for her or watched her leave the plane. Where could she go? This was an island, and the Aerons had taken the only boat.

She made it back to her room without seeing anyone, locked the door, and spent the rest of the day there, ravaging a box of tissues and hugging the stuffed rabbit Emma Carroway had given her when she was eight years old and newly orphaned. Nobody came to check on her, not even Kel. That stung, because she'd thought Kel was her friend. He was the one who'd helped Morder coordinate her rescue from Dulac captivity. He'd even saved the bag she'd brought from the Carroway house. Addie had thought it must've been blown to smithereens with the Hummer, but Kel had found it by the side of the highway.

Thanks to Kel she could hold Bunny while she cried, and she still had her favorite books. The one about the Normal girl who also had to hide or be killed. The one that got everything wrong about Merlin but was still fun to read. And the one about the princess who'd been magically hidden until it was safe for her to lead the people of Oz.

Addie took that battered old book out of her bag and cried over it, too. She'd read *The Land of Oz* many times during her years at the Carroway house. She had liked to think that she was similar to Princess Ozma, a mystery, a secret, and a heroine for her people. Didn't the very existence of the

Kin depend on her? *Some princess I am, getting people I love killed.*

But Bran had been right about the Kin being down-trodden and broken in spirit. In fact, they were only one thirteen-year-old girl away from extinction. What if Addie had been a few steps closer to the Hummer when the Dulacs blew it up? All her people would have died.

Eventually, exhaustion claimed her. Troubled dreams kept her from sound sleep, and the lurch into next week woke her up, as it often did. By the time the sky was bright pink, she'd run out of tissues and tears. She put *The Land of Oz* into her bag and Bunny under her pillow.

She knew what she had to do.

It wasn't fair that the fate of an entire race lay in Addie's hands, and the sooner she could rid herself of that burden, the better off the Kin would be. Addie was no princess, and no fit leader. The Kin should not have to depend on *her* for their survival.

She'd been given a gift by the Morrigan specifically for the purpose of negating the Eighth Day Spell, and unfortunately—no matter how much she hated him—she was going to need Bran's help. The Stone and the Sword were necessary to boost the strength of her magic, and she couldn't find them by her-self. And although she could master any spell or talent she saw wielded by someone else, Addie had never seen anyone create reality out of ideas, as Merlin had done when casting the Eighth Day Spell. For this she was counting on Bran having some arcane knowledge he would share with her when he was ready.

Addie had never felt so alone and friendless as she did now, knowing that she would have to pretend to cooperate with the Llyrs until her task was complete and *then* figure out how to get rid of them.

Bran wasn't the only one who could hold a grudge.

18

THE FLAW IN HER plan was that Addie was a terrible liar. Everything showed on her face. To pretend she was over her grief and fury was out of the question. The best she could do was pretend she was complying with Bran out of fear. Because there was truth in that. She was afraid of him now.

With the guilt of yesterday on her shoulders, Addie went downstairs feeling like a whipped dog.

Ysabel was sharpening knives in the living room, while Kel perched on the arm of a sofa, reading a magazine. "The Normals are spooked," Kel was saying. "They can't explain the hurricane. I haven't seen anything in the newspapers about the house fires in Vermont yet. But they'll start to notice if unexplainable events keep happening between every Wednesday and Thursday at midnight."

"This is good?" asked Ysabel. "That they notice?"

"They'll be frightened. They'll feel helpless. They'll panic. When Normal lives are disrupted, society breaks down. We're counting on that to help us take control of them after we're free of this wretched day." Kel saw Addie on the stairs. He threw down the magazine and jumped to his feet. "Addie, how are you?"

"Fine," she said shortly. *Thanks for asking yesterday.*

"Done crying?" Ysabel asked scornfully. Addie didn't know if the Arawen girl disapproved of tears in general, or just crying over Transitioners.

Addie ignored her and looked at Kel. "What's everyone doing?" To her own ears she sounded falsely casual.

"Working on acquiring the missing Treasures. The oracle said . . ." Kel paused, probably remembering that the oracle hadn't said this, that Ysabel had ripped it from her mind after death. He cleared his throat. "The Stone and the Sword were spoils of war taken by *the hand and the voice.* You realize, Addie, those must be the people who attacked your home. The people who killed your parents." His eyes bored into hers as if to remind her who the real enemy was.

Addie nodded. Spoils of war were items taken in battle, usually upon the death of their former owners.

"*The hand* must refer to the Bedivere hand of power," Kel said, "and we know where the head of the Bedivere clan is located. But *the voice* is kind of a puzzle. It should be the voice of command, but the Pendragon family was wiped out in a Transitioner feud years ago. They're all dead."

"Then who has the spoils of war taken from the Pendragons?" asked Ysabel. "Who are the people who defeated *them?*"

"That's a good question." Kel looked up as Griffyn entered the room. "Maybe if Griffyn hadn't killed the oracle, we'd know more."

Griffyn barely gave Kel a glance. Instead of responding to the criticism, he held up his hand for Addie to see. "It's swollen and red where you bit me," he growled. "Human bites are the worst."

He sounded as if he had experience with this, which didn't surprise Addie. Griffyn was so vile, probably every species he encountered wanted to bite him.

"Stop worrying about it." Kel tossed him a tube of ointment. "I found this for you."

Griffyn caught the tube and peered at it suspiciously. "What kind of magic is it?"

"It's not magic; it's an antibiotic." When Griffyn stared back at him blankly, Kel rolled his eyes. "It kills bacteria. Do you even know what that is?"

Griffyn sneered at Kel, but it was Addie he strode across the room to tower over menacingly. "You know what never made sense to me? If the Eighth Day Spell is carried by Emrys blood, why won't killing off the Emryses release us?" Griffyn grabbed Addie's shirt and yanked on it, forcing her to stand on her toes.

"The existence of the eighth-day timeline depends on the Emrys family," Kel exclaimed. "Even you should understand that! If they die, we cease to exist. Let her go!"

"That's what they want us to believe. That's how they

kept us from killing them back when Merlin first betrayed us. But maybe it's a lie." With Addie's shirt clenched in one fist, Griffyn drew a knife with his other hand and pressed the flat of the blade against her throat. "She cries over Transitioners and bites her own kind. Why should we keep her?"

Addie stared up into Griffyn's face, her heart pounding. She fought the instinct to struggle, because that was all it would take to provoke him. And that would be the end of not just her, but of Kin everywhere. *Unless he's right. Wouldn't that be a kick in the pants? To be useless after all?*

"Yes, Griffyn." Bran's voice startled everyone. Griffyn loosened his grip enough for Addie to turn her head and see his father standing in the doorway with Madoc behind him. "You've uncovered a ruse overlooked by hundreds of Kin scholars who've pondered our dilemma for centuries," Bran said dryly. "Undoubtedly you are the most brilliant Kin man since the casting of the Eighth Day Spell. Go ahead. Cut her throat, and we'll see what happens."

Kel made a strangled outcry, and even Ysabel flinched.

Addie looked at Griffyn, whose eyes darted between his father and his proposed victim. Then, with an angry snarl, Griffyn released Addie and stalked out of the living room and up the stairs, where they heard him slam a bedroom door. This was followed by the sounds of furniture being kicked and thrown against walls.

Addie straightened her shirt before raising her eyes to Bran. She wasn't sure what she expected from him. Another lecture on loyalty? More punishment?

"You did not appear for your lesson this morning, Adelina," Bran said.

"I didn't know I had one." She kept her voice expression-less.

"You need to practice daily. You're quick to learn, but weak in execution—and your reaction time is slow. You don't think quickly under stress."

She nodded. He was right.

Bran looked at Madoc. "Are you certain there is nothing more we can do to acquire the Treasures today? I am anxious to move forward."

"The Aerons will scout out the home of the Bediveres and determine the best way to approach it," Madoc said. "But if they're the ones who hold the Stone of Fal, they will be impervious to a direct assault. As for the Pendragons, their personal possessions were sold at auction, according to the message I received from my Normal employees after my inquiry last week. We'll have to rely on them to search the electronic records of the auction house. It's likely that another Transitioner clan moved in to claim anything of magical value." Bran glowered at the idea of relying on Normals for anything, but Madoc went on, "We should know more by their next report."

"Then Adelina and I will practice this afternoon on her spell casting. She will assist me in raising a storm." Bran's tone gave no indication that he held any resentment for her rebellion yesterday. Maybe he felt her punishment had been sufficient.

"Send it north to Canada this time," Madoc said, "or you'll hamper our efforts to locate the Treasures. My employees will need electricity and computers to get the job done."

"I'll fetch my shoes." Addie headed for the stairs, not wanting her face to give away how she felt about helping Bran raise another hurricane. What she wanted from him was a *useful* spell, not lessons on destruction.

She was almost to her room when she heard her name hissed behind her. "Addie!" Kel took the stairs two at a time to catch up with her. "I'm sorry about yesterday," he said. "I know those were people you cared about, but this is *war.*"

Addie nodded silently because she needed Kel to believe she agreed with him and she didn't trust herself to speak a convincing lie. Not with those deaths on her conscience.

Kel licked his lips nervously. "What the Morrigan said— about progeny and destiny and giving us a gift to defeat the Transitioners. Was she talking about you, Addie?"

A gift from the Morrigan wasn't an honor people aspired to. With more bravado than she felt, Addie shrugged. "I was visited by the Old Crone a year ago, and now I've seen the Girl. The only one I haven't met is the Washer Woman, which is good, because I don't think you're supposed to survive that one."

It was very satisfying to leave Kel frozen at the top of the stairs, his mouth dangling open like a fish. What a shame it had to be for something so deadly serious. Because having the Morrigan speak to you in two of her forms really *couldn't* be a good sign.

Addie opened her bedroom door just in time to catch a boy with tousled dark hair ransacking her possessions. She gasped. The boy dropped her bag and threw both hands up in a gesture of innocence. "This wasn't how I planned on meeting you," he said quickly. "But I can explain . . ."

When Addie saw the mark on the Transitioner boy's wrist, she knew better than to wait for explanations—or worse, questions. She clenched her fists and muttered under her breath, automatically preparing to defend herself against an enemy.

19

JAX COULD TELL SHE wasn't going to wait for him to explain. She muttered foreign words, and he recognized the gesture that went with them—a motion of her arms that ended with her hands curled around something invisible. "Addie, before you hit me with a fireball, listen." He knew it was her. All Kin had that silvery-blond hair and those intensely blue eyes, but something about this girl's face reminded him of Evangeline.

Plus he felt his bond to her immediately.

Her eyebrows shot up and then scrunched together. "How do you know—"

"I've seen Evangeline do that spell plenty of times," Jax said. "In fact—"

"Shut up, Dulac," Addie hissed. "How'd you get in here?"

How was he supposed to shut up *and* answer her

question? Jax settled for lowering his voice to a whisper. "I'm not a Dulac!"

"I saw you in their building!" she whispered back. "I recognize your mark!"

For a second, Jax thought she was confusing him with Dorian. They looked a lot alike, except that Dorian was shorter and a little bit geeky. Then Jax remembered the night he got a glimpse into the room where the Dulacs were keeping Addie. He'd even shouted her name, trying to let her know she had an ally in the building. "I didn't realize you'd seen me," he said. "I was trying to rescue you, but I got caught." He held up his left hand, giving her a good view of his mark. "Look at my tattoo. The Ambroses—the Dulac vassals—they have a falcon. Mine is different. I have an eagle."

The girl glared at him. "Falcon, eagle, same thing. Who cares?"

"It makes a difference," Jax insisted. "I'm an Aubrey. Jax Aubrey. Look, I hope you aren't with the Llyrs by choice but only because they got you away from the Dulacs. You haven't called for help, so I'm thinking maybe I'm right." The girl looked behind her at the partially open door. "I got here using brownie holes," Jax said. "I can get you out the same way."

"Brownie holes," she repeated.

"Watch." He crossed the room to the wall with the

brownie hole and stuck his arm in. "See? I can get you off the island this way." Addie didn't move from her spot near the door, but she clenched and unclenched her hands. "Those fireballs must sting," Jax said. "They drain the heck out of Evangeline's energy, and we're in danger the longer we stay here. So, why don't you release that spell and climb into the brownie hole. The Llyrs won't be able to reach us once we're inside. I'll prove how I know your sister, and then I'll take you to her." He hoped he sounded convincing, because the fact was, without Stink, he wasn't sure he could take her all the way back to Pennsylvania.

Thanks for abandoning me, Stink! It had to be that blasted command of Riley's to blame. Riley had only meant for Stink to stay away from Evangeline, because brownies skeeved her out, but he'd said *liege lady*. And Addie was also Jax's liege.

Meanwhile, Addie glared at Jax furiously and lifted her arms like she was going to throw her fireballs at him. "My sister is dead, you lying scum. Now I *know* you're a Dulac vassal. Dr. Morder said he was going to transport me through brownie tunnels, and if they really do exist, they connect to the Dulac building. I can't see your arm— so who knows what else is in that hole? Probably a whole bunch of Dulacs waiting to grab me."

"Whoa," said Jax, pulling his arm out of the brownie hole. "Evangeline's not dead. I just saw her a couple hours ago. Why do you think she's dead?"

"*Your people* told me. Did you not get your story straight with your superiors before you came here?"

Jax gasped, realizing where her information was coming from. "The Dulacs might've thought that when they first captured you—because we put out the story that Evangeline had been killed to prevent them from looking for her. But by the time you escaped, they'd found out she was alive. *And they didn't tell you?*" A wave of fury toward his uncle washed over Jax. It might have been a genuine mistake at first, but it had been horribly cruel for Uncle Finn to let Addie go on thinking Evangeline was dead after Angus Balin told him she was alive! "I'm *not* a Dulac vassal," he hissed, despising that clan more than ever.

"Oh, really?" Her voice was sarcastic, but her face showed uncertainty in response to his genuine expression of anger.

"I'm sworn to your sister, which makes me your vassal, too. In fact," Jax said, reaching the conclusion at the same time it came out of his mouth, "I'll bet that's why you haven't nailed me with a fireball or run out of the room to get the Llyrs. You're obligated to protect me, whether you realize it or not."

Now Addie looked truly puzzled. She lowered her arms.

"I know you have no reason to trust me, but your sister's really worried about you. We tried to rescue you from the Dulacs. We were actually in the building when the

Llyrs busted you out. We missed you by, like, minutes." His eyes wandered toward the open door. *This is taking too long. I've got to get her into the tunnel before somebody comes along.* "Evangeline's been scrying for you, but you keep blocking her. Not to mention the time you zapped her. You got me too, because I was helping with the spell." Jax pulled the papers out of his pocket and separated the one with Addie's handwriting. "We've been using this letter you left at the Carroways'."

She gasped and stepped toward him. Jax moved closer so she could see it. "How'd you get that?" Her face grew very red, and tears welled in her eyes. "The house burned!"

"No, it—" Jax looked from Addie to the crumpled tissues on the floor, then back to her face. *It just happened for her,* he realized. *And she doesn't know!* "They're okay!" he said quickly. "Mr. and Mrs. Carroway—they're okay! We got there right after you left and saved them. Mr. Carroway had a scalp wound, but that's all. And we were worried about the baby, but he's going to be okay, too."

Relief flashed across her face, and then she started crying—huge, shoulder-shaking sobs. Not what Jax had been hoping for, but maybe he could take advantage of the moment. He grabbed her arm. "Let's get you out of here."

Big mistake. "Don't touch me!" she exclaimed, yanking her arm away.

The door flew all the way open, and a Kin boy burst into the room. Jax barely had time to register that this was the first Kin he'd ever seen wearing expensive, trendy clothes and a modern haircut before he threw himself at Jax.

Jax ducked and twisted away. He'd gotten better at roughhousing while living with Riley and A.J., but they never really hurt him or played dirty, so Jax was unprepared for a blow to the small of his back and an elbow to his temple. By the time he'd shaken off the pain, he was on the ground, he'd lost the papers in his hand, and the Kin boy had him in a half nelson.

"Kel!" Addie gasped. "What are you doing?"

"Are you all right?" the Kin boy asked her. "You didn't believe this kid, did you? He's obviously a Dulac spy, come to trick you into going back." Jax struggled, and the boy tightened his grip. "Quick, Addie! Get help!"

But Addie looked outraged. "You were listening at my door?"

"Sounds like *he's* the spy," croaked Jax.

"Whatever he has from the Carroway house," Kel said, dragging Jax to his feet and toward the door, "he could've gotten it anytime since you left there. Sorry, Addie. It doesn't mean what you want it to mean. Call my dad."

"They'll kill him," Addie protested.

"No, they'll *question* him," Kel grunted. "The Dulacs are Dad's number-one suspect for who might've bought the Pendragons' possessions at auction. This kid might lead us to the Treasures."

"And *then* they'll kill him," Addie said.

"Dad! Bran!" Kel yelled, hauling Jax into the hallway. "We've got an intruder!"

Jax stopped fighting, pretending to give up. When they reached the stairs, he went limp, startling Kel with his dead weight. Then he threw himself down the steps, dragging the other boy with him. They both tumbled onto the landing where the stairs turned the corner. Jax jumped up first and mounted the stairs toward Addie, who whirled to face a huge, brawny Kin dude striding toward them on the second floor. He wore some kind of leather gear, like he'd stepped out of *The Lord of the Rings*, and he held a wicked-looking knife.

"Stay away from him!" Addie shouted, and Jax was surprised to realize she was shouting at the Kin guy, not at Jax. Addie threw both hands out, and the carpet burst into blue flames that leaped four feet into the air. Medieval Warrior Dude backed up, shielding his face with his arm.

But the magic fire and the Kin were now between Jax and Addie and Addie's bedroom door. Jax grabbed Addie's hand. "Come with me!" This time she didn't complain as he pulled her down the stairs. They'd have to run for the housekeeper's room. It had the closest

door to the brownie hole near the trash cans outside—
the one they could use to jump home.

Kel had staggered to his feet by now and met them
on the landing. Jax let go of Addie and punched him right
in the mouth. It hurt more than he expected, the pain
of impact shooting up his forearm. Kel recoiled, and Jax
dashed past him and turned the corner of the staircase—

—only to find his way blocked by an older Kin man
dressed in a long cloth tunic and carrying, of all things, a
spear. *What are these people, rejects from a Renaissance fair?*

Meanwhile Medieval Warrior Dude leaped through
the blue flames and ran toward the staircase.

"Addie, this way!" Jax vaulted over the banister, dropping to the floor six feet below.

Behind him, Addie cried out, "Griffyn, no! I invoke
my right to protect a vassal!"

As thrilled as Jax was to hear her acknowledge him
as a vassal, it obviously didn't make a bit of difference
to Griffyn, because a knife thudded into a white leather
sofa a foot away from Jax. "Holy crap!" He glanced back
and almost stopped, because Addie hadn't made it off the
stairs. She was straddling the banister, but Kel had his
arms wrapped around her.

"Run!" she screamed at Jax. "They'll kill you!"

Jax dodged, and another knife flew past him. He
turned and ran, zigzagging the way his talent prompted

179

him: left, right, duck! Downstairs, he spotted two other Kin, an Amazon Girl with more knives and an ordinary-looking man in modern clothes. He saw no sign of the children from the Carroway house.

Jax veered toward the kitchen, remembering that the housekeeper's room had been behind it. *This really sucks. I messed up big-time.* But even now, he was trying to figure out how he could still pull this off. The Kin wouldn't be able to reach him after he entered the brownie hole. He could wait for them to let their guard down and come back for Addie.

He reached the exterior door of the housekeeper's supply room and yanked it open just as instinct urged him to dodge right. But the door opened to the right. So Jax flung himself left to get outside and went sprawling. His knees hit the ground. He caught himself with his hands, scrambled to his feet, and kept going. Then the pain hit, radiating from his torso and washing over him in a dizzying wave. Jax reached backward along his own shoulder, touched something that shouldn't be there, and pulled it out.

Pain wracked him, even before he saw the knife in his hand. And the blood.

He got me. The big guy hit me.

The world spun and darkened. Jax dropped the knife, his fingers numb. He fell against the trash cans, blinking as his vision grew dim. He had to focus . . . on what? The noise and shouting behind him?

No. The brownie hole.

Clenching his teeth against the darkness and nausea, Jax searched for a weird sponginess in the air and a puckered opening. When he found it, he pitched forward and dragged himself inside, even though every movement pierced him with pain. Gravity tried to pull him to the ground, urging him to lay his head down and give up. Instead, he crawled forward. *Can't stop here. Get me home. Get me home.*

Confused images of *home* flickered in his mind. The mountain house. The house where he'd first lived with Riley. His home in Delaware.

Not home! He didn't know where *home* was, and he didn't want the brownie tunnel dumping him in an empty house. He'd pass out and no one would find him until it was too late.

Take me to someone who'll help me. Someone who cares about me. Take me—

Again there was an extended, stomach-dropping fall. Jax squeezed his eyes closed, certain that this time he was never going to open them again. Then his face struck something rough and fibrous, and curiosity forced his eyes open, so he could at least see where he was going to die.

He was lying on a carpeted floor, sprawled facedown. He couldn't lift his head, but he had a floor-side view of an unfamiliar bedroom. Everything swam before him sickeningly.

"Jax?" said someone from behind him. Then, in greater alarm: "Jax!"

He knew that voice. *Not who I was hoping for, but* . . .

Jax closed his eyes and surrendered to oblivion.

20

"I KNEW I HIT him," Griffyn exclaimed, picking up the knife. "But where'd he go? There's no blood trail past this point."

Addie stared at the blood—on the ground, on the knife—and felt sick.

Madoc had a tight grip on her arm. "How'd he get away?"

"Is there a brownie hole?" Kel asked. "The kid said he could travel by brownie holes. That was how the Morder guy found me, to tell me where Addie was being held. It's some kind of spell the Dulacs discovered."

Griffyn started kicking the garbage cans as if the boy might be hiding inside one.

"I claimed protection for him!" Addie yelled at Griffyn. "You had no right to hurt him!" Or kill him. The boy had gotten away, but did he survive a knife wound to the back? Addie shivered, overcome with worry for a total stranger. She couldn't even remember what he'd said his name was. Jack, maybe?

"How could you have a Transitioner as your vassal?" Madoc demanded. "Especially one from the Dulac clan?"

Addie shook her head, bewildered. She didn't know how she could've acquired a vassal, nor could she pinpoint the exact moment she'd known he was one. She'd wanted to hit him with her defensive spell as soon as she saw him, but she hadn't been able to. When Kel yelled for Bran, Addie had been afraid for the boy. And when he grabbed her hand on the stairs, she'd known he was trying to lead her to safety. *I should have gone with him when he asked me the first time.*

"You didn't fall for his lies, did you, Addie?" Kel asked.

She turned on him. "How much of our conversation did you listen to?"

"All of it," Kel declared. "And a good thing I did! He was trying to kidnap you." Then Kel spilled everything he'd heard the boy say. "Addie wasn't buying it," he finished. "Not until he showed her something from the Carroway house, and then she let her emotions get the better of her." He looked at her with sympathy, like he only had her best interests at heart. "Addie, you said yourself that you saw him in the Dulac building and recognized his mark."

Addie glared at Kel tearfully. The letter *could* have been taken from the Carroway house before the fire. But how had the Transitioner known about Dale's head wound and the baby? She desperately wanted him to have been telling the truth.

"He shouldn't have been able to enter the house," Madoc

insisted. "My wards repel both magical invasion and physical intruders! No one can enter who hasn't been invited."

"The boy *must be* Adelina's vassal," Bran said. "If he was bonded to her, the wards wouldn't have recognized him as an intruder. Invitation was magically implied."

"How could he become her vassal without her knowing about it?" Kel demanded.

"By swearing himself to the head of her family," Bran said. Then he looked at Madoc. "Which means she's not the only Emrys left."

Addie felt a flutter of emotion. Was Evangeline really alive?

Madoc shook her again. "What do you know about the brownie holes?"

"Nothing!" He didn't need to be so rough. It was the truth. She knew *nothing* about them. But now that she'd seen the boy put his arm into one—seen its opalescent ripple in reality— she was able to spot the one hanging in midair behind the trash cans. *Can I actually get into it?*

"There's a brownie hole in her bedroom," Kel said. "The boy stuck his arm into it, and Addie said she couldn't see his arm anymore. For all we know, there could be an army of Dulacs with him. In fact, that kid might still be here, and we just can't see him."

That was a horrible thought. Addie looked at the blood on the ground, imagining an invisible boy lying there, hurt, maybe dying.

"If there was an army of Dulacs with secret access to this island, we would already be overrun," Bran said. "And the Dulacs would not have sent a mere boy to lead their attack."

"Nevertheless, the security of the island is compromised." Madoc cursed soundly. "I *like* this house."

"They know where we are!" Ysabel called from the doorway.

"Yes, we realize that," Madoc said, dragging Addie away from the brownie hole and back into the house. "We'll move immediately."

"But now we know where they are, too." Ysabel was holding up a handful of papers. "The boy dropped these in Addie's room. They show where he came from."

Madoc passed Addie off to Griffyn. No one was going to let go of her, she realized, for fear she'd disappear just like the Transitioner. Madoc took the papers from Ysabel and leafed through them. Addie glimpsed maps of the northeastern United States. One of them had locations circled in red and a straight line drawn between the coast of Maine and someplace in the middle of either New York or Pennsylvania. Addie couldn't tell which without a closer look. Madoc frowned at Addie. "Can a brownie hole extend this great a distance?"

"I told you, I don't know anything about them," she said angrily. "Ask Kel. He heard what I said."

Bran took the maps from Madoc's hand, examining them thoughtfully even though the geography of America was unfamiliar to him. "I don't think the Dulacs are involved," he said finally. "Or any other powerful clan. This was a clumsy attempt to reach Adelina by someone with few resources—most likely the older sister. We only ever had the half-breed's word she was dead, and he was a proven traitor."

Addie trembled from head to toe. *The older sister.* Addie had buried Evangeline already in her mind. But she was alive. *I am not the last.*

"Adelina is valuable as a key to the Eighth Day Spell," Madoc pointed out. "Any number of people might want to take her from us."

"But who else would send an underage boy to do the job?" Bran replied. "A boy Adelina was compelled to protect? If he's a vassal to her sister, *this* is where she's located." He stabbed the end of the red line on the map with his finger. "Furthermore, she's repeatedly tried to observe Adelina through scrying, and given the failure of this abduction attempt, may do so again."

"We'd better leave the island at once," Madoc said. "Everyone should collect any personal items they want; we won't be returning." He looked pained.

"Very well," said Bran. "But we're also going to prepare for another scrying attempt." He waved the handful of maps. "This gives us exactly the information we need."

Addie's heart sank. Her position as ally and pupil had been precarious at best. But with her older sister resurrected from the grave, Addie had the feeling that she'd just been demoted to *hostage*.

• • •

It happened on the plane after they'd left the island—a prickling sensation that raised the hairs on the back of her neck and on her arms. Most people would never notice the touch of scrying, but Addie and her siblings had been trained by their father at a young age to be on guard against spies.

She'd hoped there would be no more attempts. There hadn't been any since the day before yesterday when Bran had sent his electrical bolt through the spell connection and the boy said they'd been *zapped*. Maybe Evangeline, if that was who it really was, had been too cautious to try again. But Bran was right. After her vassal failed to rescue Addie and was wounded—*please not killed!*—Evangeline probably couldn't resist. Addie was going to have to block the spell the same way she'd done before, this time for her sister's protection instead of her own.

The trick was to do it without giving herself away. They hadn't tied Addie to the chair, but she was under close observation. She didn't shut her eyes or give any outward sign of concentrating, but turned her head to gaze out the plane window at the clouds. *A sea of clouds,* she thought. *I am completely surrounded by impenetrable clouds.*

Unfortunately, she wasn't subtle enough to fool Ysabel, who was seated beside her and watching her like a hawk. "She's casting a spell," Ysabel declared. "A blocking spell, I think.

Someone's scrying for her now."

A hand grabbed Addie's ponytail and yanked her head back painfully. Griffyn, of course. Leaning over her seat, he placed one of his knives against her throat, the way he'd done before. Her concentration broken, she glared at him balefully. *We both know you won't do it.*

He grinned at her, as if guessing her thoughts. "Father said no lasting damage. But that leaves me a number of options."

Ysabel held up a series of signs, one at a time, for the person on the other end of the scrying spell to see—white sheets of paper with simple directions written in thick black marker.

What they wanted Evangeline to do.

What they would do to Addie if Evangeline did not follow their instructions precisely.

Bran crossed the plane to stand over them with his Spear. He motioned Griffyn away and addressed Addie. "You understand, we must show her that we mean what we say."

He said it like he regretted what was to come, but Addie didn't believe him. He enjoyed this. "I really didn't expect anything else," she told him bitterly.

For pride's sake—and for the sake of the sister who was watching—she tried to be tough. She really did. But when Bran lowered the Spear, it only took about five seconds for her to start screaming.

21

THERE WAS A WEIGHT on his chest, and at every breath pain lanced through his body. Eventually Jax was driven to force his eyelids open and investigate.

A pair of black, glittery eyes in a smushed-up face peered back at him anxiously.

"Now you turn up," Jax whispered.

Stink tilted his head and rotated his ears.

"Get off him," growled a voice from nearby. A hand swiped at Stink, and the brownie leaped from Jax's chest to the headboard of the bed. Immediately, the weight hindering his breathing disappeared, although the pain didn't lessen much. A man with carrot-colored hair leaned into Jax's field of vision. This man's face usually wore a relaxed and rather stupid smile, so it was strange to see Michael Donovan looking angry.

"Awake, are you?" Donovan crossed his arms. "Usually,

when an associate appears on my doorstep with a knife wound, I patch him up and no questions asked. But *usually*, said associate turns up on the *doorstep*. He doesn't fall out of thin air in front of my daughter. So, you wanna tell me how you landed at Tegan's feet in this condition?"

Jax licked his dry lips and tried to process the question. On one hand, it was a relief to have Donovan mad at him, because it suggested he wasn't dying. On the other hand, it was mind-boggling for Donovan—thief, con man, and all-around nuisance—to act like a protective father. *Did I really show up at Tegan's feet? How embarrassing.*

"I didn't mean to," he croaked. A flurry of activity in the doorway caught Jax's attention: a flash of orange hair, a grunt, and the sound of wrestling. There was an eavesdropper to this conversation. *Two* eavesdroppers, Jax bet. "I was traveling by brownie magic and got dumped off with someone who would help me. I didn't, uh, *specify* Tegan. I'm just grateful that"—he tried to swallow, but his mouth was like a desert—"that your family was willing to—" Jax couldn't stand it anymore. "How hurt am I?"

Donovan reached for a plastic water bottle, the kind with a straw, and maneuvered it into Jax's reach. "Drink," he said gruffly. "I had a healer come. Not the most talented guy in the world, but he does his best, and I helped stitch you up. You were lucky the knife missed all the important stuff." Donovan shook his head. "You lost a lot of blood, though."

Jax sucked on the straw while Donovan held it for him, pausing only to ask, "Did you call Riley?"

"Call him? It's the eighth day, Jax. We can't call him."

It was the same day, then. Good. Jax tried to raise himself on one elbow, and intense pain sliced through his torso. He gasped. Donovan put the water bottle aside. "Easy there. You're healing, best as my associate could do, but you need to rest. Except first, you're going to tell me what happened."

Jax told him the story as concisely as possible: how he'd used the brownie tunnels to reach Evangeline's sister and how Stink's desertion had left him unable to use the tunnel magic effectively. Stink ran up and down the headboard, chittering loudly like he was making excuses. "I thought the tunnels would take me to Riley," Jax finished. "But I was too close to passing out to focus much."

"You could use some tips on housebreaking. You made a lot of mistakes."

Mindful of the fact that this man had probably saved his life, Jax didn't mention that he had no interest in housebreaking normally.

"Sleep," Donovan ordered him. "The healing magic will keep workin' on you, but it takes time." There was another commotion in the doorway, and Donovan frowned. "Hold on . . ." He left the room, and Jax heard a whispered conversation in the hallway. "Okay, but just for a minute," Donovan said finally.

Tegan slipped into the room, then hesitated and hung back near the door. Her twin brother Thomas popped in behind her, grinning from ear to ear. "Hey, Jax!" he said cheerfully. "That was awesome. You should've seen—" Donovan grabbed his son by the collar and hauled him out of the room, leaving only Tegan.

Jax wasn't surprised Thomas thought getting knifed was cool, but he *was* startled to see Tegan with her eyes and nose all red, like she'd been crying. Jax felt even more embarrassed—and a little sick to his stomach. He must've been in really bad shape to scare her enough to make her cry. Tegan didn't scare easily, and Jax had never seen her cry. Not even when that crazy Kin lord Wylit had threatened to use her as a human sacrifice.

"You need anything?" she asked from across the room.

He could use another drink of water, but he didn't want her giving it to him through the straw like he was a baby. "Move the water bottle closer?" he asked instead.

She peeled herself away from the wall and pushed a small table closer to the bed, making sure the water was close enough for him to reach without stretching. "Thanks," he began. "I—"

"You were stupid," she interrupted him angrily. "That was a really stupid thing you did. If you'd asked *me*—"

"You said you didn't want to be involved," Jax

reminded her. "You hung up on me." Tegan scowled, but didn't argue. "I had to try," Jax went on. "It was our best shot of getting Addie away from them."

"Yes, it was," Tegan said. "But you did it *stupidly*. First of all, if you'd told Riley, he could've ordered your brownie to stay with you the whole time. If you'd brought Evangeline with you, she could've waited safely in the tunnel, completely untouchable by the Llyrs while your brownie found Addie. Then, all it would've taken was Evangeline sticking her head out and saying, 'Come here,' and Addie would've gone with her *sister* without argument. Riley could've had his allies, the Morgans, ready to assault that island the instant you had the girl safely away. And this would all be *over*."

Jax didn't know what to say. She was right.

Tegan threw up her hands and started pacing the room. "I didn't want to be involved," she muttered. "It's not our kind of thing. But you're going to get yourself killed. You're making me rethink this . . ."

Jax watched her pace and argue with herself. He heard her say *I* and *me*, and something dawned on him that should have occurred to him long ago. He'd been told that talents always ran stronger in one gender than the other and that clans were run by the oldest member of the more talented gender. His cousin Sloane outranked her father because the Dulac talent was female dominated, just like female sensitives were stronger than males. "You're in charge of your family," he said, breaking into Tegan's tirade. "You're the Donovan clan leader."

Tegan shot a look at Jax as she continued to pace. "I let Dad think he's in charge most of the time, 'cause it keeps him happy. But yeah, when it's an important decision, *I* make it." She whirled around, hands on her hips, and glared accusingly at Jax. "We're not the kind of people who save the world!"

"But you already did, once," Jax said quietly. Tegan had done her part on the pyramid to help defeat Wylit and repair the Eighth Day Spell.

"In case you haven't noticed, my father and brother aren't the sharpest tools in the shed," Tegan snapped. "And now I'm going to have to risk their lives because you and Riley can't manage to rescue one stupid girl *or* save the world without help. Thanks a lot, Jax." She stalked out of the room and, just before she closed the door, she stuck her head back in to say, "Jerk."

Same to you. That was his usual response, but Jax couldn't muster the sarcasm to say it. Because something else had finally dawned on him, and it was kind of a shock. Tegan was doing this for *him.* Just like she'd gone to New York to help rescue Billy—for *Jax's* sake, not Billy's.

And that was awkward, because Jax didn't like Tegan very much. Well, he admired certain qualities in her. She was smart and brave; he trusted her at his back in a pinch; she always had a plan—and Jax would pound into dust anyone who tried to hurt her. But he didn't *like* her.

Right?

He wasn't aware of falling back asleep, only of Michael Donovan waking him. "Sorry, Jax. But we're driving you out to Riley instead of making him come here to get you. For some reason." The last was said with a pointed glance over his shoulder and an irritated tone, so Jax guessed Tegan was issuing orders and her dad didn't like them.

Donovan was surprisingly gentle helping him out of bed and into one of Thomas's shirts. Jax didn't feel quite so weak or dizzy, and the pain had lessened. He was healing quicker than naturally possible, thanks to Donovan's "associate," but it would still take time to recover. Billy's arm, after what had been a very bad fracture, had taken a week to heal completely even with Jax's Aunt Marian's magical assistance.

Stink scampered at Jax's feet instead of riding on his shoulder as they followed Donovan out of the bedroom. "Are we in your house in Pennsylvania?" Jax asked. Then he got a glimpse out a window and, spotting a familiar city skyline, realized they couldn't be.

"We borrowed an apartment outside New York City for the time being," Donovan said.

"Borrowed, as in . . ." Jax wasn't sure how to finish his sentence. The Donovans had a strange concept of borrowing. This might be someplace they'd broken into, for all he knew.

"As in *borrowed*," Tegan said sourly. "The owner knows we're here." She was standing in the middle of a cramped living room, surrounded by over a dozen tanks of propane, stacked cases of bottled water, batteries, and canned goods.

"You guys preparing for the apocalypse?" Jax asked.

Thomas grinned proudly. "Just a little side business. After the Impossible Hurricane, we were getting fifty dollars for a carton of bottled water!"

Jax looked at Tegan, but she stared at the floor and wouldn't meet his eyes. It was the first time he could ever recall her looking ashamed of her family. "C'mon," she said. "It's going to take a couple hours to get there, even with no traffic."

Riley and Evangeline must be worried sick by now, Jax thought, checking his Grunsday watch. It was ten thirty at night, and they weren't going to make it back before Evangeline disappeared. But he could hardly complain about the Donovans taking too long at fetching a healer, stitching up his wound, and giving him time to rest before driving him home. He thanked them again and made a point of not wondering whether the car they put him in was stolen or not.

They did not, in fact, make it to the cabin before the end of Grunsday. Stink, who'd been dozing on Jax's lap, shook himself awake just before midnight and leaped through a brownie hole. Donovan pulled the car over as soon as the transition occurred and got out of the vehicle to call Riley. He stood outside of their hearing, although Thomas rolled down the window trying to eavesdrop. After a few minutes, Donovan got back in the car and handed the phone to Jax. "He wants to talk to you."

Jax glanced at the twins, wishing they weren't going to overhear him getting yelled at. "Hey, it's me," he said.

"Jax." There was a long, long moment of silence, and then Riley asked, "Why didn't you tell me what you were going to do?"

"I didn't know if it would work," Jax said. "And I was afraid you'd order me not to try it. The flaws in my plan have already been pointed out to me." He looked at Tegan. "But go ahead and yell if you're going to. Don't make me wait for it."

"I'm not going to yell." Riley sounded very subdued.

Jax glanced at Donovan, wondering what he'd told Riley and why he'd left the car to do it. *I had a closer call than Donovan let on,* Jax thought. *That's why he's not acting like himself and why Riley's not cursing and yelling and calling me an idiot. That's why Tegan was crying. I scared them all.* "I'm sorry," he said.

Riley sighed. "Based on what Donovan told me, I

think I already know the answer to this question, but I gotta ask—you don't know where Evangeline is, do you?"

Jax sat up in alarm. "Ow—what do you mean? Isn't she with you?"

"No," said Riley. "She took the Land Rover late this afternoon without telling anyone, drove off, and didn't come back."

22

WHEN DONOVAN PULLED UP at the cabin, Riley met them outside. Jax got out of the car gingerly, expecting the usual *Jax, you idiot* greeting. Instead, Riley walked up without saying anything, put an arm around him, and pulled him close for the nearest thing to a hug he could give Jax without hurting him.

"Thank you," Riley said to Donovan.

"You would've done the same for one of mine," Donovan replied.

"Come into the house—please," Riley said, walking Jax to the door with a hand on his elbow as if he was afraid Jax might fall over. For a second it seemed like Donovan was going to decline the invitation, but Tegan got out of the car and followed Riley. Her father sighed.

Inside, Mrs. Crandall took charge of Jax, helping him into the living room, planting him in a chair with a pillow supporting his back, and shoving a bowl of soup into his hands. Jax felt lucky she didn't try to spoon it into his mouth. Mr. Crandall rumpled his hair fondly with a mumbled comment about them being happy to get him back in one piece.

A.J. snorted and said, "Only an idiot with dumb luck like Jax could've survived it."

Jax grinned gratefully at A.J. for telling the truth. All this niceness was freaking him out.

"You should go to bed and rest," Mrs. Crandall urged him.

"Not until you tell me what happened to Evangeline," he said around a mouthful of soup.

"I thought for a while that she took off because she was mad at me," said Riley, "but I don't believe she'd leave *you*, Jax."

"Mad at you?" Jax repeated. "I told you to take her on a date, not make her mad!"

"Well, it didn't work out like that!" Riley retorted. "I thought she was driving around until she cooled off, except she never came back. You weren't here either, and until we heard from Donovan, we thought the two of you must be together. I was sure you'd call me after midnight and tell me where you were, but then . . ." He waved his hand helplessly toward the Donovans. The phone call he'd gotten was not what he'd been expecting.

Jax frowned. Could Evangeline have gone looking for him? No. Before jumping to the conclusion that he was missing, she would've asked the Crandalls if they knew where he was. *What would Evangeline have done after her meeting with Bedivere?*

Oh . . . no.

"She scried for Addie," Jax said. "Something she saw must've made her take off."

Riley shook his head. "She couldn't have. There's no saffron in the house."

"She had saffron," Jax said. "She made me get it and not tell you."

While Riley looked hurt, A.J. looked skeptical. "If Evangeline saw Addie—heck, even if she saw what happened to Jax—why did she leave without telling us? Is she planning to drive to Maine? Alone?"

Jax gasped. "How do you know where—"

A.J. held up his phone. "Billy. You may have blocked his number on Riley's phone, but he has my number, too. Called me right after midnight. What were you thinking, Jax? We needed that information!"

"I was afraid of what you'd do with it!"

"Deidre's on her way to that island now with a team," Mrs. Crandall said.

"See!" Jax jumped out of his chair, spilling soup, and reawakening pain all over his back. "Ow! You can't send Deidre! She'll blow the place up!"

"She won't," Riley assured him. "There's no urgency on a Thursday. She'll survey the place, but Jax—after you found them and escaped, I doubt they're still there."

"Ten'll get you twenty they've flown the coop," said Donovan.

"Blondie might not know that, depending on whether she did her witchy scrying thing before or after they hurt Jax," Tegan pointed out. "It'd be helpful if we could figure out what direction she's heading." She turned to her father. "Take Tommy to track her car."

"Dad, are you really gonna let her—" Thomas asked his father at the same time Donovan muttered, "Tegan, girl—"

"We talked about this," she interrupted them. "I made up my mind."

Donovan and his son looked at each other, then headed for the door, both of them grumbling. No one but Jax seemed surprised by how quickly they obeyed. Riley gave a relieved sigh as soon as they were out of the house. He pulled Excalibur from its sheath and laid it on the closest table. The Crandalls pulled their blades out and did the same. Jax hesitated, not wanting to intimidate Tegan with the formality of a meeting with blades on the table.

But she seemed perfectly at ease. "I don't carry an honor blade. And not because the Donovans have no honor, which is what some people might think." Tegan shot a challenging look in Jax's direction.

Jax spread his hands in a gesture of innocence. The thought had never—okay, maybe it *had* crossed his mind.

"I own one, for your information," she said. "It was my grandmother's. But it gets in the way—climbing and squeezing through small spaces—so I don't carry it. My talent works just fine without it."

"Do you think your father and brother can track Evangeline?" Riley asked.

"They have a decent chance," Tegan said. "Do you think she's deserting your side to join the Llyrs?"

"No," Riley replied. "Not for a second. This is about her sister."

"Is that what you fought about?"

"Sort of." When Tegan raised her eyebrows as if waiting for more information, Riley continued reluctantly. "Evangeline met with Calvin Bedivere to inspect the refugee lodgings he's established and discuss how to spread the word to friendly and neutral Kin. But she was more interested in circumventing the Table's decision for a preemptive strike against the Llyrs—to the point of digging up dirt on Table members to put pressure on them. I pulled her aside to warn her she wouldn't make a good impression with Bedivere that way. *A-a-a-nd* my criticism didn't go over very well."

"I bet not," said Tegan. "She's trying to save her sister any way she can."

Jax blinked in surprise. Tegan, defending Evangeline? Now he'd heard everything!

"Yeah, I know. I just . . ." Riley broke off, slumping in

his seat and rubbing his face wearily.

The Crandalls exchanged glances, and Jax guessed they were thinking the same thing he was. *Riley's trying to live up to his father's reputation as an honest leader,* Jax thought. *But if his sister Alanna was alive and where Addie is right now . . .*

"Was your family's estate sold at auction?" Jax suddenly asked. "The Kin holding Addie thought I might know who bought up the Pendragons' possessions. They wanted me to lead them to 'the Treasures.' Wasn't Evangeline talking about Treasures of the Kin?"

"She was," Riley said. "Not all my family's things were sold at auction. Maybe it's time to get one item out of storage and keep it closer." He turned to Tegan. "Billy compiled a list of properties owned by the same company that owns the island Jax was at today. Would you be willing to visit them and see if you can detect any Kin present? I'll get someone to accompany you, and it should be perfectly safe for the next seven days."

"I've committed the Donovans now," Tegan said. "I'll go."

"Tegan." Riley spread his hands. "What do you want in return? You've refused everything I've offered in the past. An alliance. Vassalhood."

Jax's mouth fell open. Riley had offered to make Tegan a vassal? Really? And when? *Why don't I know these things?*

"I don't want anything," Tegan said stubbornly. "The Donovans prefer working alone. I'm going to make an exception for now, but let's save the world and get it over with, okay?"

Jax didn't argue the next time someone suggested he go to sleep. He climbed the stairs to the second floor, then stared bleakly at his sleeping bag on the floor and wondered how much it was going to hurt to get down on the ground.

"I'll sleep on the floor," Riley said from the doorway. "You take my bed."

Jax frowned suspiciously. "You should be reaming me out, not giving me your bed."

"You *want* me to give you heck? Sure, I can do that." Riley's gaze bounced around the room before returning to Jax. "But that would let you off the hook, right? If I just yelled at you for what you did and got it over with."

"So, you're stretching it out to torture me?" Jax asked. "I screwed up and made things worse. Let me have it!"

"Everybody screws up," Riley said. "Nobody knows, when they take a risk like you did, if it will make the situation better or worse. That's life."

"Then what—"

"Here's what I want," Riley interrupted. "Get out your blade. Swear to me that you'll never leave us again to implement some plan without checking with me first." When Jax opened his mouth to protest, Riley said, "You've done it twice—gone to New York to face the Dulacs and to Maine to face the Llyrs. Both times, you narrowly escaped losing your life or your memory. How many more risks can you take before your luck runs out?"

Jax thought about his father driving his car into the Susquehanna River. Riley believed it was an accident. Balin said it was on purpose, but even if it was, Jax didn't believe it'd been an act of suicide. At most, his dad had taken a daring, desperate risk, and his luck *had* run out. Everyone said Jax was a lot like his father, but this was one area where he didn't want to follow in his dad's footsteps.

With a trembling hand, Jax pulled out his blade. "I swear," he said, "on the Aubrey name, that I will not leave the safety of the clan again without permission from you or Evangeline."

Riley helped him get into bed without hurting himself. "It's okay, you know," Riley said.

"It's not." Evangeline was missing. Addie was still with the enemy. And Jax had squandered their best advantage.

Riley turned out the light. "For what it's worth, squirt, you're way braver than I was at your age."

23

IN THE MORNING, MRS. Crandall and Tegan left to meet up with vassals of Bedivere and investigate properties that were presumably owned by the Kin family Mathonwy. Jax called Billy to apologize for lying to him and blocking his number. At first Billy responded with one-word answers, which let Jax know just how hurt his friend was.

"I did it for Addie," Jax pleaded with him to understand. "All I wanted was to get her to safety, but I messed up, and now both girls are gone."

Finally, Billy heaved a sigh and said, "Sometimes, the Doctor lies to his companions to protect them—or for some greater good. It doesn't always work out for him, either." Jax scratched his head, unsure whether the *Doctor Who* reference meant he was forgiven until Billy added, "It's cool, dude. Just get those girls back, okay?"

Meanwhile, Deidre reported to Riley that the island off Maine seemed abandoned, the plane gone. Her men had needed both magic and explosives to defeat the protective wards and enter the house, but when they got inside, the state of the place suggested the residents had departed in a hurry. The bad news of the morning was rounded out when Michael and Thomas Donovan found the missing Land Rover in the parking lot of a Poconos casino about fifteen miles away. "I don't think she's in it, though," Donovan said.

Riley had put his phone on speaker so everyone could hear the conversation, and Jax, listening in, felt his heart sink.

Donovan went on, "There's a Normal couple here makin' a report to police about their stolen car—in between arguin' over which one left it unlocked and that keepin' a spare set of keys under the floor mat was a stupid idea. I suppose somebody taught Evangeline where to look for keys when she needed a car?"

"Yeah," Riley said. "Teaching her to drive and how to steal a car—it was supposed to be for her safety, in case of an emergency. Can you track the car she took?"

"Normals don't have much of a scent to us, unless we know 'em really well. It's magic we track most easily, and that Land Rover has a unique smell—Emrys and Pendragon, not to mention a lingerin' aroma of Balin and Wylit. Finding it was a piece of cake, but we can't track the car of some random Normal couple."

"You might as well come back, then. There are

better ways to use your time."

"We don't take orders from you, Pendragon," Donovan pointed out.

"Then call Tegan and take them from her!" Riley pushed the button to end the call and looked at Mr. Crandall. "Evangeline ditched the Land Rover on purpose so we can't find her."

"What is that girl up to?" Mr. Crandall complained. "She spent years shut up in an old woman's house, out of touch with the world. She can't possibly know where she's driving."

"She's smart and resourceful," Riley defended her. "Whatever she's doing, it's gotta be part of a plan. If the Donovans turn up, send them to help Tegan search those properties. A.J. and I are going to get that Kin sword, now that we know the Llyrs want it. We'll pick up the Land Rover on the way back."

"What about me?" Jax asked.

"Can you move around? Are you in pain?" Riley asked.

"I'm feeling better," Jax said.

"Then you better come with us. I don't think I want to let you out of my sight."

The last remaining and most personal belongings of the Pendragon family were located in a facility that could've been featured on *Storage Wars*. As they left the truck, Riley fingered a set of keys in an agitated way. Jax could tell he dreaded the place.

After locating the correct shed, Riley inserted his key, rolled up the door, and peered into the dim interior. It was a large unit—deep, with two rows of stacked boxes and trunks and furniture. Riley led the way, glancing left and right at the stored items. Once, he touched a tasseled, antique floor lamp, setting all the tassels to swinging. Jax had no doubt Riley was picturing exactly where that lamp used to stand.

At the back, covered by an old tarp, was a four-foot-high safe. Riley knelt on the concrete floor to work the combination lock. He swung the door open and pulled out a short sword in a leather scabbard with straps that would go across a man's back. Standing up, he held the sheathed blade out for A.J. and Jax to see. "Doesn't look like much, does it?"

"Nope," said Jax. "But neither does Excalibur." In fact, this sword looked better than Excalibur, which was black and dull. The Sword of Nuadu was really old, like something that should be in a museum, but it wasn't corroded, at least not on the parts Jax could see.

A.J. shuffled his feet. "Maybe you should leave it locked up. I'll paint wards on the safe. They'll never find it."

Riley shook his head. "I'm thinking it'll make good bait." He tucked the Sword under his arm and bent to lock the safe.

"Bait?" A.J. repeated unhappily.

"This Sword," Jax said. "It's one of the Kin Treasures Evangeline talked about, right? And your grandfather took it from her father?"

"Her father had the Sword of Nuadu and the Stone of Fal," Riley said. "The Sword is actually the lesser of the two—a single-purpose item, a weapon of vengeance. But the Stone should have ensured a victory for the owner. When placed beneath the throne of a king, it preserves the kingdom. And placed beneath the seat of the man of any house, it preserves his sovereignty over his home."

"So how was he defeated?" Jax asked. "Evangeline's father, I mean."

"A woman surrendered both items before the battle began—just walked out and handed them over to my grandfather." Riley looked at Jax sadly. "I'm thinking it was probably Evangeline's mother."

Jax sucked in his breath. "She betrayed her husband?"

"I guess so. According to what Evangeline said, she's the one who sent her children fleeing into the woods where the Taliesins picked them up." Riley gazed at the weapon in his hands. "My grandfather said he made sure the woman was held aside, away from the battle and protected, but at some point in the confusion, she escaped. She ended up among the casualties that day, like she wanted to die beside her husband even though she'd just assured his failure. That's another thing I never shared with Evangeline. I've known for a while that I need to sit down with her and tell her everything I know about that day, but there never seems to be a good time—and how do I even bring it up?"

"Just do it. She'll want to know." Jax considered what he knew now about his own father. "It hurts, for a while, knowing what choice your parent made. But at least you know they *made* a choice, instead of . . ." He trailed off, remembering where they were standing. Riley's family hadn't chosen the manner of their death.

Riley nodded, looking miserable. "I will. If she gives me the chance." He tucked the Sword under his arm and headed for the exit. Jax and A.J. followed.

They were almost to the door when Riley paused and backed up. Jax followed his gaze to a cardboard box labeled *Photographs*.

"Hold this," Riley said, handing the Sword to A.J. He approached the box like it was a bomb and hesitantly lifted the lid. A.J. and Jax exchanged glances, neither of them wanting to interfere with the moment. Riley surveyed the interior of the box, then pulled out an album. He opened it and turned a few pages. After a second, he laughed. "Heck, I forgot about that . . ."

A.J. put the Sword down on top of a crate. "Don't touch," he cautioned Jax. Then he edged closer to Riley, peered into the album, and snorted. "That was *not* a good look for you."

"Dad chipped my front teeth with a baseball," Riley said. "Boy, was Mom mad."

Jax wanted to see too. But he remembered how painful it was when his Dulac grandmother had forced him to look through an album of family photographs that included his teenage father. He didn't want to intrude on Riley's memories.

So instead, he brushed cobwebs away from the tasseled lamp, blew dust off a roll-top desk, and finally approached the Sword. A.J. shot him a warning glare, so Jax put his hands behind his back. The handle—or *hilt*, he thought it was called—was rough hewn and curved outward, like the horns of a goat. It didn't have a guard to protect the wielder's hand, and there were no jewels on it or fancy carvings.

It was a simple, basic thing. Single-purposed. A weapon of vengeance, Riley said.

Wish I'd had something like this when that brute started throwing knives at me. What did Addie call him? Griffyn. Wouldn't I like to stick this—

Something sailed past Jax, brushing his ear. He ducked and whirled around, only to receive a glancing blow in the back of the head by another dark shape that flew by. With the vivid memory of knives slicing the air around him, Jax reached instinctively for the scabbard in front of him and whipped the Sword out. He waved it around wildly, seeking his attacker. *I'll put this through your gut, Griffyn!*

"Jax!"

He felt dizzy. His vision blurred, and his head buzzed with magic, but he held the Sword aloft, ready to deflect another attack from the air. "I'll kill you!" he shouted.

A body struck him at waist height. Jax howled as he hit the concrete floor and pain shot through his back. Hands pinned him down, and someone tried to take the Sword from him. Jax clenched his fist around the hilt and hung on.

After a moment, Riley started to holler—and continued to holler, wordlessly—an awful, agonized sound. Jax tuned in to his guardian's voice and, horrified, tried to give up the Sword, which Riley was attempting to pry from his hand.

He couldn't let go of it.

"Riley, stop it! Stop!" That was A.J.

The weight holding down Jax's arms and legs vanished as A.J. tackled his liege lord instead. Under A.J.'s onslaught, Riley released his grip on the Sword. Jax sat up and rolled away. A.J. had hold of Riley's arm, and Riley was staring at his open hand.

It was bright red, like he'd held it in a pot of boiling water as long as he could stand it.

Jax gasped and dropped the weapon. He had no trouble letting go now.

"What's wrong with you?" A.J. shouted at Jax. "We can't take our eyes off you for a second!"

"He drew it," Riley gasped. "A.J., he drew that thing. It's his now."

"I don't want it," Jax said. "Take it." He scooted backward, kicking the Sword away from him. When he realized he still had the scabbard in his other hand, he dropped that, too.

Tentatively, A.J. reached out. When his fingertips touched the weapon, he jerked back as if stung. "I can't touch it."

"Who?" Riley asked hoarsely. "Who did you draw it against?" When Jax looked blank, Riley asked more specifically, "Who were you thinking about when you drew it?"

"The guy who hit me with the knife," Jax whispered. "Griffyn."

"A Llyr?"

"I dunno." They hadn't exactly been introduced. "Maybe. Why?"

"Because the Sword is bound to you until you kill him," Riley choked out.

"Jax, you idiot!" A.J. yelled, still hanging on to Riley as if afraid his liege would try to grab the weapon again. "What part of *don't touch the Sword* didn't you understand?"

"I was under attack—" Jax tried to explain.

"From pigeons!" A.J. looked at the ceiling. "From freaking, stupid birds!"

Jax stared upward. Perched on metal struts near the ceiling were a pair of black-feathered birds. More than two, actually. Half a dozen, now that he kept looking.

"They're not pigeons," he said, scrambling to his feet. "They're crows!"

I know who did this to me—who sent crows in here to attack me and trick me!

He grabbed the Sword off the ground and charged the entrance of the storage unit. Behind him, A.J. and Riley shouted his name, but he ignored them. He skidded into the sunlight, blinking. There—several feet down the gravel walkway—he saw the girl. It was the closest he'd ever come to her, the first time he'd seen her in bright daylight, with nothing obscuring his vision.

Oh no . . .

From the doorway of the shed there was an explosion of swear words as Riley and A.J. came face-to-face with a legend they'd never believed in.

Jax threw the Sword aside, and ran straight toward the Morrigan.

"Jax!" Riley yelled. "Jax, no! Stay away from her!"

She stood on the path with blank, staring eyes, wearing an oversized T-shirt that said SPCA in faded letters, her messy, dark brown hair fanned out around her head. A crow sat on her shoulder. It lifted off with a lazy flap of its wings when Jax grabbed the girl by the arms and shook her. "Wake up! Wake up! Look at me!"

She blinked. Her brown eyes rolled around; the pupils contracted, and she focused on his face. "Jax?" she whispered. "Where am I? Help me. *Please . . .*"

Then she vanished right out of his hands.

Riley and A.J. caught up with him, grabbed him, and turned him around and around between them.

"Is he okay?"

"Jax, can you hear me?"

"Did she say his name? Holy crap, she said his name! That *can't* be good!"

Jax shook them off. "Of course, she said my name. She knows me! Didn't you recognize her?" When he saw their dumbfounded faces, he remembered. *They never met her.*

"That was my cousin!" he said. "Dorian's sister. That was Lesley Ambrose."

24

THEY TRIED TO LEAVE the Sword behind. Riley opened the safe and ordered Jax to put it inside. Jax did so, compelled by the voice of command, but when Riley started to close the safe door, Jax rammed him out of the way with his shoulder to grab the weapon back. He didn't mean to; he hardly realized he was doing it until he saw the Sword in his hands again. And he was completely oblivious to the warm wetness running down his back until A.J. pointed out that he'd popped a couple stitches sometime in the exertion of the last several minutes.

It seemed that Jax was able to put the Sword down, as long as he didn't leave its vicinity. But he couldn't hand it to either Riley or A.J., and, as Riley had proved quite painfully, no one could take it away from him.

There didn't seem to be any choice but to take the Sword with them, which they'd planned to do in the first place— just not under these circumstances. Riley held Jax by the arm as they walked back to the truck. "Do you understand what you did? By drawing that Sword, you've invoked it, and it's claimed you. No one can take it from you until you've killed the person you identified as your enemy."

"He's also protected," A.J. said. "No one can harm him until the Sword is satisfied. So, if we keep him away from this Griffyn guy, Jax is safe. Which, the way things have been going lately, is maybe a good thing. The kid's a walking menace."

"He's cursed," Riley said. "Thirteen years old, and he's cursed to kill someone. That's *not* a good thing, A.J. This is *my* fault. I shouldn't have let myself be distracted . . ." He glared at the box of family photographs A.J. was carrying. "I told you to leave those in the shed."

"Not a chance. I'm not letting you leave your family behind anymore." A.J. put the box into the backseat of his truck despite Riley's protest and removed a first-aid kit from the glove compartment.

"It's *not* your fault, Riley. The Morrigan did this," Jax said, pulling up his shirt so A.J. could replace the bandage on his back. "She's been around this whole time, pushing us this way and that. She almost got you drowned when she made me stop the car in that storm, and now she's managed to bind me to a Kin sword." Jax scowled. "How did she end up with my cousin? When Evangeline said the Morrigan *takes the body of a girl*, I didn't think she meant it literally!"

"I didn't either," Riley said. "I didn't even believe in the Morrigan until just now."

Jax was kicking himself for not recognizing her earlier. Deidre's men had seen the Girl of Crows in the ruins in Mexico and had described her as wearing a short white dress. That description had stuck in Jax's mind. But it wasn't a dress—it was the long T-shirt Lesley slept in. Jax had *seen* his cousin wearing that shirt. He'd almost made the connection when he saw Evangeline wearing one of Riley's oversized T-shirts to sleep in.

Dorian had told Jax that Lesley was prone to sleep-walking. It'd started when her father had forced her into the brownie tunnels in the hope that their magic would awaken a talent in his "dud" of a daughter. Instead, Lesley had started screaming and walking in her sleep, and this most often happened on Wednesday-into-Thursday nights.

Nights when she was supposedly skipping over the eighth day like any other Normal.

The sighting of the Morrigan at the pyramid had been on a Grunsday, and so had been Jax's glimpse of her in Central Park and during the hurricane. She'd been seen at the fall of Oeth-Anoeth on a Grunsday, too.

But today was Thursday.

"I'm calling Dorian," Jax said, taking out his phone and thumbing through his contacts without waiting for permission.

"Wait, do you think it's smart to call the Ambroses?" A.J. protested. "Riley?"

"He has to," Riley said. "We owe Dorian for getting Evangeline safely out of the Dulac building, remember? And besides, this girl is Jax's cousin. She's only what— fifteen?"

"Fourteen." Jax hit the dial button.

The call was picked up almost immediately. "Jax?" came Dorian's anxious voice.

"Where's Lesley?" Jax demanded.

There was a second of silence before Dorian answered. "How'd you know she was gone?"

Things went downhill fast from there. Uncle Finn grabbed the phone from Dorian and accused Jax of encouraging Lesley to run away. Riley took the phone from Jax and started yelling back. "I'm not keeping your daughter from you! If there was some plan to send her to me, I didn't know anything about it." Jax cringed hearing that, because he and Dorian *had* discussed the possibility of Lesley seeking sanctuary with Riley if Uncle Finn continued his experiments. "I've seen your daughter, though," Riley said into the phone, "or at least Jax says it was her."

Uncle Finn didn't believe what Riley told him. "It's true," Jax insisted, when Riley handed the phone back.

"I've seen her three times now, but the first two she was too far away for me to recognize her. Why do you think she's been having nightmares on the night when the eighth day happens? It's because she's living parts of it!"

"Jax," his uncle roared at him. "I don't know what your purpose is in spinning this outlandish lie, but if you and Pendragon know where my daughter is—"

"Where was Lesley on the night Wylit tried to end the world?" Jax shouted back. "Where was she the night the Llyrs broke out of prison? Huh? Were those the nights she had her nightmares? Holy crap, Uncle Finn, I just got away from you people! After what you and Sloane did to me, do you think I'd call you for anything less than an *emergency*?"

Uncle Finn faltered, sputtering, and then apparently lost control over the phone.

"Jax, this is Aunt Marian. Did you really see Lesley?"

Jax wouldn't have recognized his aunt's voice. She'd been crying. "Yes, I swear."

"What makes you think the Morrigan is manifesting through *my daughter*? Lesley wouldn't hurt a fly!"

"I know that, but I saw her! Her eyes were all glassy, like she's sleepwalking. There are crows with her; she disappeared into thin air—and Aunt Marian, she woke up for just a second and asked me to help her!"

"What do we do?" His aunt's voice wavered and cracked.

Jax didn't like Aunt Marian, but he felt horrible for her. He had no idea what she was supposed to do. He looked at Riley helplessly.

Riley wiped a hand across his face. "Ask them if they'll accept Bedivere's house as a neutral setting and meet us there tonight," he instructed Jax. "Because right now, I don't think we can afford to be enemies. We all have too much at stake."

25

"WHAT'S *SHE* DOING HERE?" Riley exclaimed at the sight of Sloane Dulac in Bedivere's house. Immediately, A.J. and Mr. Crandall took defensive positions around their liege lord. Jax might have thought that was an over-reaction if he hadn't experienced for himself the power of his cousin's talent.

Sloane scowled. "Lesley's my cousin and a member of my clan."

"She's right," Bedivere said. "You called on me as a neutral party, and I say the Dulac leader has a place in this discussion." They were once again in his banquet room, at the table that sometimes served as the Table. Uncle Finn, Aunt Marian, and Dorian were all there. With his relatives out in full force, Jax might've overlooked the person slouched in a chair at the opposite end of the long table if it hadn't been for her orange hair. *What's* she *doing here?* Jax wondered, not with the hostility Riley felt for

Sloane—just with the awkwardness he now felt in Tegan's company. Then he saw Mrs. Crandall and realized the two of them must have ended up here after completing their own assignment this morning.

"Jax! What happened to you?" Aunt Marian came at him like a guided missile. Before Jax could hide behind Mr. Crandall, she had her hands on him. "It's a knife wound," she told her husband.

"A knife wound?" Uncle Finn shot Riley an accusing glare. Dorian's jaw dropped.

"Is that a Kin sword he's holding?" Bedivere also looked at Riley. "*The* Kin Sword?"

"He drew it," Riley told Bedivere grimly.

"I was *tricked* into drawing it." Jax pulled out of Aunt Marian's hands and tossed the Sword onto the table. "Now it thinks it belongs to me until I kill some big Kin dude."

"What?" Uncle Finn marched over and tried to grab the Sword, but recoiled with a gasp the moment he touched it. He turned on Riley. "You let my nephew get stabbed with a knife *and* bind himself to a Kin artifact? To *kill* someone?" His hand clenched into a fist.

"The stabbing wasn't Riley's fault," Jax said quickly. "And he tried to pry the Sword out of my hand—"

"*You* let your daughter be taken by the Morrigan," Riley challenged Uncle Finn. "Torturing her in the brownie tunnels must've primed her somehow, or drew the Morrigan's attention. The stories say she likes suffering and fear."

Uncle Finn spoke through his teeth. "Pendragon, I should—" Mr. Crandall moved forward to protect his liege, and Bedivere raised his hand of power to restrain Jax's uncle.

"Finn, stop it!" exclaimed Aunt Marian. "He's right. You're the one to blame!"

Jax took a closer look at his aunt. Her eyes were red and puffy. Her hair wasn't combed into its usual talk-show-host perfection. Most surprising of all, she was staring daggers at her husband. "You did this to Lesley," she hissed. "I asked you to leave her alone. I *begged* you."

Uncle Finn opened his mouth in shock, but nothing came out.

"We're here to talk with Pendragon," Aunt Marian said, "not fight him. But first I have to take care of Jax." She turned to her nephew and said in a tearful, broken voice, "Stand *still*."

Jax didn't move. He didn't want to see her cry. Aunt Marian placed a hand on his back, and the persistent throbbing of Jax's injury faded. The pulling sensation from the stitches vanished, and he stood up straighter with a deep breath. "This doesn't completely heal it," his aunt said. "Don't exert yourself too much."

"Yes ma'am," Jax said. "Thank you."

She looked up at Riley. "Now you."

"I'm fine," Riley replied gruffly.

"Pain is like fingernails on a blackboard to a healer.

Give me your hand, Pendragon."

Riley glowered, but he unclenched the hand he'd used to grab the Sword that afternoon. Jax hadn't realized how blistered it was. Aunt Marian laid her palm over Riley's, and when she let go, the swollen blisters had deflated into loose, dead skin. Riley mumbled a grudging thanks, and she tersely replied, "Don't pick at it," without meeting his eyes.

Bedivere cleared his throat. "Now that everyone's decided to be civil, shall we sit down?"

They did so, the Pendragon clan and Jax sticking to one side of the table and the Dulacs to the other. While they settled themselves, Tegan leaned forward to peer at the Sword. "What's the deal with that thing?" she asked.

Jax couldn't help himself. "Famous treasure and *you* don't know about it?"

"My dad didn't tell us Kin fairy tales when we were little," Tegan snapped. "I know there are four of them, but not the story that goes with 'em."

Bedivere said, "There are only three now. It is believed the Arawens destroyed the Cauldron of Dagda rather than let it fall into King Arthur's hands. It was supposed to feed an army, no matter how large, to their satisfaction. This one, the Sword of Nuadu, protects the life of its owner until the death of the enemy named when it is drawn from its sheath."

"What if the owner doesn't draw it or name an enemy?" Jax asked.

"Then the Sword wouldn't really belong to him." Bedivere glanced at Riley. "Which is how it passed out of Pendragon hands without being used."

"Then there's the Stone of Fal," Dorian piped up. "It protects the owner's property from invaders, and the household will always prosper while it's there."

Sloane looked pointedly around the banquet room. "Guess who's got that one."

"It was agreed by the Table that I should take charge of it," Bedivere said stiffly. "Just as the Pendragons were entrusted with the Sword." He turned back to Tegan. "The final item is the Spear of Lugh. It also confers protection on the owner, who cannot be defeated or swayed from his purpose while he holds it. Like the Sword of Nuadu, it recognizes only one owner at a time."

"Crap," said Jax. "I think the Llyrs have that one. I saw an old Kin guy with a spear."

"*When* did you see the Llyrs?" Uncle Finn asked. "Is that how you got hurt?"

"Where was Lesley?" Aunt Marian begged him.

Jax held up his hand. "Wait. Let me tell it in order." He started to explain his plan to contact Addie via brownie tunnels but was interrupted by Uncle Finn almost at once.

"How did you know you could jump locations using brownie magic?"

"Uhhh . . ." Jax tried not to look at Dorian.

His cousin raised a hand voluntarily. "That would be

me. I told him how to do it."

"How would you know?" Uncle Finn turned on his son.

"I've been experimenting."

"Since when?" demanded his mother.

"Since I first found the tunnels," Dorian declared in a tone of defiance Jax had never heard him use before. "About six weeks *before* Dad told me about them."

While Uncle Finn stared at Dorian in disbelief, Bedivere addressed Sloane. "You told the Table your clan had ended its experimentation with brownie holes."

"This was unauthorized. You heard him." Nevertheless, Sloane looked at Dorian with a combination of speculation and pride.

"Where does Lesley come into this?" Aunt Marian asked impatiently.

Jax continued his story, including how he got hurt, and eventually how he came to draw the Sword. When he told them about Lesley begging for help, Aunt Marian put both hands over her mouth and Uncle Finn paled. Dorian looked like he might cry, but he was the one who asked, "How can we save her?"

Bedivere sighed. "After Riley called me and apprised me of the situation, I did some research. Legends about the Morrigan are often contradictory, but most agree that she takes Normals as hosts for her three incarnations—one girl, one middle-aged woman, and one elderly woman.

I'm sorry to say, there are *no* stories of her hosts returning to their former lives."

"Lesley spoke to Jax as herself," Riley said. "I saw that. For just a couple seconds, she woke up—or snapped out of her trance—or whatever. She's not gone."

"Not yet," Bedivere said. "But the Morrigan has been borrowing Lesley Ambrose for months to influence events. Until this week, the girl was returned home after each appearance. Now, it seems the Morrigan has taken her and kept her. Why?"

"I'm more interested in why she took Lesley Ambrose in the first place—out of all the Normal girls in the world," said Mrs. Crandall. "What Riley said is possible: the Morrigan might've been attracted by the girl's distress, especially if she was suffering in a magical environment." Here, almost every person in the room shot an accusing look at Uncle Finn, who stared at the table. "Even so," Mrs. Crandall continued, "it's an astounding coincidence."

"I thought the Morrigan was all about coincidences," Jax said.

"Warfare is her primary goal," Mr. Crandall replied. "And that's coming."

"With *both* Emrys heirs helping the Llyrs," Sloane said, "we can expect another attempt on the Eighth Day Spell. The Morrigan is probably behind that, too."

"Evangeline is *not* helping them," Jax protested. "She's trying to rescue her sister. If your clan hadn't kept Addie locked in a cell, neither of them would be with the Llyrs. So, it's your fault, Sloane—or at least your grandmother's. Here's your chance to make up for it. Do you still want to blow them up if we find out where they're hiding? I know you don't care about Addie or Evangeline, but what about Lesley?"

"Sloane," Aunt Marian said urgently. "What if Lesley is with the Llyrs? What if they have her? You can't authorize a preemptive strike now!"

Sloane stared back at her clanswoman and licked her lips in an uncharacteristic gesture of uncertainty. When she didn't answer immediately, Aunt Marian planted both hands on the table and leaned forward. "You held Lesley on the day she was born. You came to the hospital with your father and asked to hold her. You were four years old. Do you remember?"

"I remember." Sloane sat very still. Her expression was the same one Jax had seen on Riley's face a few days ago, when he was weighing the lives of billions against the safety of one. Finally, Sloane blinked and scanned the table. "Dulac and Bors are changing their vote," she announced, speaking for her uncle and vassal Oliver Bors as if it wasn't necessary to consult him. She removed a phone from her purse and apparently sent a group text—if the notifications Jax heard on his own phone and several others in the room were any indication.

Bedivere nodded approval. "The idea of a sneak attack

that could result in genocide never sat well with me. Of course, I don't know if we're any nearer to finding the Llyrs. The Donovan family is working with us now, checking properties owned by that Kin company. But there were quite a lot of them."

"And I think they're on to us," Tegan spoke up. "Some of the places I was taken to had Kin living there recently, including the kids from the Carroway house. I recognized their scent. But every place I saw had been abandoned, probably just this last eighth day. Because Jax tipped our hand. They know we've discovered their hiding places."

Jax cringed, remembering the papers he'd dropped while fighting Kel.

"The Emrys girls could escape pretty easily, if they only knew it," Dorian said. "They can both travel by brownie magic."

"I could send the Ganners to try and snatch them," Sloane volunteered. "My men would stand a better chance than Jax did." Her vassals, the Ganners, served as a security team for Sloane's clan, and, like the Dulacs and Ambroses, they'd been granted access to the brownie tunnels by Dr. Morder's spell.

But Jax objected. "As far as Evangeline and Addie know, the Ganners are enemies." In fact, as far as Jax knew, they still might be. Sloane was devious enough to double-cross them. "They'd fight back. Someone could get hurt."

"And thanks to Jax spilling the beans about the brownie holes, the Llyrs might have precautions in place," Tegan added. Jax gave her a look. Yeah, he'd messed up. But did Tegan have to remind them every two seconds?

"What about Lesley?" Aunt Marian asked plaintively.

"I don't know what we can do about her," Mrs. Crandall said as gently as possible. "The Morrigan goes where she wants."

"The Morrigan goes where there's a battle—*which is coming*," Mr. Crandall stressed. "Not to diminish the importance of the girls, but if we're going to face the Llyrs head-on in warfare, we need to have a plan. Sheila Morgan will be furious when she finds out you're voting down her military strategy. Let's have an alternative ready to suggest to her."

"Do you have one in mind?" Bedivere asked.

Mr. Crandall nodded. "The Llyrs want the Treasures. Riley was thinking of using the Sword of Nuadu as bait, but it seems to me the more powerful item is the Stone of Fal. What if we lure them into a battle *here*, where their own Kin magic will work against them?"

They bounced the idea around, but Jax kept finding flaws in their plans. Evangeline wouldn't know what they were up to, and there were very few people she'd completely trust. His talent nagged at him, pestering him with a fragment of an idea, until suddenly it clicked into place. "You're missing something obvious," he said, interrupting a suggestion from Mr. Crandall. "Something we need for this to work. A man on the inside."

"No!" exclaimed every adult in the room.

Jax guessed they knew what inside man he had in mind.

Riley grabbed Jax by the front of his shirt and lifted him out of his chair. "If you'll excuse me a minute, I need a few words alone with my ward." He hauled Jax out of Bedivere's banquet room and shut the door behind them before letting go of his shirt. "You will not do this. You swore an oath to me. No more stupid risks."

"I swore I'd get your permission first. I'm doing that now." Jax clutched the Sword of Nuadu with both hands and stared up at Riley. "This won't be a stupid risk." He didn't want to die the way his father had, doing something reckless and poorly thought out. "This is going to be a very carefully calculated and planned risk, because every smart person in that room is going to help me figure it out. You'd do it if you could."

"Yeah, but I'm eighteen. An adult. You're *thirteen*."

"When you were thirteen, you took charge of a whole clan."

"And went into hiding," Riley reminded him. "I didn't walk into the Dulac stronghold and dare them to kill me. I *hid*, Jax."

"Hiding was what you needed to do right then," Jax said. "You kept Evangeline safe all those years—until I showed up. I messed you up again and again."

"Jax—"

"Hiding won't do us any good now. Look, you know only I can do this." Jax lifted the Sword. "I've got something the Llyrs want, but they can't take it away from me, and they can't hurt me while I've got it."

"Unless you use it."

"What?"

"Unless you actually kill that guy," Riley said. "Then the Sword dumps you. It's done with you. No more protection."

"I'm not going to kill anyone," Jax scoffed.

"You were tricked into drawing it. You might be tricked into using it." Riley paced the hallway. "I don't like the way you've been pulled into this. I didn't believe in the Morrigan, but you've seen her again and again, which means—"

"She chose me to play this part," Jax said solemnly.

"She's a force of chaos and destruction. What kind of part do you think it'll be?"

"I'll do it my own way," Jax said. "And surprise her." He held up the Sword again. "I have this. And I have a liege to serve. You dragged me into this hallway so you can tell me how much you wish you could take my place. But I'm the only one who can do this."

"I'd do anything to keep you safe," Riley said. "You and Evangeline."

Jax realized, to his shock, that his guardian was pretty choked up—which immediately put Jax in the same state. But he blinked away the tears and said, "You have to let me do this. It's the only chance we have of getting Evangeline and Addie back alive and maybe Lesley, too. This is my *talent*, Riley. I *know* it."

Riley nodded reluctantly. "I know it too," he whispered.

26

"AGAIN," BRAN DEMANDED.

Addie called up wind for the third time, sending Condor Aeron stumbling, but Bran wasn't satisfied. "You use the same spell over and over. It's predictable. Your execution is weak, and you're not aggressive enough." He thumped the Spear on the warehouse floor, which lurched beneath her. Addie lost her balance and her rear end hit the concrete. Laughter came from above, where Griffyn and Ysabel were leaning against a railing on the second floor, watching the action.

He does earthquakes now, too? Then Addie saw Condor coming for her. He was a grown man fighting a thirteen-year-old girl, but he had no qualms about hitting her. She'd already learned that. Scrambling to her feet, Addie reached out mentally to the white, intense magic of the Spear in Bran's hand, then waved her arms at the stacked boxes around them. *Here's some aggression for you.*

The boxes exploded. Hunks of plastic and metal pierced

the air like shrapnel. Something winged Addie's face. *Whoops. Next time I should duck.* Condor had already dropped and covered his head. He had plenty of practice dodging things that exploded, imploded, and collapsed. It was *his* talent Addie was copying.

The Aeron magic had been hard for Addie to get a handle on, like a greasy, black oil slick. But Addie was finally getting a feel for it. *Mayhem of any kind. Whatever will make the greatest mischief.*

Bran had forced her to continue training last night even after torturing her on the plane. He'd woken her early to start again today. Addie understood that he held no ill feelings for her defiance in Vermont or her defense of the Transitioner boy, and he expected the same lack of resentment from her. *You were punished for your errors. Learn from it.* That was Bran's motto.

Addie was willing to play along. If this bizarre training unlocked the key to casting the spell she needed to release the prisoners of the eighth day, Addie intended to invoke her own motto: *Remember every insult and injury.*

She was preparing to utilize the Aeron talent again to burst water pipes above her head while simultaneously throwing up a shield spell she'd learned from an orphan at the Carroway house when Kel and his father, Madoc, burst out of one of the offices on the second floor. "What are you doing?" Madoc yelled, pushing Griffyn out of his way and running down the metal staircase to the warehouse floor. "There are computers in those boxes worth thousands of dollars!"

"I thought this wasn't your warehouse," Addie said.

"Money is money," Madoc exclaimed. "You can't wantonly destroy everything you see!"

Madoc had been distressed to discover that the papers carried by the Transitioner boy had the name of his company written on them. If Transitioners knew about Madoc's company, none of his holdings were safe. The Aerons making use of his properties had been forced to vacate. Madoc had hidden the plane, and they'd all taken refuge here—in a place owned by Normals who were used to secrecy, fond of money, and close to the point of origin marked on the Transitioner boy's map. It also brought them nearer to the Bedivere property, where they believed one of the missing Treasures might be found.

Just then, the huge loading-dock door at the front of the warehouse began to roll up. One of Condor's clansmen waved a Jeep into the warehouse.

On the plane yesterday, Addie had not known for sure if it was her sister viewing her through the scrying spell. It would've served Bran right if it'd been the Dulacs after all—if *they'd* been the ones to receive Bran's message and if they'd planned an ambush for today. But the Aeron men emerging from the Jeep looked triumphant. And they were followed by a girl.

Five years had passed since Addie had seen her sister, but there was no mistaking this for anyone but Evangeline.

She'd grown quite pretty—*of course she had*—although she wasn't very tall. Addie, at thirteen, was about the same height. *I'll end up taller, even if I'm never as pretty.* Then she was ashamed that her first thought, after all this time, was to compare them.

By contrast, Evangeline's face lit up when she saw Addie, proving that she was the better person, just like Addie remembered. She started toward her little sister, but one of the Aerons caught her by the arm.

Griffyn hurried down the stairs from the second floor to get a closer look at the new captive, while Ysabel followed more slowly. Two of the Aerons escorted Evangeline to Bran under guard, although their lax demeanor suggested they didn't consider her much of a threat. *They should.* Now Addie was noticing what she should have seen *first*—how her sister glowed with an ominous, simmering light. No one but Addie would be able to see it, but everyone else ought to have paid attention to how her sister was walking with bouncy, jittery steps and how her hands shook.

Evangeline had come here holding uncast spells inside her—big ones, by the look of it. Unlike Addie, who'd been able to cast spells without symbols or rituals since her first visitation from the Morrigan, Evangeline would've had to set this up in advance. *Her skin must feel like it's trying to crawl off her body.* Grudgingly, Addie had to admire her sister's ability to hold all that unreleased power, probably for hours. Evangeline glanced over her shoulder at Addie and mouthed, *Be ready.*

Addie chewed on a fingernail, wondering what message to send back. *No, don't!* or *Yes, please!*

"Did she turn herself over willingly?" Bran asked the Aeron men when they brought Evangeline to a halt a few feet in front of him.

"Yes. She was wearing this, and I thought you'd want to see it." One of them handed Bran an engraved dagger—an honor blade, the Transitioners called them. Bran examined it. From across the room, Addie saw that the dagger had its own curious glow, which, like the illumination around Evangeline herself, was invisible to everyone but her.

"You've been hurting my sister," Evangeline accused Bran. "Against your word."

"I'm not hurt," Addie called, knowing her face was bruised from Condor's blows and scratched from the explosion she'd caused. "Don't worry about me."

"This bears the mark of the Pendragons," Bran said of the dagger. "Why do you carry it?"

"It was a gift." Evangeline raised her chin.

Bran looked at Madoc. "It's not a very old blade. Perhaps the Pendragons are not *all* dead. That would explain the words in the prophecy." Evangeline's eyes widened, realizing she'd given away something they didn't know, and Bran smiled at her reaction, which confirmed his theory. "Does an Emrys perform powerful magic on a Pendragon blade?"

Evangeline's eyes flickered from Bran to Griffyn, who was approaching from the staircase, then to Addie and back to

Bran, as if noting everyone's position and distance from her. "I killed Wylit with it," she said proudly. The Aeron man restraining her had released his grip, and Evangeline used this new freedom to step closer to Bran and extend her index finger toward the dagger.

Addie realized what spell her sister was holding and stepped back.

Somehow, Bran also guessed—or saw something in Evangeline's eyes that warned him—because he flung the Pendragon blade away just as her finger brushed against it. If he hadn't, he would probably have lost his hand. As it was, a percussive blast threw him off his feet and sent Griffyn ducking for cover. Evangeline and her guards were also flung backward, but Evangeline's additional stored spells must have been protective in nature because she alone managed to keep her feet. She whirled, her long hair swinging in an arc, and started running toward the warehouse's open bay door. "Addie!" she yelled.

For a second, Addie froze in indecision. Evangeline was going the wrong way. She would never outrun the Aerons, with or without their vehicles. "No!" Addie shouted. "This way!" Condor grabbed for her, but Addie thrust him aside with a gust of wind and bolted for the back of the warehouse. Out of the corner of her eye, she saw her sister's flight path falter and zigzag. To Evangeline it must have seemed like Addie was running toward a dead end. But Addie had been eyeing an opalescent glimmer beside a Dumpster all day, waiting for a chance to examine it unobserved. The opportunity had never come, and now she'd have to rely on the word of a Transitioner boy and a half-breed traitor that she could actually enter a brownie hole.

But her sister wasn't going to make it. As soon as Evangeline changed course and ran toward Addie, Ysabel Arawen launched herself down the stairs, sprinting like a deer. With her long-legged stride, she intercepted Evangeline, grabbed her around the waist with a brawny arm, and hauled the slighter girl completely off her feet.

And Addie, watching this over her shoulder as she ran, never saw the broken metal computer panel Condor Aeron hurled at her like a discus until it slammed into her side. She hit the concrete hard—knees, chest, and then her head. For a second, Addie knew what it meant to *see stars*. By the time she'd shaken off the pain, Condor had her by the shirt collar, and Ysabel was pushing Evangeline in front of Bran Llyr, who was now on his feet again, his tunic scorched but his face impassive.

"Two halves of a detonation, contained within an object and your person," Bran remarked without emotion, as if evaluating Evangeline's work. "Clever in conception. But you wasted the strength you could have put into it by providing protection for yourself and preserving the object." He glanced at the dagger, still intact on the floor where he'd thrown it. "And your timing was off." Then he backhanded Evangeline across the face contemptuously, as if punishing her for *failing* her assassination attempt. Bran turned to his son. "Well, Griffyn? Can you handle her?"

"What do you mean, *handle* her?" Ysabel repeated, scowling.

"Scrawny girl like this?" Griffyn scoffed. "Of course."

Bran returned his attention to Evangeline. "You're as spirited as your sister, I'll give you that. But you're a traitor, as your ancestor Merlin was. You ally yourself with the Pendragons and boast of killing Wylit, then attempt to kill *me*—"

"Wylit was insane," Evangeline said, staring up at him unafraid even while the mark of his hand on her face reddened. "No doubt you are, too."

Bran continued to list what he saw as her inadequacies without reacting to the insult. "Your spells were wrongly proportioned and as ill planned as your vassal's attempt to abduct Adelina."

At that, Evangeline blinked rapidly, then looked at Addie, obviously alarmed. *She doesn't know what happened to him,* Addie realized. *He didn't make it back.* Addie was surprised by how hard that hit her.

"The only hope for the Emrys line is to bind it to my own and breed something worthwhile into it," Bran went on. "Therefore, you will speak the Handmaiden Oath to my son and marry him when you come of age."

"I will not!" Evangeline exclaimed in horror, while Ysabel protested, "But *I* am promised to Griffyn!"

"Condor," Bran said. "Break Adelina's wrist—to start with."

Addie yanked her shirt out of Condor's grasp and invoked the spell she'd been thinking about during their sparring match minutes ago. A translucent barrier sprang up between them.

While she was focused on Condor, Madoc seized her from behind, pushed her to the floor, and put a knee on her back. Addie hadn't been expecting an attack from Kel's father, and by the time she realized she needed to fight back with another spell, he had her arm pinned on the concrete, preparing to snap her hand the wrong way.

"Dad, wait!" Kel yelled.

The pressure on her arm eased. Addie heard Evangeline screaming, "I'll do it! Let her go!"

"No, Evangeline!" Addie shouted back. "You don't have to! They can't—" Madoc clamped a hand over her mouth. She bit him, but he hung on.

Evangeline got down on her knees. "Don't hurt her!"

Griffyn kicked the Pendragon blade across the floor toward Evangeline. The spell bound to it had been released, but Griffyn was obviously wary of touching it. "Rid yourself of this, first!"

Picking up the dagger, Evangeline braced its tip against the concrete, then jammed the hilt down with both hands. The blade snapped in two, and Evangeline sagged with a sob. Then Bran took a handful of her hair and wrenched her head back, forcing her to stare up at Griffyn while still on her knees.

"*I was promised to Griffyn,*" Ysabel repeated. "From birth."

Addie made a muffled protest. She tried to think of a spell

that would dislodge Madoc from her back, but Evangeline was already speaking. "I, Evangeline Emrys . . ."

"Pledge yourself as handmaiden to Griffyn Llyr," Bran prompted her.

"Pledge myself as handmaiden to Griffyn Llyr."

"His word is your sole command, to be obeyed without question," Bran continued. "His will and his safety are your only object, until death part the two of you."

Evangeline faltered here, but Bran yanked her head around to face Addie, and Condor grabbed Addie's arm, ready to help Madoc break it. Hurriedly, Evangeline repeated the rest of the oath, and when Bran let go of her, she bowed her head in defeat. Ysabel's hands moved toward her knives, as if she wanted to implement the death option immediately. When Bran gave her a baleful glare, Ysabel turned and stalked away.

Madoc released Addie. She scrambled up and ran across the room, flinging her arms around Evangeline as her sister rose shakily to her feet. "Why'd you do that?" Addie gasped.

"Addie," Evangeline whispered. Her shoulders shook as she hugged Addie back. And suddenly who was prettier and who was taller and even the fact that they didn't know each other after five years didn't matter.

Griffyn picked up the broken honor blade. "I'll hang on to this," he said, slipping the two halves into his leather vest with a nasty grin. "Maybe I'll return it to its owner. Personally."

When Addie felt Evangeline shudder at his words, anger

bubbled up inside her. *Griffyn has total control over my sister.* Addie pulled out of Evangeline's embrace. "You shouldn't have come here after me, and you shouldn't have sworn yourself to that barbarian! They can't kill us. They *need* us. You know that!"

"Addie, they were torturing you." Evangeline wiped away the blood on Addie's face.

"It's just pain. It doesn't mean anything. Watch!" Addie put her hands to her face, and when Evangeline gasped, Addie knew the scratches had vanished. She brushed her fingers against the red mark on Evangeline's cheek, where Bran had hit her, and watched that fade to nothing.

"How'd you do that?" Evangeline asked in astonishment.

"Get away, little beast." Griffyn shoved Addie aside and surveyed his newly sworn handmaiden, swaggering with his power over her. "You will not try to escape or vanish into brownie holes, do you understand me? And you'll prevent your sister from doing so." Evangeline nodded. "You won't let your vassals act against me, either, if you have any more besides that runt of a boy."

Tears were running down Evangeline's face now. "How do they know about Jax?" she asked Addie in a hoarse whisper.

Jax. That was his name. Addie felt her cheeks flush. "I'm sorry, Evangeline."

"I put a knife in his back," Griffyn bragged. "He's dead."

Evangeline made a wheezing, gagging sound, like she was choking.

"Who's dead?" a voice called out. "Me? Think again."

Addie whipped around, her mouth falling open.

The Transitioner boy climbed out of an opalescent hole in the air right before their eyes. He wasn't dead, but he looked *ticked off.* A large brownie was clinging to his shoulder, and he was wearing—of all things—a sword strapped across his back.

27

EVANGELINE GASPED AND COVERED her mouth in relief. Addie gaped at Jax before breaking into a grin, like she was happy to see him. *Guess she doesn't think I'm a Dulac anymore.* After assuring himself that both girls were unharmed, Jax turned his attention to the enemies.

One of the men Jax had seen at the island house shouted for someone to lower the warehouse's loading dock door. "It's like having a missing wall. The wards aren't complete with it up!" he yelled. "Condor, take your people outside to look for others."

Men with tattooed faces scrambled to follow his directions. One began rolling down the giant warehouse door. Jax knew that when it closed no one else could arrive using the brownie tunnels or observe him through scrying. He was tempted to wave good-bye, but he didn't want to give away that someone was watching. So he kept his hands at his side and surveyed the rest of the group. Was there anybody else here he recognized?

Yup, there was the old man with the Spear, and Kel, the teen with the boy-band haircut. There were more tattooed people, and—

When Jax's gaze landed on Griffyn, it was as if a veil of red fury fell over the room. The shouting and the sound of the metal door crashing shut vanished behind a buzz of rage. Griffyn grabbed Evangeline to keep her away from Jax, and the sight of that brute digging his fingers into her arm made Jax reach for the hilt of the Sword sticking up over his right shoulder.

"Jax, don't!" Evangeline's voice, full of distress and fear, snapped his attention from his enemy to his liege. With a surge of willpower, Jax forced his hand away from the Sword and down to his honor blade, calling upon the most recent oath he'd made on it.

No matter how he and Riley had tried, it had proved impossible for Jax to swear *not* to draw the Sword. The best he'd been able to do was to swear to keep the safety of his lieges foremost in his mind, an oath that enhanced and renewed his original vassal bond. Because it did not serve the girls to draw the Sword now, their need superseded the compulsion of the Kin weapon, which dwindled to a throbbing in the back of his mind, like a persistent headache.

A second later, he was surrounded by Kin—surrounded, but untouched. Stink chattered nervously, clinging to Jax's shoulder. "Is that the Sword of Nuadu?" one of the men demanded.

Jax looked at the circle of tattooed faces. Some were decorated with spirals and geometric designs. Others resembled animals. It was like being captured by a tribe of cannibals. "Go ahead and take it," Jax suggested. "If you can." Now that Griffyn was blocked from his sight, the plan returned to him: what he was supposed to say and what he was supposed to do.

But holy crap . . . I didn't realize how it was going to affect me when I saw him . . .

One of the Kin grabbed the strap crossing Jax's chest. The man's lips peeled back from his teeth in a grimace of pain even though he wasn't touching the actual weapon. He didn't hang on as long as Riley had—just fumbled at the buckle, then stumbled backward with a wordless snarl, staring at his burned hands.

"Sorry," said Jax, "but it seems to think it belongs to me."

"Jax!" Evangeline gasped.

There was a thumping sound, like wood striking concrete, and the circle of tattooed men parted to make way for the old man with the Spear. Jax guessed he was the head Llyr. Oddly, Jax felt less worried about him than about Griffyn. *This old man can't hurt me, even if he is the Llyr leader, no more than I can take that Spear away from him. But Griffyn . . . the Sword wants me to kill Griffyn . . .*

"Do you have any idea what sort of power you've invoked, boy?" the old man asked. Jax thought he'd sampled a taste of it a few seconds ago, but he didn't say so. The man continued, "Your liege lady was allied with the Pendragons. I assume you stole the Sword from them? It's hard to imagine them giving it to a boy."

His use of the plural didn't escape Jax's notice. The Llyrs didn't know the Pendragons were reduced to one person, and they weren't going to find out from Jax. "The Pendragons never drew it," he said, "so it didn't really belong to them. It was pretty easy to claim it."

"Against whom did you draw it?" the Llyr leader asked.

Jax's answer had been carefully thought out and analyzed for flaws before he came here. He stated it precisely as he'd been told to. "I drew the Sword of Nuadu against all enemies of my liege lady and her family. Anyone and everyone who threatens to harm an Emrys is targeted." He felt the lie thrum through his body as the Sword tempted him to look at Griffyn. Instead, he finished his scripted lines. "Considering how many people have tried to hurt them so far, the job should keep me busy till I die of old age. You guys are stuck with me."

"Can he do that?" someone asked. "Invoke the Sword of Nuadu against an unnamed enemy? *Multiple* enemies?"

The Llyr leader turned to the man who'd ordered the

warehouse door closed, the one Jax thought might be a Mathonwy, the Kin with all the money. "Madoc?"

Madoc shook his head. "I don't think—"

"It's happened before!" Jax said before they could start doubting him. "Malcolm the Long-Lived did the same thing in the seventeen hundreds. I looked it up on the internet to make sure before I drew the Sword and named my enemy that way."

Madoc looked less certain now. He might have been rich and well connected, but he could only access the internet through remote employees. "You want the Sword of Nuadu," Jax repeated, "you've got to have me along with it."

The old guy turned toward Griffyn. He raised his eyebrows in a wordless question, gesturing toward the dagger held in the young man's hand.

Griffyn stared at Jax with a mixed expression of disgust and anger. He still had Evangeline by the arm, but he put his dagger away. "I can't touch him," he admitted grudgingly. "I can't even think about it."

That was ironic, because killing Griffyn was all Jax could think about. His muscles coiled, and his hand twitched involuntarily.

"I wouldn't handle my sister so roughly if I were you, Griffyn," Addie said loudly. "Or Jax will take you for one of our enemies and run you through."

Run him through. Jax's stomach turned over. He blinked and drew in quick breaths to clear his head. *I don't want to kill anyone—not even him. And a stupid sword can't make me!*

Maybe Griffyn sensed danger because he let go of Evangeline's arm. "Tell your vassal he's forbidden to leave by brownie holes," he snapped. "Tell him to obey our orders."

"You may not leave by brownie holes," Evangeline repeated to Jax in a strained voice. "Obey their orders." Then she glanced at Griffyn for permission, and when he grunted, she dashed across the intervening space and hugged Jax tightly. Stink scrambled to the floor, out of her way. He was no longer under orders to avoid her, but he knew when he wasn't wanted.

Evangeline pressed her cheek against Jax's. "I'm Griffyn Llyr's bound handmaiden," she whispered in his ear. "Don't tell me anything you don't want him to know."

Bound handmaiden? What the heck was that? But Jax got the last bit loud and clear. Evangeline guessed he'd come here as part of a plan and wanted him to keep it secret. That threw a monkey wrench into things—as did her direct order not to leave by brownie holes. Not that he could do that while they were warded, but it was definitely on his to-do list.

"Bran, we should leave," Madoc said to the Llyr leader. "We're at risk of attack here." He glared darkly at

Jax. "This boy has cost me most of my safe houses."

The tattooed man named Condor returned with a report. "There's no sign of anyone in the vicinity, but I've sent men further afield to make sure we don't get cut off. There must be other Transitioners coming behind him."

"There aren't," Jax insisted. "The brownie magic took me to my liege, but I didn't know *where* I was going ahead of time. I still don't know where I am. This warehouse could be in Timbuktu for all I know."

"Make him tell you the truth." Griffyn glowered at Evangeline.

Evangeline looked at Jax miserably. "Are you alone?"

Why is she doing everything he says? "Yes. No one is with me."

"Is someone watching us?" Griffyn pressed. "From the brownie holes? Or scrying?"

"No one is watching," Jax said through clenched teeth, keeping his eyes averted from the big, ugly Llyr. But Griffyn's voice set his nerves on fire, and he had to grip his honor blade again for strength. "The wards are complete now, aren't they? We're shielded from scrying, and brownie holes can't transport anybody in from the outside." Uncle Finn had wanted to come with Jax, backed up by members of the Dulac clan security force. But the Llyrs had defeated the Dulacs on their home ground once already, and Sloane had chosen not to risk her men's lives by sending them blindly into an unknown situation. They needed to face the Llyrs with a combined Transitioner force in a place of their choosing—during a battle that would attract the Morrigan.

That was the plan.

Jax turned back to the Llyr leader. "I came to serve my liege lady, and if she wants me to, I'll tell you where to find the last of those Treasures you're looking for."

Bran Llyr stared at him through narrowed eyes. "The Bediveres have the Stone of Fal."

Jax sagged a little. "Oh, you know that already?"

"It's a trap," Madoc proclaimed.

"Of course, it's a trap," said Bran. "Isn't it, boy?"

"Uh." What was he supposed to say? "Yeah. But what do you care? You're like a weather god, aren't you?"

Bran turned his back on Jax and faced Madoc. "We will assault the Bedivere house. The Transitioners' plans do not concern me."

"The house is protected," Madoc said. "A direct assault will be fruitless. It would be better to go into hiding until they've lowered their guard. The Aerons have one or two hiding places we can reach before midnight if we leave at once, and I know of abandoned properties out west where we can . . ."

"Madoc Mathonwy, I have not asked you to take a vow of loyalty," Bran interrupted him, "out of recognition for your service in freeing us from Oeth-Anoeth. However, as we head into battle against our ancient enemies, there can be only one leader of the Kin."

Madoc stiffened. Across the room, Kel looked shocked. Into this hesitation jumped Condor. "I'll swear my allegiance to you, Lord Llyr," he proclaimed loudly, dropping to his knees.

Way to suck up, thought Jax, *and make Madoc look bad at the same time.* All the tattooed men started clamoring to swear themselves, but Bran held Madoc pinned in his gaze. "Yes, of course," Madoc said belatedly. "You had only to ask."

"But you were not willing to *offer,*" Bran finished. "I have wondered why it took five years after Elwyn Emrys's death for you to assault Oeth-Anoeth. Perhaps it was because you were looking for a way to accomplish your goals *without* freeing me?"

Madoc didn't try to make lame excuses. He got down on his knees, looking sick. "I, Madoc Mathonwy, do swear my allegiance . . ."

Jax felt Evangeline's hand on his arm, pulling him away. A moment later, Addie was on his other side, and the three of them huddled together, watching Madoc swear himself to Bran Llyr. "How'd you end up with the Sword of Nuadu?" Evangeline whispered.

"Same as usual," Jax replied in an undertone. "I did

something stupid while Riley wasn't looking. What about you? What's this handmaiden stuff?"

"I'm magically bound to marry Griffyn Llyr," Evangeline said hoarsely.

"What?" A blinding rage overcame Jax, and if the girls hadn't each had one of his arms, he would've reached for the Sword again. Their touch grounded him, enabling him to protest with his voice instead. "You can't be *engaged* to him!"

"Worse than engaged," Addie hissed. "The handmaiden oath is for captured brides from enemy clans. The point is to humiliate her and break her spirit. It's an oath more binding than vassalhood; she's practically his slave." Addie leaned across Jax to whisper fiercely into Evangeline's face. "I can't believe you did it!"

"Was I supposed to watch them break your bones one by one?" Evangeline shot back.

Geez. The sisters couldn't have been reunited more than a few minutes, and they were already arguing? "How do we get her out of this?" Jax asked Addie. He needed to focus on what to do next, not on what had already happened. Because this was a huge kink in his plans.

"You could take your big old sword and kill Griffyn," Addie suggested snarkily. "That would do it." Then the sarcasm drained from her expression, and her eyes got wide. "He's supposed to die by an innocent hand. That was the oracle Aine Corra gave him. It's why he killed her." Addie looked at her hands. "Maybe I'm supposed to do it," she muttered.

Jax tried to swallow, but his throat had gone dry. *No, it's me. To free Evangeline, I'm really going to have to kill Griffyn Llyr.*

28

COULD I DO IT? Addie asked herself. Of all the magical talents she'd imitated during her practice sessions with Bran, the one she'd never attempted was lightning. It was the most lethal spell she knew, and she was afraid of accidentally striking someone dead. *But what if I wanted to do it on purpose?*

"Neither of you is going to kill Griffyn," Evangeline whispered. "And not just because I'd be compelled to stop you if you tried. You're both *children*. You aren't going to plot to murder anyone. Do you hear me? *I* took the oath. *I'll* find a way out of it."

Evangeline hadn't changed much. She was as bossy as ever. If Jax had been Elliot's age, this would've been like old times at the Emrys house. "The Dulacs told me you were dead," Addie said. "You and Elliot both. But you're alive, so could Elliot be . . . ?" She saw the answer on her sister's face even before she finished the question.

"He's gone," Evangeline confirmed sadly. "A long time ago. Wylit tried to make him break the Eighth Day Spell, and it killed him."

Addie's eyes stung but she blinked the tears back stubbornly. *Nothing's different from what I thought before. Hearing it from Evangeline doesn't change anything.* "That's what they said happened to you," she said, stuffing the memory of her little brother way, way down inside. "That you and Wylit tried to break the spell and failed."

"What?" Evangeline exclaimed. "No! Wylit was crazy. I almost got killed preserving the eighth day!"

"You had the chance to end the spell and you *preserved* it instead?" Addie gaped at her sister.

"Of course I did!" Evangeline stared right back at Addie. "These people can't be unleashed on the Normal world. What if they were free to create hurricanes *every day?*"

"What are you whispering about?" Griffyn growled. "Get over here." Evangeline shot a worried look at Addie, then went to stand where Griffyn told her to. "Keep your mouth shut and don't move," he ordered. Obediently, Evangeline pressed her lips together, but her eyes blazed with fury. Addie doubted Griffyn was going to break her sister's spirit no matter how he humiliated her.

Addie turned to say this to Jax and found him staring across the warehouse at Griffyn and Evangeline with a glazed expression, breathing heavily. He twitched as if he was having a fit. The Sword on his back pulsed with an ugly red glow, like it had been doing on and off since he'd arrived, and his hand was clenched around his honor blade. "What's wrong with you?" Addie asked. When Jax didn't respond, she grabbed his arm. "Hey!"

Jax shook himself. "Thanks," he muttered.

The Sword's glow faded to the dullness of dried blood. Addie looked Jax up and down, and then her gaze passed on to Griffyn with speculation. *Jax isn't telling the truth about the Sword.*

The final Aerons were making their loyalty oaths to Bran, and as each one was accepted, the rest of them cheered. Watching their excitement build, Addie realized that Bran could have called on them to pledge themselves days ago, but he'd deliberately saved it until the eve of his planned assault to rouse their passion and ferocity. The Aerons were too disorganized and wild to maintain focus for very long. Madoc—who'd apparently thought himself on equal footing with Bran—had been entirely blindsided by this, as had Ysabel, who'd returned from wherever she'd been sulking only to have Bran cast an expectant gaze in her direction, too.

The Arawens had enjoyed the status of being allies with the Llyrs for two millennia. But Ysabel was the last of her line, with no family left to back her. Her eyes swept the room, which was now full of enthusiastic Llyr vassals. She glared at her former betrothed and his new, unwilling bride-to-be—but in the end she came forward and knelt before Bran as if it were her own idea. As if she had a choice.

"Now," Bran said to Madoc when Ysabel had sworn her allegiance. "Your son."

"Kel's only fourteen," Madoc protested.

"His age is irrelevant."

Kel crept forward like he was going to his doom. Bran accepted his vow with disinterest, not even looking at him. Instead his eyes passed over the crowd and fell on Addie—the only uncommitted person in the room. The Aeron clan, Ysabel, and the Mathonwys were sworn to the Llyrs. Evangeline was bound to Griffyn, and Jax was pledged to Evangeline. Addie was obligated to protect Jax, an Emrys vassal, and had a family loyalty to her sister, but compared to everyone else here, she was relatively free.

If he expects me to kneel down, he's going to be disappointed. Addie didn't care how much pain Bran inflicted with his Spear. He might make her scream, but he couldn't make her swear. And if he hurt her *or* Evangeline, Jax might unleash the Sword on him.

Bran surveyed her with calculation, then turned away. It occurred to Addie that he wasn't going to ask her to swear her service to him—not because of her stubbornness or because he was worried about Jax's Sword, but because he'd already heard someone else claim her as an agent, someone even he wouldn't dare oppose.

The Morrigan.

• • •

Addie had been twelve when the Old Crone first appeared to her. At the time, she'd been peering through the window of a candy store, her eyes fixed on a display of colorful sweets.

"Do you want what you see in there?"

Addie had jumped and whirled simultaneously. A stranger was watching her from the street—an old woman with a bent back and snow-white hair, wearing a shapeless dress more appropriate for sleeping than for walking around in the daytime. She didn't look threatening, but appearances were deceiving where Kin were concerned—and the woman had to be Kin, because she wasn't marked with a tattoo.

Addie had glanced up and down the street. They were alone, but the Carroway house was on the next block. If a stranger had gotten this close, Emma would know. Dale would've blown the whistle to call all the children home. This woman must have been expected. "You're new here," Addie said.

"I come now and then."

Her eyes were weird—heavy lidded, as if she were half-asleep—and there was something else strange about them that Addie couldn't put her finger on. "Do you need help finding the house?" Addie asked. Usually Dale or his son led new refugees in, because it was impossible to locate the house otherwise. Perhaps this woman had arrived early.

The stranger shuffled closer. Instead of answering Addie's

265

question, she repeated her own: "Do you want what you see in there?"

She meant the candy. "Yes," Addie said. Why deny it?

"Why don't you take it then?"

It was strange to hear an adult encourage a child to steal, but not all Kin respected the property of Normals. Honesty wasn't what prevented Addie from breaking into the store, and it wasn't the punishment she'd get from Dale, either. Addie turned and pressed her face against the window, trying to put her feelings into words. "It would be cheating and not as good," she said.

"You don't want the candy," the old woman concluded. "You want the right to walk in and acquire it like a Normal person."

Was that it? Addie turned around to answer—and jerked backward. Somehow the old woman had got right up behind her, and now that she was closer, Addie could see what was wrong with her eyes. They were brown. Kin eyes were always blue.

Before Addie could push her away and run, the stranger touched a finger to Addie's temple. Stars exploded in her head; fire coursed through her veins. Then everything went black.

In the darkness, she heard the old woman's voice: "Adelina Emrys, the Eighth Day Spell that binds you to an alternate timeline runs in your veins. You come from a line of spell casters known for the flexibility of their magic. I grant you the ability to combine this talent with the limitless power in your blood to *see what you want and take it*."

When Addie's vision returned, she found herself sitting on the sidewalk, propped against the candy store wall, alone.

She had told no one what had happened. She didn't know how to describe it, first of all, and she thought she might get in trouble somehow. She'd quickly determined that no new visitors were expected at the Carroway house, and Emma had detected nothing out of the ordinary. It wasn't until the next day—the following week for the Carroways—that Addie learned about the death of Mrs. Stanwell, the elderly Normal who lived next door. According to Emma, the old lady had died of a heart attack on the night between Wednesday and Thursday. Mrs. Stanwell's obituary photograph in the newspaper left no doubt in Addie's mind that she had met a Normal woman on the eighth day—and that the poor woman had died from the strain of whatever she'd experienced.

Even back then, Addie had suspected who'd *really* spoken to her through Mrs. Stanwell's mouth, although she wasn't absolutely certain until the Girl of Crows confirmed it. And by that time, she'd long since realized how the Emrys talent had been altered inside her so that she could see the magic of others—and take it.

Bran ordered them to vacate the warehouse. Because Madoc still believed Dulacs could be tracking Jax through the brownie tunnels, they made the move in warded vehicles.

Wards protected the cars from magical detection but didn't make them invisible. So in the early evening, when Bran commanded the vehicles to stop and everyone to get out on a bridge overlooking a river valley, Madoc argued. "This is madness. We're highly visible here and vulnerable. Two of Condor's men didn't report in today. If they were captured, who knows what they—"

Bran flipped the Spear in his hand and struck Madoc in the head.

The pain of contact with the Spear must have hurt as much as the blow, but Madoc didn't make a sound. He staggered toward the edge of the bridge. "Dad!" Kel screamed. For a second, Addie thought Madoc was going to tumble backward into the river, but he caught the railing, and a moment later, Kel was there to steady him.

"Gather everyone, hand to hand," Bran said to Condor, turning his back on the Mathonwys.

Addie followed the crowd gathering on the center of the bridge. Griffyn stood beside his father with Evangeline at his side and Ysabel glowering at them from nearby. Jax was pushed into the lineup. When Condor ushered Addie forward, Bran shook his head. "Let Adelina stand aside to watch and learn."

Evangeline's head whipped around. *Watch and learn what?* Addie could see the question on her sister's face.

"Tomorrow," Bran called out, "we assault our ancient enemies. But our tomorrow is eight days hence, and knowing those adversaries will be preparing for our arrival, I wish to send them *a gift*. Vassals, lend me your strength."

Bran began to speak in Welsh. The sky churned, clouds thickening and darkening overhead. Moments later, Addie felt rain droplets strike her face. Then Bran raised the Spear to the heavens, and power ignited like a bonfire. Griffyn took his father's free hand and mumbled his own incantation. He grabbed Evangeline, drawing her in against her will.

Magic was invisible to most people, but ever since the Old Crone had touched her, Addie had been getting glimpses of it in colors and images. Never before, however, had she seen it so vividly. Bran was a white spear point of intention; Griffyn, a tightly coiled steel spring of fury; and Evangeline, a brilliant orange star of passion and spirit. Addie watched the Aerons join in one by one, some of them mischievous sparks of malice and others destructive balls of fire. There was Ysabel, dark and jealous and deeper than Addie expected. Jax's power flickered as if he was holding back, but then he lost control—his loyalty given over to Bran's spell in a burst of sapphire brilliance while the Sword on his back pulsed with crimson purpose. The brownie on Jax's shoulder leaped off and bolted back to the cars, ears pressed flat against its head.

The rain intensified, drumming against the bridge. It ran down Addie's face, and she put up a hand to shield her eyes. This was not a hurricane. Bran was calling for rain, using the Spear to magnify his power. It was going to rain over this mountain range—*hard* and *for days.*

By the time Bran lowered the Spear, they were all drenched. Rain was coming down so heavily, the water beneath the bridge looked like it was boiling. Jax pushed wet hair out of his eyes, gaping with a stricken expression at what he'd helped create. Evangeline seemed just as upset. As soon as Griffyn let go of her, she pulled Jax into a hug. She looked back at Addie and held out an arm to include her.

Addie didn't move. She didn't need comforting, and she didn't want to answer the questions Evangeline would no doubt ask. *Why did he leave you out? What did he want you to learn?*

Her heart was racing. Addie had been seeing and copying talents for a year, but in the presence of the Spear and the Sword, she perceived so much more. Even the oath bonds had been visible to her: the ropes lashing vassals to Bran, the chain that fettered Evangeline to Griffyn, the fierce friendship between her sister and Jax.

This is what Bran wanted me to learn—how the Treasures enhance my gift from the Morrigan. Addie had already noticed it was easier to copy talents since the Morrigan had repaired the Spear of Lugh, and when she borrowed magic from the Spear, her spells were stronger. Now, Jax had brought her the Sword.

Is Bran going to finally show me the counterspell to the eighth day, now that I might have the strength to cast it?

Bran looked at Madoc, who had joined hands at the end of the line of vassals. Kel hid his sullen expression behind his father's back, but Madoc faced his liege with defeat and servitude.

"*Now* we will seek shelter," Bran said. "Make sure it's on high ground."

29

THE KIN SELECTED a house they thought was suitable for waiting out the seven-day timeline. Most of them went in immediately, but Jax was told to stay in the car while Madoc warded the house. Kel's father was convinced people must be scrying for Jax.

Madoc was right, of course; there *was* someone keeping tabs on him. But the only occasions Jax would've been open to scrying were the first few seconds after his arrival in the warehouse—and on the bridge. Jax cringed. Not only had he helped Bran Llyr summon the mother of all rainstorms, Tegan Donovan might have watched him do it.

Why'd it have to be her, *of all people?* But Riley had proved too impatient to master scrying, or maybe Jax wasn't a very good teacher. Jax himself had only cast the spell under Evangeline's instruction. But Tegan had taken to it right away, maybe because she was such a talented sensitive. Jax had been mortified. What if she caught him at an embarrassing moment—scratching his butt, picking his nose . . . or worse? But having someone monitor Jax had been one of the conditions the adults had set for letting him take this mission, and Tegan had been the one assigned to the job. *She can't do it too many times in a row, though. The spell will exhaust her just like it did Evangeline. Maybe she missed the part on the bridge.*

It wasn't Jax's proudest moment. He'd tried to fake participation, but it was as if an ocean wave had knocked him over. Instead of drowning, he'd ended up riding the surf, and it had been *exhilarating.* That was the worst part: that he'd enjoyed the incredible surge of magic.

Jax scratched Stink behind the ears and eyed the man with the tattooed face in the driver's seat. The guy had been told to wait with Jax, but he wasn't paying close attention, so Jax took a rubber band from his pocket and slipped it onto Stink's right front limb. He and Riley had worked out basic messages in advance. Stink's right front limb meant Jax had hit a snag, and they should be prepared for deviations in the plan. Riley would probably consider Evangeline bound to a Llyr and Jax forbidden to use the brownie tunnels more than a *snag,* but Jax didn't have a way to convey details. *Just as well. Because I'm the only one who can* un*snag us.*

Kel opened the car door. "Out," he ordered. Stink jumped off Jax's lap, hit the ground running, and scampered away from the house. "Hey!" Kel yelled. "Where's that thing going?"

"I dunno." Jax climbed out of the car. "He never leaves an itinerary."

Kel grabbed Jax by his shirt and hustled him through the door and into an ordinary-looking kitchen. This wasn't an established Kin "safe house." It was some poor Normal's home, invaded by the deadliest people on earth.

"The residents are *not* to know anyone's been in here," Madoc called out. "Touch nothing. Move nothing." Then he did the exact opposite and helped Condor shove a refrigerator back into its alcove. Jax caught a glimpse of a ward inscribed in ink on the wall before the refrigerator slid into place. He realized Madoc had hidden the wards behind objects in the house, so the Normal homeowners wouldn't see them.

"His brownie ran off," Kel said.

Condor glared suspiciously at Jax. "Where'd it go?"

Jax shrugged. "To look through garbage cans or off to poop."

"Forget the vermin," said Madoc. "Secure the boy."

"How much time is left?" asked Kel, removing a length of twine from his pocket.

"Two minutes."

Jax looked around for his liege ladies. Evangeline had come in with Griffyn, and Addie had been sticking close to Bran. Evangeline didn't have a choice, but Jax didn't understand what was going on with Addie. She acted like she was the Llyr lord's apprentice or something.

"Give me your hand," Kel demanded.

Jax turned. "Sorry, dude, I don't wanna hold your hand."

With a sneer, Kel looped the twine around Jax's wrist and bound it loosely to his own. Then they stood there awkwardly. "You know," Jax said, leaning his arm on the back of a chair, "the singer you stole that hairstyle from is a real . . ."

The world lurched under his feet, and Jax's vision whirled, like he'd taken an unexpected spin on a merry-go-round. He lost his balance and might've fallen if Kel hadn't yanked him upright. The chair he'd been leaning against was now a foot away from where it had been with a raincoat draped over its back. Being physically bound to a member of the Kin race had dragged Jax straight from one eighth day to the next, like it had done to Riley last month when he and Evangeline had experimented with tying themselves together.

For Jax, seven days had flown by in the blink of an eye.

"What's the matter, Transitioner?" Kel unwound the twine. "Didn't like the jump?"

No, he didn't. Jax hadn't paid close attention to his surroundings before, but he was pretty sure there hadn't been a mop and a bucket beside the back door a second ago, and he was betting the towels stuffed along the windows were new, along with the water stain on the ceiling. It'd been raining hard here for days, just like Bran wanted. *This place is pretty high up in the mountains. What happened to the houses down in the valley?*

Madoc looked at his companions. "*Now*, you can do whatever you like."

And they did. The Kin trashed the house, eating whatever they wanted out of the fridge and stealing anything they found useful. Jax didn't like what they were doing, but he *was* hungry enough to grab a package of deli ham and eat it all. "Are we leaving immediately?" Madoc asked Condor. "They'll know we're coming."

"Bran says it doesn't matter what they know or what they've planned," Condor replied.

Madoc lit up a cigarette, looking worried. Jax knew how he felt. Why didn't Bran care that he was walking into a trap?

Griffyn dragged Evangeline over to Jax. "Remind your vassal that he's forbidden to leave through brownie holes and that he's to make no attempt to assist the enemy today."

Evangeline repeated his orders as a direct command, liege to vassal, while Jax clenched his teeth, hung on to his honor blade, and stared at her, mentally repeating the words of the oath he'd made to Riley. *I will think about the needs of my lieges before anything else.* The Sword on his back practically quivered with hunger this close to its target, and it was a relief when Griffyn stomped off to commandeer food out of his vassals' hands.

Evangeline lowered her voice. "I'm sorry, Jax. I know I made things worse, going to meet them and getting myself forced into this oath. But they were torturing Addie!"

"You saw that while scrying?"

She nodded. "They told me where to turn myself over." Then she bit her lip and asked, "Is *he* angry?"

Jax didn't have to ask who *he* was. "He's worried. And he's hurt you didn't tell him."

"They said if I brought anyone with me or let myself be followed, they'd kill whoever it was and hurt Addie more. I couldn't tell him, Jax! He would never have let me go on my own." Evangeline wrung her hands. "I had no idea it was possible to travel long distances through brownie tunnels or track someone with them. Otherwise I would have figured out a better way."

Jax grimaced. It all came back to him keeping his plan a secret, just like Tegan had pointed out to him. *Not that she was around to give me advice at the time.* "I messed up," he confessed. "It's my fault they knew you were scrying for Addie and even that you were still alive."

Evangeline squeezed his arm. "I messed up too, Jax. But I'm not beaten yet."

Jax whispered quickly, not knowing how much more

time they'd have. "About Addie—she doesn't *look* like she's been tortured. I'm sorry to say it, but she seems buddy-buddy with ol' Bran."

"I see that." Evangeline glanced over her shoulder, looking for her sister. "I don't know what he's teaching her, but I've seen her do something she shouldn't have been able to do. And what she said about the Eighth Day Spell . . ." Evangeline didn't finish the sentence, but she didn't have to. The fear was evident in her eyes.

Addie wanted the spell broken, just like the Llyrs did, just like Wylit had.

Just like her father.

Griffyn grabbed Evangeline's arm. "This way, hand-maiden. We're leaving."

As quickly as that, the Kin vacated their hideout. They'd been there all of ten minutes by Jax's counting, but a week had passed in the Normal world. When the homeowners reappeared on Thursday, it would look like their house had been wrecked in a split second by invisible poltergeists.

Jax was pushed through the back door toward the same car, which had returned from wherever they'd stashed it for a week. Before he got in, Stink came running from behind the house. Jax held an arm out for him. But Condor intercepted the brownie midleap and held him up by the scruff of the neck.

"What are you doing?" Jax demanded.

Condor shook Stink and looked him over while Jax watched anxiously. "Checking for messages." Since Jax had been with them, these Kin had tried to kick Stink or chase him off, but when they did, he simply vanished and reappeared somewhere else. This time Condor didn't bother trying to hurt the brownie and tossed him back to Jax.

Jax caught him. Stink twisted around in Jax's arms and bared his teeth at the Kin. "Yeah, he's a jerk," Jax agreed. *And not very observant.* Condor might have suspected Stink was carrying a message, but he hadn't spotted it. The brownie was still wearing a rubber band on his right front limb, but a different color one. It was a return signal from Riley.

Things weren't going the way he hoped either, but Jax was to stick to instructions and be prepared to improvise as needed.

Yeah, no problem, Jax thought, getting into the car. *'Cause making stuff up as I go along is pretty much all I ever do.*

30

WITH THE MOON HIDDEN behind clouds, the mountainside was very dark. Since, by Bran's command, they were deliberately heading into Transitioner territory and certain ambush, the Kin drove without headlights to avoid being seen as long as possible. It made Jax nervous. *The Sword of Nuadu's supposed to protect my life, but will it prevent broken bones if this car plummets off a cliff?*

After about forty-five minutes, the vehicles came to a stop. Condor walked up the road, waving the drivers to steer their cars off the asphalt and into the woods. Jax watched out the window as his car bumped over uneven ground and between the trees as far as it could go. Then they all got out. "We're walking from here," Condor announced.

Walking? Was he kidding? Jax had no idea how much farther it was to Bedivere's mansion, but it was *down the mountain*. Last week's torrential rains had left the slope a slick and swampy mess. Jax's clothes hadn't had the chance to dry, and now the trees dribbled cold water on his head. He grumbled, hanging on to trees and rocks and trying not to let his sneakers get sucked off in the mud. Stink avoided the situation by popping out of sight and reappearing every fifty feet or so.

Evangeline slipped on a particularly muddy incline, but grabbed a sapling tree to save herself. Quick as a snake, the Arawen girl gave her a shove while she was off balance, and Evangeline's feet went out from under her. She slid down the hill on her behind, while Griffyn laughed nastily. "What is *wrong* with you?" Jax snarled at the two Kin, hurrying after his liege.

It was a long drop, but Evangeline managed to stop her fall about twenty feet down. Jax braced himself and pulled her upright.

Addie made her way down to them. "Are you hurt?" she called.

"Just my dignity, but I think that was the point." Evangeline glanced uphill. "Does she really love that big, ugly lout?"

Addie shrugged. "He *belonged* to Ysabel, and Bran stole him from her and gave him to you."

"She can have him back anytime," Evangeline muttered.

A few of the Aerons also slipped on the hill, but to Jax's disappointment, the Llyrs and Ysabel acted like gravity dared not interfere with them. Griffyn grabbed Evangeline's arm as he passed and hauled her along with him, keeping them both on their feet.

Addie watched, and Jax saw hatred flicker across her face. "You want her freed from him, don't you?" Jax whispered.

"Of course I do," Addie snapped.

"Then—" Well, why not just ask her? "Are you on *our* side or *theirs*?"

Her pale eyebrows shot up. "Who says there's only two sides?"

Fair enough. He hadn't thought about it that way. "Another question. Do you trust me?"

"Yes." Addie frowned, like she'd surprised herself with such a prompt answer.

Jax pointed at the brownie crouched on a branch above his head. "That's Stink," he said. "If I send him to you at any point, will you follow him?"

"We're forbidden to leave by brownie tunnels," Addie reminded him.

"No." Jax made sure his voice was low. "Evangeline has to obey Griffyn, and I have to obey Evangeline. But you're not *compelled* to obey either one of them. Right?" Addie was Evangeline's *sister*, not her vassal.

Addie smirked. He'd nailed it.

"Well?" he asked. If worse came to worst, at least one of them could escape.

"I'll think about it." Then she deliberately moved away from him, so he couldn't question her anymore.

The slope leveled off at another paved road. Now Jax could see the river—and Bedivere's mansion on the opposite hill—but the town in the valley was unrecognizable. The Lehigh had overflowed, especially in the curve of the river, where it looked like a shallow lake full of buildings. The town was dark, although there should have been leftover light from the seven-day timeline. Jax could only assume there'd been no electricity in the town on Wednesday to leave any image of light.

A rustle of leaves and the cracking of a branch made Jax whirl around. A band of tattooed Kin emerged from the woods, herding a bunch of children before them. When Jax recognized the pint-sized toddler being carried by a young boy, he realized who these kids were.

"What are *they* doing here?" Addie gasped. Of course, she recognized them, too.

"Shields," Madoc said, brushing mud from his sleeve. "Transitioners are notoriously reluctant to fire on children. Besides, some of them have useful talents."

Addie's mouth fell open. She looked both horrified and guilty.

"Where's the boy with the talent for barriers?" Bran demanded.

"Gawan Ratis!" someone called.

The boy holding the toddler was pushed forward. He stared up at the Llyr leader with frightened eyes. "Give the baby to someone else," Bran said. "You'll need both hands free."

Addie jumped forward, but the baby twisted away from her, crying and reaching for Jax instead. Jax gulped. He wasn't used to babies, but he grabbed the little girl under the armpits and lifted her. She quieted at once, wrapping her arms around Jax's neck. By luck or instinct, she avoided touching the Sword.

Addie seemed embarrassed. "Brigit is hard to handle. And she's never liked me."

Jax glanced at Evangeline, who chewed on her lip and stared back at Jax. At the Carroway house, this baby had held up her arms invitingly to both of them. *Brigit likes you and your liege lady,* her mother, the oracle, had said to Jax. *I take great stock in that.*

What did it mean, if the child of an oracle liked Jax and Evangeline, but not Addie?

Bran pointed across the river. "Our goal is to take the Bedivere house, no matter the cost."

"Our people hold the bridge south of town," said one of the Aeron men. "We can cross there and approach through the cover of the forest."

"Adelina," Bran prompted. "What do you see in the forest?"

Addie hesitated before answering, "Pockets of blankness where magic is suppressed. They're waiting for us. If we go in that way, we could have our talents cut off from us." Jax stared at her. That would be Sloane's uncles, the Bors men, with their talent for magic suppression, but how did Addie *see* them? Evangeline seemed perplexed too.

Condor flicked open a cigarette lighter, producing a flame. "Fire will drive them off."

"The forest is too wet to burn," Madoc said.

"It'll burn for Aerons," Condor said with a smile, causing a ripple of malevolent chuckles from the shadowy figures in the woods.

"Send your clansmen to burn as much of the forest as they can," Bran directed. "You, Condor, will stay with me. I'll lead a small group in a different direction while the Transitioners are forced to fight the fire on the mountainside."

The Aerons raised their voices in whooping war cries. Tattooed men and women snatched up kids and carried them off or dragged them by the hand. A few of the children went voluntarily, shouting in glee. Jax didn't know if they'd been brainwashed into cooperating, or if they had no understanding of the situation.

He hoped Tegan would catch this development through her scrying and warn the Transitioner forces. Jax knew she wouldn't see everything. The exhausting nature of the spell would force her to choose wisely who she looked for and when. But she'd had seven days to rest—seven days Jax had skipped over—and there would be people lending her strength. *Please, Tegan, see the children!*

Madoc's mind was also on scrying spells. "My lord, I suggest we leave the Transitioner here. Tie him to a tree, if necessary. Our enemies can spy on our movements through him, and, frankly, I don't trust him with that Sword."

"The Sword of Nuadu must come with us. Leaving it behind is not an option," Bran said. "If *you* wish to carry it, Madoc, by all means, go ahead." Madoc shrunk backward, knowing he couldn't take the Sword from Jax. "As for spies," Bran continued, "Adelina . . . ."

Addie glanced guiltily at her sister, then raised her hands like a preacher at a pulpit and closed her eyes. Evangeline stirred, her brow furrowed, and Griffyn put out an arm to prevent her from interfering.

White wisps gathered in the air. The tendrils thickened, wrapping cold, clammy arms around the group. Jax turned, watching, as the mist grew into a massive, impenetrable blanket of fog. Within seconds, the river and the opposite bank disappeared. Jax could barely see Kel and Condor and the boy, Gawan, standing ten feet away. Evangeline appeared stunned. Jax had never seen *her* cast a spell this way—without symbols and incantations. Her repair of the Eighth Day Spell had required the magical artifact Excalibur, the mummy of Niviane of the Lake, and a long impassioned speech. Not to mention a kiss.

Addie looked up at Bran as if seeking approval, and he nodded. "Let them spy on us now, if they can."

Jax would never have admitted it to anyone, but marching down a winding road in the middle of the night, through thick fog, in damp clothes and squelchy shoes, was made a little more tolerable by carrying a small child. It didn't make sense, because his arms got tired, but Brigit's warm embrace around his neck and the sound of her soft thumb-sucking in his ear made him feel a little stronger, a little braver. There wasn't much else about the situation to cheer him. Addie was walking double time to match pace with Bran. Evangeline's eyes were glued with suspicion to her sister's back. Even Stink seemed nervous, darting ahead of Jax and then waiting for him to catch up before taking off again.

At first, Jax didn't pay attention when Brigit lifted her head off his shoulder. It was only when she didn't put it down again that he noticed her staring in the direction of the river. Then she pulled her thumb out of her mouth and pointed. Jax slowed his pace. The fog was as dense as pea soup, but a clear patch had appeared over a formation of rocks in the middle of the river. At the same moment, the moon slipped out from behind the clouds to illuminate that spot.

"What the heck is that woman doing?" Jax blurted out before he thought better of it. But really, she couldn't be part of the Transitioner defense, could she? A lone woman standing on rocks in the river? Washing clothes by hand?

Everyone stopped, and Jax was surprised by their reaction. Griffyn's eyes bugged out of his head. Ysabel nearly tripped over Jax, getting between Griffyn and the river. "Don't look!" she snapped at him, grabbing him by an arm and making him turn around.

"Jax, don't you look either!" Evangeline cried.

"Let him," said Condor, his eyes steadfastly averted from the river. "He's the only one of us who's immune. He's protected by the Sword."

"Unless both Emrys girls are killed and the Sword no longer has a target. Then he's as vulnerable as the rest of us," Madoc corrected. "And if that happens, we'll never know it. We'll just be *gone*. It was madness to bring them both here! One good sharp-shooter could annihilate our entire race!"

"Silence, Madoc," Bran roared. But he didn't strike his complaining vassal again, and Jax noticed he didn't look at the woman in the river, either.

But Jax did, now that he realized who it was. During the week he'd had to prepare for his role as the "inside man," he and Billy had collaborated to dig up every bit of information they could find on the Morrigan over the internet. There were supposed to be three aspects to this force of nature—or deity—or whatever she was: the Girl of Crows, who manipulated events toward great battles; the Old Crone, who changed the fate of individuals; and the most dreaded of the three, the Washer Woman, who washed the bloodied clothes of fallen warriors *before* they fell.

"Legends are unclear on whether seeing the Washer Woman means she'll wash your clothes," Billy had concluded from his research, "or if she'll wash your clothes whether you see her or not. But all the legends agree it's best not to look."

Jax couldn't help himself. He had to make sure it wasn't Lesley. But this was a heavy-set woman with speckled black and gray hair, wearing yoga pants and a cardigan. She bent awkwardly to rinse a white shirt in the water. *Whose shirt?* Jax glanced around, trying to place it.

"Jax!" Evangeline pleaded, and for her sake, he sighed and turned his back on the river.

"Don't worry," he told her. "I've seen the Morrigan before. This is like the fourth time."

"Me too," Addie boasted. "I've seen all three incarnations of her now."

"You got me there," Jax replied. "I've only seen two of them. You win—if you call it *winning* when you've been chosen by an evil goddess of destruction and chaos."

"Addie," Evangeline gasped, as if suddenly under-standing something. "What did the Old Crone say to you? What did she *do*?"

Addie didn't answer. Jax looked back once more, but fog had closed over the gap, hiding the Washer Woman from view.

31

THE ROAD BOTTOMED OUT in an industrial complex beside the river, where they had to slog through an inch of floodwater in the street. Jax saw Addie whirl around in response to nothing he could detect and peer up at the mountainside. He looked, too. The fog was too thick to see anything, but after a moment, he smelled smoke. Then they heard gunfire. The Aerons must have crossed the bridge south of town. The battle had begun.

"Gawan." Madoc's voice sounded strained. "Do you know who these girls with us are?"

"I know Addie," the boy replied.

"Addie is an Emrys," Madoc said. "She and her sister are the last of the Emrys family. Do you know what happens if they die?" Gawan nodded, his mouth hanging open. "Use your talent to shield all of us from bullets, but especially them."

"Shield the Emrys leader," Bran corrected. "And the

people with her. Adelina and I will be leaving you here."

"No! Where are you taking her?" Evangeline exclaimed. Of course, Bran didn't bother to answer. Evangeline grabbed Addie by the shoulders. "Whatever you think about the eighth day, you're wrong! Whatever he tells you, it's a lie!"

"Shut up," Griffyn snapped at his handmaiden, pulling her away from her sister. "And do what you're told." Evangeline pressed her lips together, compelled to silence, but stared at Addie plaintively, conveying her message without words.

"Take the railroad bridge to cross the river," Bran instructed his son. He pointed a finger at Evangeline. "Put *her* to use, attacking Transitioners. That should invoke the Sword of Nuadu."

Evangeline's eyes grew wide in horror. Jax guessed what she was thinking—that her oath to Griffyn might compel her to attack Riley, which would identify Riley as her enemy and also set Jax against him with the Sword. Jax wished he could reassure her, but he couldn't tell her the plan. Not with her sworn to obey Griffyn.

Bran walked away, and Addie turned to follow him. She didn't seem surprised that he was separating her from the group, and that worried Jax as much as it did Evangeline. "Addie!" he called out. When she looked back, Jax mouthed, *Remember,* and jerked his head toward Stink.

Addie gave a barely perceptible nod, then disappeared into the fog.

Griffyn led Evangeline, Jax, Gawan, and the Mathonwys to the railroad tracks, which they followed onto a trestle bridge. Jax couldn't see the river, thanks to the fog, but he heard it gurgling not far beneath his feet. *I can't believe I'm carrying a toddler into a flooded town and a war zone.* But there was no safe place to leave Brigit, even if Griffyn allowed it.

In the distance, an explosion rattled the valley. Jax's skin prickled with apprehension. *Bran sent his vassals and a bunch of kids to attack a house that's magically protected by the very artifact he wants to capture.* There was something wrong with that strategy. Not to mention, as soon as the battle began, Bran had taken Addie and left. *What is he up to?*

On the other side of the bridge, the tracks led to an elevated platform outside a railroad station. Jax glanced around apprehensively. He couldn't see more than a couple feet or a few seconds ahead, and he fingered his honor blade, seeking information. His talent warned him only a couple seconds before Condor's head jerked toward a rumbling sound. "On your right, Griffyn!" Condor called.

Out of the fog bank, a gray armored vehicle rolled toward them. Griffyn reacted by throwing a bolt of electricity from his hand. Instead of hitting the vehicle directly, the sizzling bolt struck a rod on the armored roof and was deflected away.

This, Jax knew, was a lightning rod with magical enhancements crafted by Mr. Crandall, whose artisan specialty was working in metal. But Griffyn tried a second time, as if he didn't understand why his bolt of lightning was hitting the metal rod on top of the vehicle instead of electrocuting the people inside. Jax wondered if news of Benjamin Franklin's invention had never penetrated Oeth-Anoeth.

Meanwhile, a gun mounted on the armored jeep rotated and blasted the railroad bridge. Debris rocketed in all directions. Jax bent over to shield Brigit and ran downhill, away from the railroad station and toward the town with Stink on his heels.

They could have done that while we were on *the bridge, but they waited for us to cross and then cut off our escape route.* Griffyn was being coaxed into a prepared trap. The Transitioner forces expected Jax to jump out of the area with the Emrys girls if the danger became too great, whether or not their plan for the Morrigan—and Lesley—came to fruition. *But they don't know I'm forbidden to use the brownie tunnels. I'm gonna be caught in the trap, too.*

The armored vehicle advanced on Griffyn, who changed his tactics. He waved his arms, and tendrils of fog whirled in a tight circle, coalescing into a funnel-shaped cloud that sucked in debris from the bridge. The mini-tornado roared as it grew taller, dispersing the fog enough for Jax to see railroad ties yanked from the ground, vinyl siding ripped off the station, and utility poles thrown at the Transitioner vehicle, which reversed and retreated. Flying bits of metal drove Jax to seek shelter around the corner of the first intersection he came to, even though the street was flooded with three inches of water. Stink squeaked in protest and clambered up a street sign.

Out of range of the tornado, fog closed in around him again. Shadowy buildings on either side muffled the sounds of destruction at the train station. Jax counted his companions as they joined him. Gawan was there, along with Kel and his father—and then, thankfully, Evangeline.

He was less pleased to see Condor, Ysabel, and Griffyn right behind her. The tornado could've sucked any of *them* up, as far as Jax was concerned.

"Which way?" Madoc asked.

Griffyn pointed. "Toward the house on the hill. As my father commanded."

Madoc shook his head in frustration. He knew it was a trap, too.

"Are you all right?" Jax asked Evangeline. She nodded mutely, and Jax's jaw clenched as he realized that until Griffyn rescinded his order to *shut up*, Evangeline couldn't speak. The Sword throbbed on his back, magnifying his fury. "Take Brigit," he growled from between his teeth, his fingers itching to draw the Sword and end her servitude.

But Evangeline's eyes were focused on something behind him. She grabbed Jax and turned him around.

Dark shapes appeared out of the fog at the end of the street. Something unnatural about the way the shadowy figures moved made Jax recoil. Backing up, he found himself shoulder-to-shoulder with Kel, while Griffyn and Ysabel strode forward to meet the new threat. "Get over here and do your part," Griffyn snarled at Evangeline when she hung back.

"No lightning!" Madoc yelled. "We're standing in water!"

Griffyn swore in Welsh. At least he understood that much about electricity, Jax thought gratefully. The Transitioners had probably driven Griffyn this way on purpose to prevent him from throwing lightning, but the strategy wouldn't have done Jax and Evangeline any good if the barbarian had electrocuted his companions out of medieval ignorance.

The things coming out of the fog didn't look human. Their arms were long enough for them to move on four limbs like orangutans. Their faces were elongated, their jaws and teeth jutting forward like the muzzles of dogs. Condor stationed himself beside Ysabel, and Evangeline summoned invisible balls of fire to defend Griffyn whether she wanted to or not. Two of the creatures charged Griffyn and Condor, while the third peeled away from the group, dodged a fireball from Evangeline, and went right for Jax. Brigit screamed and hid her face.

Gawan stepped in front of Jax and threw up his hands. A shimmering, transparent barrier appeared between them and the creature, which jerked to a stop with inhuman reflexes. Wild eyes in a bearded face surveyed Gawan and Brigit before settling on Jax—who gasped in shock. Somewhere in that twisted, savage version of a human face, Jax recognized the features of the Transitioner lord, Ash Pellinore.

You've heard of werewolves? Sheila Morgan had replied when Jax asked about Pellinore's talent. *If you ever have the chance to see him in action, you'll never forget it.*

Pellinore sniffed, his nostrils flaring. Then he bared his pointed, wolflike teeth and turned to join the fray behind him. Griffyn had struck one of the wild men in the throat with a knife, dropping him short of his target, but the other had tackled Condor, and Ysabel jumped in with her knives to assist him.

Drawing a dagger to replace the one he'd thrown, Griffyn faced Pellinore, crouching with his weapons held low. Pellinore dropped to all fours and charged, but it was only a feint. He leaped over Griffyn and barreled toward Evangeline.

Evangeline hit him full in the face with her remaining fireball.

Pellinore howled, his beard and hair igniting in blue flames. He stumbled to a halt, trying to beat out the fire with his hands, and Griffyn hurled both his knives into the man's back. Evangeline covered her mouth in horror as Pellinore collapsed at her feet.

The magic barrier Gawan had thrown up to defend Jax broke apart into shimmering pieces, and the little boy sagged.

"Nice work defending your liege with the Sword," Kel said to Jax, attempting sarcasm in spite of the tremble in his voice. "Oh, wait. You were hiding behind a baby."

"And you were hiding behind me," snapped Jax. But Kel was right: carrying Brigit would prevent Jax from serving Evangeline properly. He dumped the child into Kel's arms. *"Don't* let anything happen to her, or you'll be sorry."

Ysabel wiped her knives on the shirt of the man who'd assaulted Condor. She looked uninjured, but Condor's face and arms were bloodied. *"He* seemed to be the leader," Ysabel said, pointing at Ash Pellinore, and Griffyn nodded agreement. Ysabel knelt beside Pellinore's body, placed a hand on his head, and closed her eyes. "His objective was to capture the Emrys heirs unharmed."

Jax sucked in his breath. "What's she doing?"

"Talking to the dead," Kel replied. "That's what Arawens do."

"The Transitioners know about the children in our company," Ysabel went on, pulling information from the dead man's mind, "and that's preventing them from using lethal force."

"This wasn't meant to be lethal?" Condor muttered, his fingers pressed against a jagged bite wound.

"The scryer tracking Jax Aubrey has been hampered by the fog. Individual operatives, like these men, are scouting for him instead."

Jax swallowed, feeling sick. Pellinore had been trying to *find* him and *rescue* Evangeline. If Jax had recognized the man in time, if he'd alerted Evangeline that he was a friend, not a foe . . . she still would have been bound to follow Griffyn's orders. Jax told himself it wasn't their fault Pellinore had been killed, but it still felt like a betrayal and a failure.

"Where's the leader of the Pendragon clan?" Griffyn grinned at Evangeline nastily. "I want to return the pieces of his dagger." Evangeline's face flushed red.

Ysabel's eyes remained closed, her hand on Pellinore's head. "He's at the Bedivere house," she said after a moment, "not involved in the fighting."

Griffyn laughed. "Your former ally is a coward," he told Evangeline. "Hiding behind the lines."

Evangeline looked relieved to hear Riley was safely out of the fighting, but Jax bristled with anger. Riley wasn't a coward. When Sheila Morgan had banned him from the battlefield, he'd argued bitterly against her decision. Much to the relief of Jax and the Crandalls, however, he'd been forced to submit to Sheila's logic and the vote of the Table. Riley was incapable of using brownie tunnels; he wasn't trained on most of Sheila's weaponry, and in this battle his skills were better put to another use. Riley's talent was the voice of command, but instead of commanding men, he was in charge of an army of four-legged vermin. They were essential to the Transitioners' strategy, and they obeyed no one else.

"As for you . . ." Griffyn marched over to Evangeline. "I notice you only hit your target when defending yourself. Otherwise, you conveniently *miss*." He slapped her across the face.

That was it. Jax didn't think. Not about the plan. Not about his oath. The *smack* of Griffyn's slap hadn't finished echoing in the fog before Jax's hand closed over the hilt of the Sword. Yanking it out of its sheath and over his head, he ran toward Griffyn, filled with rage and magic.

He never saw what hit him or even felt the blow. One second his eyes were on Griffyn's back; the next, his body slammed into the street with a splash, the Sword of Nuadu flew out of his grip, and he was facedown in the water. A hand grasped his hair and pulled his head back. Ysabel leaned over him, her knife hovering near his throat.

By the look in her eye, Jax thought he was a goner. Then Ysabel tossed the knife aside and dug her knee into his kidney while she grabbed his hands and wrenched them together behind his back.

Jax barely registered Griffyn, who was glowering at him in disbelief, or Evangeline's shocked and frightened expression. He was too busy staring at the Sword of Nuadu, lying in the flooded street out of reach, and wondering how he could possibly have failed when he had a magic sword that was supposed to guarantee his success.

TRUDGING THROUGH THE DARK and the fog behind Bran Llyr, Addie kept picturing the horrified expression on Evangeline's face when she realized that the Old Crone had visited her little sister—had, in fact, *changed* her. In the legends, things rarely ended well for those favored by the Morrigan. *But I was chosen to break the rules and take what I wanted. Maybe I can break the curse of the Morrigan, too.*

Evangeline was a rule follower. Addie shouldn't have been surprised that her sister had preserved the Eighth Day Spell when it was almost broken by Wylit. Neither Evangeline nor their mother had been happy when their father was working on a counterspell all those years ago. Addie figured she was the only Emrys with the same rebellious temperament as her father, which was ironic, because she'd been his least favorite child. Evangeline had been the perfect one, and Elliot had been the boy . . .

Remembering Elliot, she should have resented how Jax

seemed to have taken her brother's place with Evangeline, but Addie had to admit he was growing on her, too. She didn't know if it was the magic of the vassal bond, or if Jax was just that likeable. Nevertheless, she wasn't going to jump into a brownie hole on his say-so. Jax's idea of safety probably meant running back to the Dulacs, who'd locked her up and stolen her blood, or to the Pendragons, with whom her sister had been inexplicably allied even though they'd killed Evangeline and Addie's parents.

No, Addie needed to stick to her plan, which meant following Bran a little longer.

Bran led her to the base of the town's water tower and, after using a gust of wind to blow open a security fence, climbed the ladder up the tower with remarkable agility for his age. Addie tipped her head back to check out the height of the platform around the water tank, then regretted it. She stared straight through the rungs as she climbed, looking neither up nor down, and by the time she made it onto a wooden platform that was wet and slippery from days of rain, she was breathless. It bothered her that Bran was not. *Tough old man.*

The moon was out in full now, and the water tower stood above the fog. She couldn't see the river or the town below, as they were blanketed in white, but Bedivere's huge house was visible on the opposite hillside. Off to the left, in the dense trees on the mountain, she saw flames.

Addie could also see the powerful magic at work tonight.

The Spear of Lugh carried by Bran was an intense white beam of focused intention, guaranteeing that he would never be swayed from his course. The Stone of Fal cast a golden glow around the Bedivere mansion like a fire on a hearth—fire that would warm the inhabitants of the house and sear the skin off invaders. Comparing the two Treasures, Addie thought the Stone was probably superior. Bran could be as single-minded as he liked, but unless the Stone was willingly given up, it would protect its owner's property until the end of the earth. "Your people are never going to take that house," Addie said.

"No," Bran agreed. "They will never take the house."

Addie blinked in surprise. "Then why—"

"We don't need the Stone itself. Any spell caster besides you, Adelina, would require the physical presence of the Treasures to make use of them. But *you* only need proximity to magic to claim it as your own. The Stone's power is yours for the taking *here and now*."

"You mean the attack is a diversion? You sent your vassals into battle for nothing?" Addie couldn't imagine doing such a thing to Jax.

Bran stared across the breadth of the valley at the house. "Launching an assault on Bedivere's home awakened the magic of the Stone, just as the Spear became active the moment the Morrigan repaired it. When your vassal draws the Sword, you'll have the magic of all three relics alive at once and at your disposal. You need not have your hands on them to break the Eighth Day Spell."

"But I don't know how to cast a counterspell! I can copy any spell or talent I see, but no one has ever shown me the Spell of Making that Merlin used to create the eighth day. I thought *you* were going to teach it to me!" She'd been waiting all this time for him to instruct her on the ancient spell or introduce her to someone who knew it.

"You don't need the Spell of Making, and you aren't casting a counterspell." Bran leaned down to look Addie directly in the eye. "I have seen you master any magic performed in your presence, and the Eighth Day Spell is all around you. It runs in your veins. You've been tapping into it ever since the Morrigan gave you that ability, but you lacked the strength to *master* it. Your magic was weak." He snapped his fingers contemptuously, mimicking the trick she'd first shown him. "You were playing with *matches* instead of learning to create *conflagrations*. But when you absorbed the power of my Spear to create this fog, look at what you did!" He waved a hand at the white carpet lying heavily in the narrow valley as far as they could see and beyond.

He knew she'd drawn on his Spear for that? Addie had thought he wasn't aware of it. "My brother died trying to break the spell," she reminded him. "If I get it wrong . . ."

"Your brother was a child, and I assume he didn't have the Morrigan's gift. Adelina Emrys, you already know everything you need to set our race free." Taking her by the shoulders, he turned her to face the valley. "Feel that power. Draw it into yourself. Use it."

Was it really as simple as that? Addie gripped the railing to steady herself. *When the Old Crone told me to take what I wanted, this is what she meant.* With growing confidence, Addie reached out to the blinding-white light that was the Spear. The liquid fire of its ruthless power sharpened her senses and fortified her. It was like *becoming* fire.

This much she'd done before.

"This is what we've been training for, Adelina," Bran said, encouraging her. "You had versatility, but lacked the aggression and strength necessary for this task. It was only once you started stealing power from my Spear that you developed a capacity for this level of magic."

Addie's skin tingled and itched. She turned her attention to the glow across the valley—the power of the Stone, defending its home. The Spear was like an old friend now; she'd been sneaking sips of magic off it ever since Bran had tortured her with it. Not as secretly as she thought, apparently, but with Bran's awareness and tacit approval. The Stone was new to her, but she understood it. It offered protection, just as the Spear represented intention. Addie drew on it with her newly defined purpose, devoured it, felt herself swelling almost to the bursting point with it. But she didn't burst; she *expanded*.

"That's my girl," Bran said in her ear. "Focus now. Do you

see the Eighth Day Spell? It's always been there; you just didn't have the discernment to see it before."

Yes, she could see the clouded barrier in the heavens that separated her from the moon and the stars of the seven-day world. But the Eighth Day Spell was more than an encapsulation of time. It was also an intricate tapestry. All the individual Transitioners and Kin were woven into it—the Transitioners only loosely, but the Kin were bound like flies in a spiderweb. And every single one of those people was tethered to Addie Emrys, the anchor for the Spell.

There was a second anchor too. Addie could pinpoint Evangeline's exact location in the foggy valley by the glittering strands of magic. If Addie had been able to access this magnitude of perception earlier, she would never have believed the Dulacs when they told her Evangeline was dead. She could have found her sister by following the threads of the spell.

Addie could *see* it now, but could she break it? Even with the power of the Spear and the Stone thrumming through her body, the strands of the Eighth Day Spell were like cables holding up a suspension bridge—flexible, but inconceivably strong. This was not the kind of magic Addie could reach out and *take*.

Suddenly an angry crimson light flared in the fog bank below—a blinding, searing explosion of rage and vengeance.

Jax had unsheathed the Sword.

33

GRIFFYN REMOVED THE LEATHER laces from his vest, and Ysabel used them to tie Jax's hands behind his back. They left him lying in the water-filled street while they argued about what to do with him.

"Leave him here," said Madoc. "He's been a threat to us all along. I told you he was."

"No," Griffyn argued. "You heard what Ysabel got from the dead man. People are looking for him. If we leave him, the Transitioners will find him. They'll take the Sword back."

Jax wriggled forward on his belly, trying to reach the Sword even with his hands tied behind his back. The compulsion was irresistible; he couldn't help himself.

Ysabel planted a foot on his back, pinning him down. "He tried to kill you!"

"No child is going to defeat me with a sword," Griffyn growled. "Magic or not."

That was the problem. Jax didn't know how to use a sword. Even if he was magically compelled to *try*, he had no skill at fighting. Ysabel had jumped him from behind and disarmed him in half a second.

What would Riley do in this situation? *Riley wouldn't have drawn the Sword. He would have resisted.* Jax hung his head. Giving in to the Sword's desire left him and his liege in a worse position than before. He'd just blown a big part of his mission here.

Stink ran around frantically, up to his belly in water and squeaking. Griffyn kicked at him, but Stink dodged out of the way. Meanwhile, Evangeline tugged on Griffyn's arm. "What?" he said, just as annoyed by her as by the brownie. "Speak."

"Let him up," Evangeline said. "He won't use the Sword if I order him not to."

"Don't trust her," Ysabel snapped. "She may be bound to you, Griffyn, but she's fighting you every way she can. Maybe we should . . ." She pushed Jax with her foot. "Roll him downhill toward the river and—" Her voice petered out as if she'd forgotten what she wanted to say.

"The Sword isn't going to let him drown," Madoc said. "Even if you did give him a push, which I'm betting you can't."

"I made him drop the Sword," Ysabel boasted.

"But you can't kill him. His life is protected by something stronger than you."

"Father wanted the Sword drawn," Griffyn said. "This had to happen."

That piece of information broke through the red haze of the Sword's compulsion. "Why?" Jax asked, lifting his head and calling on the inquisition part of his talent.

"The magic of all three relics must be active for his plan to work," Griffyn said, not seeming to realize he was answering Jax. Nobody did. They kept arguing until Griffyn shouted over all of them, "We will make our stand *here*. Let Transitioners come for the boy if they will. Father wanted the Sword drawn, and now it is. We stay near it, defend it, keep the boy from sheathing it. It'll give Father the time he needs."

Facts clicked through Jax's mind like numbers punched into a calculator. *Bran has the Spear. I drew the Sword. The Stone is protecting the Bedivere house. And Bran took Addie away.*

Add those things together and what did he get?

Bran and Addie were attempting to break the Eighth Day Spell. *Right now.*

Crap! Trying to break the spell had killed Elliot Emrys.

The Sword of Nuadu's hold on Jax faded in the face of danger to one of his liege ladies. Jax turned his head, seeking Stink. "Addie's in trouble," he whispered.

Stink stood up on his hind legs and cocked his head with an expression that clearly said: *You're the one in trouble!*

"Help Addie!" Jax commanded.

Instead, Stink yanked the rubber band off his front

limb with his teeth. "No!" Jax hissed. "Don't!" But it was too late. Stink popped out of sight. Riley had ordered the brownie to pull off all rubber bands and return if Jax needed immediate help. Now Riley was going to send a rescue party for Jax instead of getting help to Addie. Worse, Griffyn and company were going to be waiting for them.

Jax was hauled to his feet and away from the Sword, which still lay abandoned in the street. Griffyn kept him close as the Kin arranged themselves in defensive positions. He and Condor and Ysabel stood with their backs to one another. Gawan chose a spot near them, his eyes darting everywhere apprehensively. Evangeline took a defensive position beside Griffyn, even though her eyes burned with hatred for him. Kel and his father hung back and looked nervous. Jax bet their talent for prosperity would be of little use in a fight.

Proximity to Griffyn made Jax grit his teeth in frustration. He worked his hands against his bindings, trying to focus his attention on loosening his bonds rather than running this Llyr idiot through with a sharp blade. His hands were wet, and the leather was slippery. While he struggled, he kept his eyes peeled in all directions. Rescue would come for him via brownie tunnels, he was sure, which meant Dulac vassals—odd as that seemed after being their enemy not that long ago. They would be guided by Riley's special-ops troops, and they might show up anywhere, without warning.

In fact, when the attack began, it came from several angles simultaneously. Gawan Ratis was the first to sense danger. "They're here!" the boy yelled, holding up his hands.

Tranquilizer darts fired from the rooftops of buildings on both sides of the street hit Gawan's shields and fell to the ground. Sloane had vassals with a talent for perfect aim, but Jax was happy to see they weren't taking unnecessary chances with Jax and Evangeline and innocents like Brigit present. That meant darts instead of bullets, but Jax suspected nothing would get past Gawan's magic barricades.

Griffyn shoved Jax toward Ysabel and threw out both his arms. Wind whipped along the buildings, breaking glass, ripping off rain gutters and shingles. Anyone perched on those roofs would've had to flatten themselves and hang on or be blown off. At street level, the water in the street surged upward, rising from a few inches to a foot.

Condor Aeron pointed at the buildings, one after the other, calling out in Welsh. An explosion shattered the windows in one; flames ignited in two of the others. Jax didn't know if he was rupturing propane tanks or gas appliances or what, but the destruction seemed effortless.

Once again, Jax understood why Transitioners had been forced to imprison the Kin in an alternate timeline, with some of them suppressed even further in a magic-proof fortress. He'd thought Transitioners were a force to be reckoned with, but how could anyone fight this kind of formidable power? Even denied the use of lightning, Griffyn wielded air and water for both attack and defense. Condor detonated anything combustible. Little Gawan blocked shots from Sloane's vassals even after they apparently jumped to new locations. Ysabel, while holding on to Jax, used her free hand and her throwing knives to take out two Transitioners who didn't duck out of sight quickly enough.

Only Madoc and Kel had nothing to contribute. "Defend the Mathonwys!" Griffyn ordered Evangeline. Obediently, Evangeline trudged through the water to stand in front of Madoc and Kel, who still held Brigit.

That was when Jax noticed Brigit watching him expectantly. The toddler pointed up. Griffyn's winds had dispersed the fog, and when Jax followed Brigit's finger, he saw dark wings gliding overhead.

The crows landed half a block away on a lamppost. On the street beneath the streetlight, their mistress stood. She still wore only that long T-shirt and running shorts, her legs bare in the cold floodwater. Her loose dark hair whipped around so wildly, it was impossible to see her face.

Jax and Brigit were not the only ones who witnessed her arrival. Seconds later, a figure stepped out of an invisible hole in the middle of the street—a man with a brownie riding on his shoulder. "Lesley!" yelled Uncle Finn.

Jax didn't know if Tegan had seen the Girl of Crows when the fog thinned and sent him here, or if Uncle Finn had been waiting in the brownie tunnels for this moment all along. The Morrigan, unlike regular humans, could be seen from inside the tunnels. Jax had shared that information when he, Riley, Bedivere, and the Ambroses had planned the steps of this confrontation:

Lure the Kin to battle.

Wait for the Morrigan to appear.

Send Finn Ambrose to rescue his daughter.

Jax had begun to worry that the Girl of Crows wouldn't show up, that the Washer Woman was the only aspect of the Morrigan they'd see today. But here she was, and Uncle Finn slogged toward her through shin-high water despite the wind flinging broken glass and other debris at him. Jax's eyes dropped to his uncle's wrist and spotted what he hoped to see there: a metal ring.

Uncle Finn was wearing one half of a pair of handcuffs, with the other ring open and ready to snap closed around his daughter's wrist. If everything had gone as planned, they wouldn't be ordinary handcuffs. Oliver Bors had a talent for magic suppression. Arnold Crandall had a talent for working magic into metal. And Roger Sagramore had the ability to bind the talents of other people together. When Jax left them a week ago, the three Transitioner men had been cooperating to create handcuffs that might prevent the Morrigan from working her magic and force her to vacate Lesley's body.

"Lesley!" Uncle Finn shouted. "Lesley Evelyn Ambrose, do you hear me?"

Ysabel noticed Uncle Finn and reached for one of her knives. Immediately, Jax flung himself sideways and jammed his elbow into her gut. To his surprise, he caught her off guard, and they fell into the street together with a splash.

The Girl of Crows surveyed the battle through tangled dark locks. The wind buffeted her, and water swelled around her legs. She didn't seem to notice the elements, nor did she acknowledge her father's approach. "Lesley, sweetheart. Look at me!" Finn called again.

"Lesley!" That was a new voice, chiming in.

"Dorian!" Uncle Finn roared at his son, who'd just appeared. "What are you doing?"

Dorian was supposed to stay safely in the Bedivere house. His arrival was definitely not part of the plan, and he didn't have a brownie guide with him. Before Jax could see if Lesley would react to her brother, Ysabel got to her knees. With a wrench that probably took off a layer of skin, Jax slipped his hands free of the wet leather thongs and grabbed Ysabel's arm to prevent her from throwing knives at his relatives.

At that moment, Uncle Finn lunged at his daughter with the open handcuff.

Instantly, the girl switched from a statuelike immobility to fluid motion. She turned and caught Finn by the front of his shirt, lifted him off the ground, and flung him aside as if he were a life-sized rag doll. The brownie with him leaped off and disappeared a second before he struck a lamppost and slid down.

"Dad!" screamed Dorian, running toward him.

Keeping one hand locked around Ysabel's wrist, Jax reached desperately for the Sword of Nuadu, still lying abandoned in the street. He was hauled back by Ysabel, who had given up trying to throw her knife and instead wrapped one of her brawny arms around Jax's neck. "Griffyn, get that other boy!" she yelled.

Dorian dragged his father out of the water and propped him against the lamppost. "Dad, wake up!" He looked over his shoulder. "Lesley, don't you know us?"

The Girl of Crows showed no sign of hearing Dorian's plea. But Griffyn did. He waded over and grabbed Dorian. "I know you can see me!" he shouted to the enemies watching with guns from the rooftops. "Deliver the Stone of Fal to us!" Then Griffyn pushed Dorian to his knees and plunged his head into the water.

"Stop!" Evangeline screamed. Jax thrashed, trying to pull himself free from Ysabel.

Griffyn yanked Dorian's head up. The boy choked and

coughed and gasped. Griffyn looked at Ysabel and muttered, "I don't think they'll do it. Not for a single boy."

"No," Ysabel agreed. "Just drown him and be done with it."

Griffyn grinned, shoved Dorian back into the water, and held him there.

34

THE CRIMSON LIGHT OF the Sword was wicked and spiteful and strangely compelling. Filled with the power of the other two relics, Addie resisted the allure of this third one. It was hard to hold all that magic and also concentrate on rational thought. The Kin Treasures were wild and ancient; they encouraged reaction, not reason. And Addie needed to think very carefully now.

She stepped sideways and put a little distance between herself and Bran.

He didn't seem to notice. His eyes were alight with ambition. "This is a momentous occasion. I'm not aware of any other time these Treasures were employed all at once."

It sounded like he was claiming credit, but Addie suspected the Morrigan had more of a hand in it than he did.

Bran turned to Addie. "Merlin Emrys needed the assistance of dozens of Transitioners to create the Eighth Day Spell," he said. "But you and I alone will shatter it."

"Or maybe just me." Addie backed up and called on the Aeron talent for mayhem to rip away the bolts attaching Bran's section of the walkway to the structure encircling the tank.

Metal screeched; wood splintered. The walkway tipped but, still attached to the neighboring sections, did not fall. Bran leaped off the collapsed area with more speed than Addie had counted on. Realizing she'd made a grievous error, Addie scrambled around the side of the water tank away from him. With the power of the Treasures at her disposal, she could have torn the entire platform off the tower, but she'd tried to be delicate, seeing how she was standing on it herself. *A mistake.*

Addie pressed herself against the tank, trying to sense the location of the Spear and Bran. He was, at most, twenty feet away from her around the circumference of the tank. She hadn't planned on confronting him in a place like this! She'd thought he was bringing her up the tower to get a view of the battlefield—maybe share his strategy for capturing the Stone. She hadn't realized he wanted to make his assault on the Eighth Day Spell from here.

"You turn against me *now*, girl?" Bran roared. "When I've brought you this far? Given you access to this kind of power?"

"Well, *after* I broke the Spell would be too late, wouldn't it?" she called back. "Since you were planning to kill me." Addie had figured out days ago that her value as an Emrys would disappear the instant the Eighth Day Spell was vanquished.

The existence of the Kin would no longer depend on her life. She'd simply be a spell caster with a unique access to powerful magic—and a threat to Bran. *He probably picked the tower so he could toss me off afterward.*

She sensed the Spear moving toward her around the tank. The ladder was on his side. Another mistake! If she kept circling away from him, she'd run into the broken section of the walkway. *Think, Addie!* she chastised herself. No lightning. The tank was made of metal. No more attacking the walkway. What if the whole thing collapsed?

Addie's hold on the magic of the Spear and the Stone wavered under her panic. This was the part she'd never been good at. Picking the right tactic at the right moment. Thinking quickly under attack. In all their practices, Addie always ended up on the floor at Bran's mercy. She looked at the ground—far below and invisible under the fog. There would be no mercy this time, and *flying* was not one of her many stolen talents.

Wind.

She grasped at the idea and called it up desperately, summoning gusts of wind to assail the man approaching her along the circumference of the tank. *Stop him coming closer. Knock him off.* The blast of air caught her, too. She gasped, struggling to hold on.

As suddenly as it started, the gale cut off. "You can't use my own talent against me, Adelina!" Bran called. "And you cannot defeat me while I hold the Spear."

"You can't break the Eighth Day Spell without me," Addie shouted. "And if you knock me off this tower, there's only Evangeline left. Maybe you shouldn't have sent her into battle with your stupid son. What if she gets killed down there? If we both die—you go poof!"

"I admit, I considered eliminating you after you'd served your purpose," Bran said. "But you're too clever a girl to waste. If you'd been a little older, I would have pledged you to Griffyn instead of your traitorous sister. You'd make a better daughter to me than she ever will."

"That's not winning me over!" Addie felt disgusted on both counts, and she didn't believe him anyway. *Whatever he tells you, it's a lie,* Evangeline had said. But that was too simple. What Bran did was combine truth and lies to manipulate the listener. Addie remembered his twisted tales about Merlin and his speech about the future of their race—right after he left Aine's baby to die in a fire. Probably Bran *did* see value in Addie—but he would kill her anyway, just to eliminate any challenge to his power.

He was seeking her location now. She felt the prickling sensation that usually meant someone was scrying for her. But in this case, it was more likely Bran using her connection to the Spear to pinpoint her exact spot.

"You don't trust me," Bran acknowledged. "And now I can't trust you. There's only one solution. Swear your allegiance to me, Adelina. Become my vassal, and we will proceed as planned."

Oh, sure. Because being his vassal meant he'd protect her. She could ask the Aerons he'd sent into a pointless battle about that. Addie shuddered, partly at the thought of swearing to Bran and partly because of that creepy, crawly sensation of being sought after through magic. Her link to the Spear was going to get her killed.

Or . . . maybe not. *You cannot defeat me while I hold the Spear,* Bran said. And no one could take it from him, according to legend. Of course, the legends had never included anyone like Addie.

Now she had a plan. It was risky, and she'd better do it before she chickened out. Taking a deep breath, she prepared to charge around the tank straight toward Bran.

Thump.

That was the sound of the Spear striking the wooden planks of the platform. She had only a second to remember the time Bran had rocked the warehouse floor. Then the walkway dropped beneath her. Addie's chest hit the slick boards, and she slid backward on her stomach. She scrabbled frantically with her hands, her fingers catching the gap between two wooden planks just as her legs went over the edge.

The walkway dangled brokenly from the framework, with only a few bolts still supporting it. Her body had slid underneath the railing, and her arms were stretched to their full length to hold on. Addie dug her fingers between the boards. Every shred of stolen magic fled her.

Bran stared down at her from an intact section of the platform. "Swear to me, Adelina," he said. "And I will pull you up."

All Addie's bravery and defiance vanished with a hundred-and-twenty-foot drop beneath her feet and her fingers slipping. Even knowing that she couldn't trust Bran didn't matter. "I'll swear!" she sobbed. "Please!" Another bolt popped. The walkway jerked down a bit farther, and although Bran reached for her, Addie's precarious hold was jarred loose.

She fell, screaming.

Clouds caught her.

That was what it felt like. Squishy, bouncy clouds.

Addie jerked, like she did when she had a dream of falling and woke up in her bed. She was *not* in bed waking up from a dream, however, but suspended in the sky a few yards beneath the water tower. Shrieking, she flailed her arms, desperately seeking something to hold on to and finding nothing but squishiness.

And dark, furry bodies that squeaked and scurried around and over her.

She wasn't falling. It took a few seconds for Addie's brain to accept that, and when she did, she grew very still, afraid to break the spell. She was nestled in a pocket of opalescent magic, sharing the space with half a dozen brownies. Now that she'd quit thrashing around, they'd stopped squealing and were all staring at her.

This was a brownie hole. The brownies had opened

a hole beneath her in midair, and she'd fallen into it. "You caught me," she said.

Some of the brownies cocked their heads. Others rotated their ears.

"Did Jax send you?" Addie looked for the one with the goofy white tuft of hair—Stink—but he didn't seem to be here. "Can you—" She felt stupid, asking questions of brownies, but Jax talked to his like he expected the creature to understand. "Can you get me out of here? Without letting me fall?"

One of the brownies leaped excitedly around in a circle. Addie took that for a *yes*.

She looked up at the water tower and inhaled a couple times, screwing up her courage.

"Can you get me back on that platform?"

35

DORIAN'S STRUGGLES GREW WEAKER as Griffyn held him under water. Ten seconds . . . fifteen seconds. Evangeline sobbed and pleaded for Griffyn to stop. Jax bucked and strained against Ysabel's headlock, but the girl had hands of iron.

Twenty seconds.

The Girl of Crows shuffled forward as if she wanted to see the drowning close at hand. Her black-feathered companions, perched on the lamppost, watched their mistress with glittering eyes. She bent over, reached into the water—

—and emerged with the Sword of Nuadu. When she looked up, it was with the pale face and trembling lips of a frightened girl.

"Let go of my brother," Lesley Ambrose said in a shaky voice.

Griffyn froze with his mouth hanging open. Perhaps

he was too shocked at being addressed by the Morrigan to respond to her command. His hand remained on the back of Dorian's head.

"Let him go!" Lesley hefted the Sword over her shoulder. *"Now!"*

"Griffyn," said Condor. "You'd better do what she—"

Lesley swung the Sword like a baseball bat and smacked Griffyn in the head with the flat side of the blade. He howled in pain and surged to his feet, releasing Dorian, who floundered before getting his head above water. Jax watched anxiously while his cousin gulped in air, gagged, then doubled over and vomited up water.

Griffyn backed away, holding one hand to the side of his face. Lesley stepped between the brawny Kin and her brother, breathing rapidly and holding the Sword awkwardly in both hands. Her eyes darted around like she was trying to figure out where she was. She gasped when she saw her father, motionless and propped against a lamppost, and her eyes grew wide at the sight of all the Kin watching her. Then her gaze fell on Jax. "Am I dreaming?" she whispered.

"No, Lesley," Jax called. "This is real. It's good to see you back!"

But was she? How could she touch the Sword if she was just Lesley Ambrose, a dud without even Transitioner talents? It had burned Riley and anyone who'd tried to take it from Jax. He had a bad feeling that only something as strong as a force of nature could hold it.

Griffyn, on the other hand, was coming to the opposite conclusion. He looked Lesley up and down. "This isn't the Morrigan." He lunged for her. Lesley shrieked and jumped backward.

Ysabel let go of Jax and stood up. "Griffyn, don't provoke her."

"It's just a girl. An imposter sent to trick us." Griffyn made another grab for her.

Lesley tried to hit him again, swinging the Sword like it was a wooden prop in a play. He caught her arm and twisted her around until her back was against his chest. His left hand locked on her right wrist, immobilizing the Sword, and his other hand closed around her throat. He looked at Ysabel and laughed. "The Transitioners keep sending us children. These must be the best warriors they have." He wrenched Lesley's head back until she was staring up at his face. "What shall I do with you?" he taunted her.

"Griffyn, watch out!" yelled Ysabel.

A crow had launched itself from the lamppost. It stabbed its beak at Griffyn's face, missing his eye by an inch. He let go of Lesley to shield his face from a second crow—and a third. They swirled around his head, jabbing at him with their beaks and raking him with their claws.

"Jax!" Evangeline cried. She had summoned her fireballs and was moving reluctantly toward Griffyn, compelled by her handmaiden bond to defend him. But her expression said, *Stop me!* Jax didn't need a second hint. He leaped to his feet and tackled Evangeline before she could come between Griffyn and the Morrigan.

It was a good thing he did, because Lesley whirled on Griffyn with a cry of rage—an inhuman screech Jax didn't think his cousin was capable of making. Her clumsy grip on the Sword changed suddenly to something far more competent, and with expert precision, she thrust the blade into Griffyn's chest. He had time to register the shock of being skewered by a fourteen-year-old girl. Then the Morrigan yanked the Sword out, and Griffyn dropped like a stone.

Jax felt Evangeline shudder in relief as her handmaiden bond dissolved.

Ysabel screamed in grief. It was the first time Jax had seen the girl show any emotion. But when she started to run toward her fallen boyfriend, the Morrigan turned, eyes burning with fury, and Ysabel froze.

Dorian, who didn't seem to have the strength to stand or move away, stared up at his sister in terror.

This was not Lesley.

The Morrigan's eyes passed over the group with calculation, as if she was considering using the Sword on the rest of them. When she came to Jax, she held out her free hand.

"The scabbard," Evangeline whispered. "She wants the scabbard."

Jax unbuckled the strap across his chest, his fingers fumbling with nervousness. He glanced at Uncle Finn, but it seemed unlikely the Morrigan would allow him to retrieve the magic-suppressing handcuffs. So he approached the Morrigan with only the scabbard—held at arm's length because he didn't want to get any closer than necessary. When she took it from him, he said, "Thank you."

"Do not presume to thank me." Her voice was as cold and dark as the grave.

Got it. Jax dropped his eyes. *Can we have my cousin back?* was probably out, too.

With a rush of air, the Morrigan vanished, taking the crows and the Sword with her.

"Lesley," Dorian whispered hoarsely.

"That wasn't Lesley," Jax said, helping him up. "Are you okay?"

He nodded, coughing. "But she's still in there, isn't she?"

"Yeah, she saved you, dude." Jax pounded his cousin on the back.

Dorian looked at Jax miserably. "I wanted to save *her.*"

A moment later, five of Sloane's vassals burst out of three different brownie holes on the street. They dropped poor Gawan with a tranquilizer before he could react. Condor Aeron, left unprotected, roared like a madman, hurling a fire hydrant and a signpost at the newcomers with his destructive talent before three darts took him down.

Madoc threw up his hands in surrender. They shot him anyway. One man targeted Kel, but didn't shoot, probably because he was holding Brigit. Another one aimed at Evangeline.

"No!" Jax cried, stepping in front of his liege. "Not her!"

"She was fighting with them."

"Not by choice, and she's free of them now. But—" Jax looked around. Where was Ysabel?

Evangeline pointed down an alley. "The Arawen girl ran that way, as soon as the Morrigan vanished." Two of Sloane's men took off after her, while another bent over Uncle Finn, feeling for a pulse and looking under his eyelids. Dorian splashed over to check on his father for himself, but Jax could see that his uncle was beginning to stir. He'd been knocked unconscious, but he was alive.

"The Morrigan vanished?" repeated Albert Ganner, leader of the Dulac security force. "You mean we missed her? What happened?" He looked at Griffyn's body lying facedown in the street and nudged it with his foot. The sleeves of Griffyn's white shirt billowed in the water.

That's what I saw the Washer Woman rinsing in the river. A shiver ran up Jax's spine. "He tried to kill Dorian, and Lesley stopped him. Why didn't you guys show up sooner?"

Evangeline looked down at Griffyn with revulsion. Then, to Jax's surprise, she rolled his body over and started searching his pockets.

"We jumped here through the tunnels as soon as the Morrigan attacked Finn," Ganner said, "but it looks like there was a gap in time for us." He pointed a thumb at the brownie riding on his shoulder. "I'm not convinced these things are as smart as Pendragon says they are."

Oh, they were smart all right. They knew better than to show up while the Morrigan was in a murderous fury. They had jumped Ganner and his men ahead to a time when she was already gone. Which reminded Jax . . .

No sooner did Jax think of him than Stink dropped onto Jax's shoulder from nowhere. "Well, thanks for sending in the rescue team. But I told you to go to Addie!"

Stink cocked his head quizzically.

"Take us to her, now!" Evangeline had found what she wanted on Griffyn's body—the hilt of a dagger and a broken-off blade that went with it—but when she stood up, Albert Ganner took her arm.

"You're not going anywhere," he said. "Sorry, Jax. Now that I've got one Emrys heir out of two, I'm not letting her go back to the Llyr leader—or you, either, for that matter."

"Stink will do it," Jax said with more confidence than he felt. "Go get her, Stink. Bring Addie to us." Stink leaped off his shoulder and vanished, and Jax tried to summon a reassuring smile for Evangeline.

I'll think about it, Addie had said when Jax asked if she'd follow Stink. He hoped that was just Addie being Addie— that she'd welcome the chance to escape Bran Llyr.

Because he was really worried about what she might be doing right now.

36

THE LAST PLACE ADDIE wanted to be was back on the water tower, but—here she was. There'd been a lurch, and instead of sitting in a bubble of magic, she was standing on what was left of the walkway around the tank.

The brownies had deposited her behind Bran, who was looking over the railing where Addie had fallen. Had he seen her drop into a brownie hole, or did he think she was dead? It didn't matter. She had maybe two seconds before he turned around and saw her.

Addie concentrated on locating the Stone and the Sword, rapidly drawing in their magic. The Stone of Fal was familiar now, passionate and protective. The Sword of Nuadu was hateful, tasting like fury and hungry for blood. Their combined potential staggered her. *I am vengeance,* Addie thought. *I protect the Kin.*

She saved the Spear for last. As soon as she called on its

focus and obsession, Bran sensed her presence and whirled around. "Miss me?" she asked.

His face darkened with anger. "That was a clever trick," he said, "but vermin can't save you if you cross me again." Bran held the Spear out in preparation for calling something new and terrible down upon her. "You *will* submit to my authority!"

She laughed. Submit? With the stolen power of three Treasures, Addie thought she was more than a match for a Kin lord who fancied himself a weather god. She rushed forward and clamped her own hand on the Spear of Lugh.

Bran's eyes widened. He tried to pull it away from her, but Addie willed the Spear to stay where it was, and *it obeyed.* "Thanks for torturing me with it so many times," she said, grinning. "The pain doesn't bother me anymore."

Then she yanked it out of his hands.

Five minutes ago, she hadn't been positive she could do it. But with the magic of the Treasures vibrating inside her, it was impossible to imagine failing. Addie had attuned herself to the Spear through repeated contact. It was confused, no longer sure of its true master. She backed away from the Llyr lord as the new possessor of the Spear of Lugh.

For a second, Bran looked shaken, but he recovered quickly. "You are a presumptuous child, swollen with stolen magic like a blood-filled tick, but still a child. You don't know who you're dealing with."

Bran held up his hand as if to call lightning down upon her. Addie didn't know if he meant to kill her or frighten her into submission, but the biting power of the vengeful Sword of Nuadu prompted her to defend herself. She snapped her fingers. It was the same gesture that had caused Bran to mock her for *playing with matches*. This time, all the coarse, woolen clothing on his body caught fire.

The old man howled. He beat at the flames with one hand. With his other, he summoned rain. But neither act was going to do him any good, because he also staggered backward off the edge of the broken walkway, his face frozen in disbelief as he went over. Addie watched him fall through the fog. No brownie hole opened up to catch him.

Intention. Protection. Vengeance. That's me.

Power thrummed through her body, demanding her attention. Addie dismissed the Llyr lord from her mind and surveyed the river valley with her enhanced sight. The woven strands of the Eighth Day Spell were more visible than ever, although they didn't look as unassailable as they had before. Not with the magic of *three* Treasures inside her. Not with the Spear of Lugh in her hand. The only question was where to start.

Should she unravel the spell—pick it apart thread by thread?

Or punch a hole right through it?

Addie smiled grimly. *Let's face it. I'm not very patient.* The

Spear was heavy and several inches taller than she was, but she raised it over her head, preparing to tear the hated spell to pieces.

Above the water tank, half a dozen black crows circled against the backdrop of a purple eighth-day sky, then dropped one by one to perch on broken pieces of the wooden railing.

The Morrigan, wearing her Girl of Crows body, had appeared on the platform near the place where Bran had gone over. She'd come to see the Spell dismantled, which wasn't surprising, considering how she'd overseen almost every step that had brought Addie to this point. What made Addie's heart lurch, however, were the objects in the Morrigan's hands—a scabbard with a leather harness and the Sword of Nuadu.

Jax's Sword.

Whirling around, Addie sought out the individual strands of the Eighth Day Spell and saw that her sister's anchor was still there. But what about the boy who was supposed to be guarding her? Addie couldn't pick him out among the strands of hundreds of Transitioners.

Addie turned back to the Morrigan. "Where's Jax?" she demanded. "How did you get the Sword?" Jax had drawn it and then lost it somehow. What did that mean for Evangeline? "Is my sister in danger?"

"You have the power of three Treasures within you, Adelina Emrys. Just as planned." The Morrigan's dark eyes were vacant and hollow in the face of her girl host. "The time has come for you to fulfill your destiny."

"Not until you answer my questions!" Addie had never handled a spear before, but she knew what to do with the pointy end. She swung the heavy thing down and held it level with her hips, aimed at the Morrigan. The Sword's desire for vengeance churned inside her. If the Morrigan had hurt her sister or their vassal . . . well, deity or not, she was going to see what *Addie's* vengeance looked like!

"You dare to threaten me, presumptuous girl?"

It was chilling to hear the dire warning in that voice while the body and face of the speaker remained blank, like a sleepwalker's. But Addie refused to be cowed. "The last person to call me that went over the side," she snapped. "I'm going to ask you again: What happened down there?" The Morrigan had made Addie into a vessel for the power of all the Treasures combined. Now she was going to have to deal with what she'd created!

"The boy completed his task." Addie thought it had to be a measure of her own importance that the Morrigan actually answered her. "You must complete yours. The power of the Sword will fade now that it is satisfied. Act quickly, before it is too late."

The Sword was satisfied? Then, as Addie had suspected, Jax hadn't really invoked it against a nameless parade of enemies. There'd only been one target all along, and based on how the Sword had pulsed in the presence of one particular person—and how hard Jax had fought against its allure—Addie knew who it must have been.

Griffyn Llyr was dead, and Evangeline was free.

Addie grinned, rotating the Spear back to its upright position. "Good riddance to the Llyrs," she said. "The world is better off."

"Break the Spell now, and your people will have all the happiness you desire for them," the Morrigan said. "You will be their savior."

Addie liked the sound of that. The Kin could come out of hiding. They could have everything Normals had—libraries and candy stores and lives that didn't skip across time like a stone skimming a pond. The protective instincts of the Stone of Fal swelled within her. Addie had been the one chosen to end the exile of her people and win them the happiness they deserved.

If you call it winning when you've been chosen by an evil goddess of destruction and chaos.

Addie blinked. Jax had said those words back when they saw the Washer Woman. Why was she remembering his sarcastic comment *now,* when she was on the verge of getting what she wanted?

Because it wasn't like the Morrigan to deliver happiness. That wasn't her function.

Addie gripped the Spear tightly and narrowed her eyes at the being sharing this platform with her. It wore the body of a teenage girl, some Normal probably stolen from her bed the same way old Mrs. Stanwell had been stolen when the Crone appeared to Addie in Vermont. Poor Mrs. Stanwell hadn't survived it. What was going to happen to this girl? For the first time, Addie wondered who she was, who was missing her, whose lives would be bereft without her.

Behind the blankness of those eyes, was she screaming silently in terror? In warning?

On the other side of the river, the mountainside was in flames. Addie assumed the Aerons were still wreaking a path of destruction through the forest, and by the gunfire rumbling in the distance, the Transitioners were fighting them. Down in the valley, Addie's sister was alive and free of Griffyn, but what about Condor and Ysabel? Was Evangeline at their mercy? And the Morrigan hadn't actually said Jax was okay, just that he'd done his job.

The Morrigan was sounding more and more like Bran, manipulating Addie with a mix of truth and lies. There were no candy stores and libraries on offer here. The Morrigan was the Morrigan and she always wanted the same thing. Death. Chaos. Turmoil.

The powers of *protection* and *intention* warred within Addie, and her uncertainty must have shown on her face, because the Morrigan's words grew more forceful. "Break the spell, Adelina. The time has come for you to pay for the gift you were given."

"You're not supposed to pay if it's a *gift*," Addie argued.

The Morrigan snarled like an animal, contorting the face

of the Normal girl. As the howl wound down, her lips peeled back against her teeth, and she hissed, "Do as you are told!"

Addie had heard that command many times in her life, and her reaction to it was always the same. "No."

For once in her life, it was more than just contrariness prompting an automatic response. This time, Addie understood that if she did what she was told, the Kin—and the Transitioners—and the Normals—were *all* going to suffer for it.

The water tower shook with the Morrigan's rage. The crows launched themselves upward in alarm, their wings flapping frantically. Addie braced herself with the Spear to keep from losing her footing.

"You *want* to break the Spell!" the Morrigan exclaimed.

"Yes, but not if *you* want it this much," Addie said. "I guess you should have picked someone more obedient. Or more easily fooled." *Although I was fooled. For way too long.* Her hand ached from gripping the Spear tightly in anger and disappointment. After all she'd been through, she wasn't going to get what she wanted! Or what she *thought* she had wanted . . .

"You *are* a fool." The Morrigan's expression had returned to a deathlike vacancy that was somehow all the more foreboding after her display of fury. She sheathed the Sword of Nuadu.

With a sinking feeling, Addie realized that the vengeful magic of the Sword had left her. It had gone dormant now. And her hand was stinging not because of how tightly she was gripping the Spear of Lugh, but because it was starting to reject her. She had stolen it from Bran when she thought she wanted to break the Eighth Day Spell, but she wouldn't do that on the Morrigan's orders. She didn't know what she wanted anymore, and the Spear would never accept an owner without a purpose.

As for the Stone of Fal—Addie tried to cling to its warm power, but who was she trying to protect? Her people? Her sister? Her vassal? It occurred to Addie, as the Stone's magic slipped away, that she'd be lucky if she could protect herself. Moments ago, she'd been full of limitless potential, capable of taking on the Morrigan. Now she was just a foolish girl who hadn't thought things through before defying a goddess.

The platform jerked beneath Addie's feet and the entire water tower started to shake like it was coming apart. Addie hung on to the Spear in spite of the pain radiating up her arm and grabbed the railing for balance. Over a hundred feet below, the stagnant floodwater she'd trudged through to get here had become a raging torrent beating deliberately against the support legs of the tower.

Addie backed away from the Morrigan, who simply watched her with a knowing smile and a malevolence as old as time. The ladder was on the other side of the tank, but Addie couldn't climb down into that churning water, even if the structure lasted long enough for her to do so. The tower was coming down, and Addie was trapped.

Then the air shimmered above the walkway, and a

single brownie dropped onto the wooden planks and bolted straight for Addie, ears plastered unhappily against his head as if he knew exactly what was standing behind him. Addie didn't need the telltale white tuft to recognize him. Jax had sent his pet for her, just like he promised he would.

The Morrigan didn't stir, but one of her crows dived for the brownie, its outstretched claws narrowly missing his head. More of the crows flew at him, trying to spear him with their beaks while Stink darted back and forth, dodging them. He could have popped out of danger the same way he'd arrived. Addie had seen him do that before. But he didn't do it now. Stink was coming for Addie because Jax had sent him, and the brownie was as loyal as his master.

Addie charged forward. "Get away from him, you filthy crows!" She swung the Spear of Lugh at the hovering birds, hoping to bash them out of the sky. But the Spear was too heavy, and the pain of holding on to it had become too great. When the wooden shaft knocked against the water tank, her hands, numbed and clumsy, lost their grip. The Spear slipped between the tank and the walkway and vanished into the water below.

Addie barely registered its loss before Stink leaped into her arms. She squeezed his warm body—a welcome antidote to the cold, searing pain of the Spear—and the brownie squealed in protest. Or maybe he was squealing because the water tank was looming over their heads . . . and the platform was tilting wildly . . . and the Morrigan's crows were flying straight for them. "Get us out of here, Stink!" she shrieked.

The brownie tried to twist free of her hands. But Addie was afraid to let go. She hung on, closed her eyes, and pitched into the empty sky with him.

37

JAX STOOD ON THE flooded street in his soaked clothes next to Evangeline, whom he'd led away from Griffyn's dead body, and stared up at the mountainside. The fog was finally dissipating—only to be replaced by smoke from the fire. Jax watched the distant flames worriedly while Albert Ganner radioed for help transporting the unconscious Condor, Madoc, and Gawan—and the fully awake and glowering Kel—to a secure location. "You know there's innocent kids out there in the fighting, right?" Jax asked one of the Dulac clansmen.

The man nodded. "The Morgans are doing their best to extract them."

"I'm sending Jax and the Emrys leader back to headquarters via the brownie tunnels," Ganner reported into the radio. "Under guard. Jax seems to think the other Emrys might arrive on her own. Keep an eye out for her." He signed off.

"Evangeline's not a prisoner," Jax objected. "She doesn't need a guard."

Ganner was unapologetic. "With one Llyr still on the loose and a whole lot of crazy Aerons trying to burn down the mountainside, it's for the protection of both of you."

Ganner's man didn't let go of either Jax or Evangeline as they entered one of the brownie holes on the street and jumped, with brownie assistance, back to the Bedivere house. The high-ceilinged entry hall was a beehive of activity centered around Sheila Morgan, who wore full combat gear in spite of being stationed at the mansion. Their guard tried to direct them toward her to give a report, but Jax resisted. "I need to see Riley first, let him know we're okay. Then we'll tell you guys anything you want to know."

"He's in the banquet room," the man said, pointing. "Make it quick. We still have people in the field needing any intelligence you've got."

Jax took off in that direction with Evangeline right behind him. "You're sure Addie will meet us here?" she asked.

"Stink will bring her," Jax insisted, faking confidence, because he really wasn't sure—not until he threw open the banquet-room doors and heard the commotion inside. Riley was bellowing and slapping at his leg. His jeans were wet, and Tegan held an empty metal pan in her hands.

"Really?" Riley exclaimed indignantly at the Kin girl

on the other side of the room. "We save your life, and *you set my pants on fire?*"

"Where are my sister and Jax?" Addie shouted back, clenching her hands like she was preparing to call up fireballs.

"Addie, we're here!" Evangeline rushed into the room and flung her arms around her sister. Addie cried out and returned the hug enthusiastically.

Stink scampered up Jax's clothing and onto his shoulder. Jax grinned at Riley and offered him a fist bump. "Got 'em back. Told you I would."

Riley knocked his knuckles with Jax's. "Don't get cocky, squirt. Things didn't go exactly as planned."

"When do they ever?" Jax shot back. But it'd been mostly *his* plan—and *most* of it had turned out the way he wanted. He'd gotten everything he wanted . . . except for Lesley.

"Bran Llyr is dead." Addie pulled out of her sister's embrace. "And Griffyn is too, right? Jax killed him?"

"What?" Riley looked stricken. "Jax—"

"I didn't!" Jax protested. "The Morrigan took the Sword. She's the one who did it." Jax didn't know Addie well enough to hug her, so he punched her lightly on the shoulder in greeting. "Hey, I'm glad you're okay and everything, but did you *have to* set Riley's pants on fire?"

"They were only smoldering." Addie punched Jax back. "Your brownie dropped me in a room with strangers instead of taking me to you and Evangeline! And one of them was a Pendragon. What was I supposed to think?"

Riley approached Evangeline. "Are you all right?" He could see she was unhurt, so Jax suspected he was really asking: Are *we* all right?

Evangeline looked up at him. "Riley, I'm sorry I left without telling you. I did what I thought I had to do to reach my sister."

"I know you did," Riley said quickly. "I never doubted it. I overstepped my bounds, keeping information from you, and I—"

He froze when she held out the pieces of his dagger. "I didn't want to do this," she said. "But they were hurting Addie, and they made me break it." To Jax's surprise, she burst into tears.

"Whatever you needed to do to save your sister was the right thing to do." Looking panicked by her tears, Riley whipped out Excalibur and extended it toward her, hilt first. "I can offer you another blade to settle things between us."

Evangeline shook her head vigorously. "I'm not going to take Excalibur from you! I don't need a blade to represent our . . . *alliance* . . ."

"Then . . . what's wrong?" Riley looked at Jax for help. Jax shrugged. *You're on your own, dude.*

"This was your childhood blade," Evangeline explained, holding out the broken pieces. "I know it had to be a gift from your father. It was important to you and maybe a family heirloom."

Riley nodded, understanding her at last. *"This,"* he said, waving Excalibur, "is a family heirloom." He chucked the ancient dagger onto Bedivere's table, where it spun around and almost went over the edge. *"You're* important to me."

Dropping the broken pieces of his dagger, Evangeline gave a little leap and threw her arms around his neck. Riley lifted her right off the ground and kissed her.

Jax retrieved Excalibur from the edge of the table before it fell off. "That was pretty smooth," he whispered to Addie. "But I'm betting he actually wants this back." Then he noticed Addie's mouth hanging open in astonishment. "Oh, you didn't know about those two?"

"No," Addie said faintly, staring at them. "Emrys and Pendragon . . . that's not possible."

"Sure it is. Why not?" Jax glanced at his friends, then looked away and said loudly, "But I wish they'd knock off the PDA. Nobody wants to see that!"

"You can say that again!" snapped Sloane, flinging the banquet-room doors open. Riley and Evangeline broke apart reluctantly as Sloane stalked across the hardwood floor, followed by Bedivere and someone Jax thought must be part of Sheila Morgan's mercenary crew. "Jax, we need a report *now* on what happened out there and—" Sloane broke off when she spotted Addie and called back over her shoulder to the Morgan vassal. "The other

Emrys *is* here. Inform Sheila."

"Tell her Addie says the Llyr lord is dead, too. At the water tower, I expect." Riley held a hand out to Jax, and Jax wordlessly passed Excalibur back to him.

"How'd you know that?" Addie asked as the Morgan vassal stepped aside to speak into his radio. Her eyes scanned the pans of water on Bedivere's table, the packets of labeled hair, and Tegan, who looked bleary-eyed. "*You.* Were you scrying for me?"

"You were the hardest one to reach," Tegan said. "But yeah, I spotted you on the tower."

"I stole hair from your room when I was on the island," Jax explained. "Tegan's been keeping an eye on all three of us—you, me, and Evangeline."

"I sensed someone watching," Evangeline said, "and made sure not to fight it. But you must be exhausted." It was the first time Jax had ever heard Evangeline praise Tegan.

Tegan shrugged and rubbed her eyes. "I had support, first from Gloria Crandall and then Riley, or I wouldn't have been able to keep it up as long as I did."

"You sent the brownies," Addie said to Tegan. "The ones that caught me."

"Well, I saw you were in trouble, and Riley sent the brownies."

Bedivere, who'd been speaking to the Morgan vassal during this exchange, turned to Addie. "Are you sure the

Llyr lord's dead? We sent military forces to that tower as soon as Riley and Tegan reported your location, and they witnessed unnaturally turbulent water knocking it down. That has to be weather-working magic, and if there's a Llyr out there, we need to know. There are still many of our people out on that mountain."

Addie shook her head. "It was the Morrigan. She knocked the tower down."

Sloane slapped both her hands on Bedivere's table in frustration. "The Morrigan was at the tower *and* on the main street? Can anyone explain to me *why we didn't get her*? Finn has a concussion, a dislocated shoulder, and very little memory of events. Dorian looks like a drowned rat, and he's practically incoherent. Jax, what happened?"

So Jax told the story as briefly as he could, explaining how the Morrigan had tossed Finn Ambrose aside and used the Sword of Nuadu to kill Griffyn.

"You were trying to *capture* the Morrigan?" Addie asked incredulously.

"We were trying to rescue the girl she stole," Jax clarified.

"That accounts for one Llyr," Bedivere said. "What happened to the other one? If he had the Spear of Lugh, wasn't he protected?"

Everyone looked at Addie, who quickly said, "It was the Morrigan. The Treasures don't affect her, right?" Her eyes darted around at everyone. "She, um, threw Bran off the tower."

"Why would she do that?" Bedivere asked doubtfully.

Addie shook her head and shrugged at the same time. "Well, I guess she was angry things weren't going her way. She thought Bran could break the Eighth Day Spell while the Treasures were all active and they had me prisoner. But he couldn't, and she got mad. If Stink hadn't rescued me, she would've killed me next."

Jax and Evangeline exchanged dubious glances, but Bedivere seemed to accept her explanation. "We have an Arawen on the run, and an unknown number of Aerons to subdue," he said to Sloane. "But no one can damage the Eighth Day Spell if we have both the Emrys heirs, and Sheila will be relieved to know we won't be dealing with any more tornadoes and lightning."

"As long as there's fighting, we might still see the Morrigan," Sloane said. "We can't send Finn, but she didn't respond to him anyway. She did react to Dorian . . ."

"You can't let him go after her again!" Jax exclaimed.

"Of course not," Sloane snapped. "I'll just have to hope someone on my security team will have better luck—move faster, get that cuff on her. Something!" She strode toward the doors, her face like a thundercloud and her hands clenched at her sides. Bedivere followed her.

Addie shuffled nearer to Jax. "Do you know *she*"—Addie

pointed at Sloane's back—"is one of the Dulacs who held me prisoner?"

Riley beat Jax to an answer. "We know. But she's also the reason you're still alive. She's trying to save Lesley Ambrose, and thankfully that meant protecting you, too."

"My dad sniffed you out," Tegan said. "He found where all of you were hiding over the last week. That house in the mountains. Sheila Morgan wanted to bring out the bulldozers and demolish the place."

"But Sloane voted with us to lure the battle here instead of taking action at that house," Riley explained. "Normally, I wouldn't trust Sloane Dulac as far as I could throw her, but where Lesley's safety was concerned, she was unmovable."

Jax sucked in his breath, realizing he and Evangeline and Addie could have been snuffed out of existence without ever knowing what happened—if it hadn't been for the Morrigan taking Lesley. "She wasn't there, you know," he said. "It's not like the Morrigan *hung out* with us."

"Doesn't matter," Riley told him. "She might've been there. That was enough to sway the vote, because Lesley was the one Sloane cared about."

"You could have wiped us out." Addie's eyes were big with shock. "But you let the battle come here, let the Aerons burn the forest and the Llyrs destroy that town— to save one girl?"

"No," Riley said. "To save three girls, one boy, and an

entire race." He reached out to Evangeline, and she took his hand in hers.

Jax opened his mouth to make another complaint about public displays of affection—just to lighten the moment—but Evangeline turned suddenly on her sister. "Now that we have a moment alone," she said, "how about telling us the truth? Because that was a whopping pack of lies you gave Bedivere."

38

"YOU'RE CALLING ME A liar? I haven't seen you in years, and as soon as we're back together, you call me a liar?" Addie found that an attack was often a good first line of defense.

"I know your 'lying voice,' even after years apart," said Evangeline. "And I've seen that your talent has changed. What did the Old Crone do to you?"

"I'll leave," the Pendragon boy offered. "If you want to speak privately."

"I won't," said the girl with the orange hair, putting her chin in her hand. "I want to hear this."

Addie saw Evangeline squeeze her boyfriend's hand, encouraging him to stay. Feeling like everyone was ganging up on her, Addie turned to Jax, who nodded. *It's okay. Talk.*

"*I* was the one who was supposed to break the Eighth Day Spell, okay?" she said. "I can copy any spell I see. I can use magic that doesn't belong to me. I didn't need to *have* the Treasures. I only needed them active so I could use their power to boost my own. Is that what you wanted to hear?"

"What happened?" Evangeline asked.

Addie crossed her arms sullenly. "I didn't do what I was told to do."

With a gasp and a laugh, Evangeline let go of Riley and threw her arms around Addie. "*Of course* you didn't! When do you ever?"

Addie should have been offended by that, but even she had to admit it was true. Still, she added over Evangeline's shoulder while her sister hugged her, "They would have killed me when they were done with me. I'm sure of it. But I *hate* the Eighth Day Spell! I *wanted* to end it!"

"We all hate it," Riley said. "But it's our burden to preserve it."

Evangeline drew back and took Addie's face in her hands. "Did you kill Bran?"

"He fell," Addie insisted. Then she admitted, "He attacked me. I defended myself. *Then* he fell."

"He fell off the tower while he had the Spear?" her sister probed. It shouldn't have been possible.

"I had the Spear," she confessed. "For a little while, it was mine. But I lost it. I'm sorry. I know it was valuable."

"Not as valuable as you are," Evangeline said, hugging her again.

• • •

Over the next few hours, the Transitioners rounded up the remnants of the Aeron marauders and put out the fires. The town and all the neighboring residences had apparently been evacuated of Normals during the seven-day timeline. "The original plan," Jax told Addie, "was for Sloane and her Dulac relatives to plant a false emergency in the minds of the mayor and the police and fire chiefs. But thanks to all that rain and flooding, they had a real emergency on their hands."

Jax dragged Addie around the Bedivere mansion and grounds, checking on his friends. He seemed to have a lot of them. They ruffled his hair, patted him on the back, and congratulated him for pulling off a successful "extraction."

Addie, of course, was the thing he'd *extracted*. Like a rotten tooth.

A dark-haired Morgan girl who seemed to know Jax pretty well filled them in on the details of the Transitioners' military defense. "We were trying to keep the casualties low," the girl said. "But they weren't making it easy. They set half the mountainside on fire, and they didn't care very much about preserving their own lives. Believe it or not, having the Donovans with us made a big difference. I don't know how Thomas and Michael could smell out people through all that smoke, but they did. Michael even saved a couple Kin kids who got separated from their captors and were trapped by fire. He was a real hero."

"You take that back, Deidre Morgan!" shouted a red-headed man who was being tended by a healer for burns. "You'll ruin my reputation!"

That made a lot of people laugh. Addie smiled faintly, pretending she got the joke. Although these Transitioners came from different clans, they seemed united by a common enemy—and elated by their victory. Addie felt out of place, having been, for a time, one of the enemy, but the Transitioners didn't seem to object to her presence. Apparently the story she'd told Bedivere, painting herself as an innocent victim, had been accepted.

Not even Evangeline and Jax knew how close she'd really come to destroying the Eighth Day Spell.

Addie and Evangeline were the only Kin present for most of the morning, but around noon, a group of Kin adults were escorted into the house. Evangeline hurried to greet the new arrivals, while Addie craned her neck trying to see them.

"Who are they?" Jax asked.

Addie started to tell him she didn't know and realized the question was addressed to Riley Pendragon, who'd come up behind them. "Some of them are people who voluntarily took refuge with Bedivere, but you recognize the last two guys, don't you? The Taliesins?"

Addie stood on tiptoe to take another look. The Taliesin brothers had been the ones to pull her kicking and screaming out of Evangeline's arms on the day their parents died.

"They're special guests at our Table meeting," Riley went

on. "We'll be talking about what to do with the prisoners, and these Kin representatives have been invited to take part in the final discussion. Which is kind of a big step forward in Transitioner-Kin relations."

Evangeline caught sight of Addie and gave a little wave, mouthing the words *See you later.* Then she disappeared into Bedivere's banquet room.

"How'd you pry the Taliesins out of their library?" Jax asked Riley.

"The Taliesins are record keepers for the Kin. They're going to help place those orphans. Some will go back to the Carroways, but the Taliesins may be able to reunite long-lost family members." Riley looked down at Addie. "That reminds me. We need to get you back to Vermont. Not to stay, I mean. Just to visit."

Addie hesitated. "I don't know if they want me to visit."

"Are you kidding? Dale phones me every Thursday to get an update on your whereabouts."

Addie felt her cheeks flush. "I wasn't sure Dale would forgive me."

"Sure he will. Jax set me up to be shot by his evil relatives and fed to a wyvern, and I forgave *him.*" Riley clapped Jax on the shoulder and slipped into the meeting room before the door closed.

"That's a totally unfair version of what happened," Jax muttered. Then he turned to Addie. "I bet you wish you could have some time with Evangeline without all this going on."

Addie shrugged. "When you're invited to be a special guest of the Round Table . . ."

"She's not a guest. She's a member. Evangeline took Merlin's place at the Table."

Of course she did, was Addie's first thought. Then she quashed it. "Good for her," she said—and meant it. She was proud of her big sister. "*I* couldn't do it."

"Sure you could. Why not?"

"Is that your attitude about everything?" Addie demanded. "*Why not?*"

He grinned. "Why not?"

She laughed. "I knew you were going to say that."

"Seriously, Addie, I sat in for her once. If I can do it, so can you." Jax looked across the mansion's massive entrance hallway. "While we wait for her to get out of there, I really should say something to my so-called evil relatives."

When Addie followed his gaze and saw who he was looking at, she drew back, putting Jax between her and them. It was the Dulac inquisitor who'd captured Addie and taken her blood for experimentation, along with his wife, the falsely smiling woman who had decorated Addie's prison cell with Hello Kitty junk—although she wasn't smiling now and seemed quite upset. "I knew you had his mark!" Addie gasped. "You *are* one of them!"

"He's my uncle, yeah. But my mark's slightly different, which means I'm not part of his clan," Jax explained. "He's a jerk, but I feel bad about Lesley. I want to tell him and Aunt

Marian how sorry I am. You can come with me. They won't bother you."

"The last time I saw that man," Addie said, staying behind Jax, "I bit him."

"Erg." Jax grimaced. "Okay, wait here. I'll just be a second."

"Can your brownie wait with me?"

"Sure. Stink, stay with her."

The brownie hopped from Jax's shoulder onto Addie's. When Jax turned his back to walk across the room, she waited about two seconds before slipping around two camouflaged soldiers and losing herself in the crowd. Stink made a squeaky protest. Addie ignored him. There was something she needed to do, and it had to be done before the Table meeting ended, because Evangeline, the rule follower, would never approve.

Addie found a staircase at the rear of the house and slipped upstairs to a hallway that was quiet and empty. "Where's the nearest brownie hole?" she asked Stink.

Stink scolded her.

"Fine, I'll look for myself." Addie scanned the wall at base-board height. "Brownies like food and trash, but there's too many people near the kitchens for me to go there. They also like soft places to sleep, so maybe a linen closet . . ."

Stink made an aggravated noise and leaped down from Addie's shoulder. He jumped through one of the walls, then popped back out again. "Why, thank you, Stink," Addie said, squatting down to push her way into the invisible hole.

Jax had told her that all the people jumping in and out of

the Bedivere mansion with brownies on their shoulders were Dulac vassals who'd been given access to brownie holes by the deceased Dr. Morder. "But humans can't jump accurately unless they have a brownie guide—which is where Riley came in today because brownies obey Pendragons. He assigned a brownie to everyone who'd be using the tunnels—except my cousin Dorian, who wasn't supposed to go anywhere but got lucky when he did. When we're done here, Riley can order the brownies not to take Dulacs anywhere, which will hopefully shut down any plans Sloane has for using the tunnels to her advantage."

Addie didn't think Jax was right about that. If this kid Dorian had managed to jump without brownie guidance, then it could be done. She bet *she* could learn to do it, given her talent for working with other people's magic. But right now, she was glad for Stink's help because time was of the essence. According to Jax, the Transitioners had been preparing holding cells for prisoners for almost two weeks, but if what Addie had overheard while accompanying him around the mansion today was true, the captured Kin wouldn't be occupying them anywhere near that long.

She told Stink where she wanted him to take her, and although his ears flattened in disapproval, he did what she asked. After a dizzying jump through space, Addie found herself standing in the hallway of another building. She had to trust that Stink had taken her where she asked—the place Jax had pointed out to her earlier from their vantage point on the Bedivere grounds. It was an office building, located safely above the flood zone.

When she tried to find a hole to exit the brownie tunnel, Stink squealed, stopping her. He stuck his head out, and it disappeared as if sheared clean off his body. Then he retreated back into the tunnel with alarmed squeaking, and Addie realized the problem. The tunnel was contained in an alternate timeline, and people outside it would not be visible to her.

So, she waited until Stink signaled the coast was clear before climbing out of the tunnel. The brownie scampered a few steps down the hallway, then stopped to sniff at one particular door. The ward painted on it was of Kin origin, with unique alterations made by a Transitioner artisan. It would keep the occupants securely inside, but did not prevent physical entry from the outside. Addie touched the lock, and it clicked open silently. *Thank heavens for Aeron mischief.* Stink scrambled up her pants leg and shirt onto her shoulder, and she slipped inside, closing the door behind her.

Kel was lying on a cot in the bare, windowless room with his arms crossed over his face, but he sat up at her entrance. "Addie! Did they get you, too?" Then he saw the brownie on her shoulder, with its unmistakable white-topped head. Jax's brownie. "Oh . . . I guess you're . . ."

"Here by choice," she agreed.

"You've gone over to their side," he said resentfully, "like your sister, the traitor."

"Don't call her that!" Evangeline might be annoyingly perfect, but she was a better person than Addie had ever been. She was Merlin's heir, upholder of the spell, and most importantly, *Addie's sister.*

"What happened to my dad?" asked Kel.

"He's not hurt. The adult captives are under sedation, locked up, and warded. The children are being held separately. The Transitioners aren't sure what to do with you and the Aeron teenagers. Evangeline is arguing in your favor"—*in spite of what you think of her*—"but there's a good chance they're going to send you with the adults."

"Where?" If he was trying to sound defiant, he failed. Kel was scared.

"Oeth-Anoeth," Addie said bluntly. Kel flinched. "They're going to put you into coffins for transport before midnight, fly you to Wales during the seven-day timeline, and when they let you out, you'll already be there." In a medieval fortress of magical suppression, cut off from the world.

For a moment she thought Kel was going to cry. If he did, she wouldn't blame him. Unlike most Kin, he'd lived his life in luxury, and now he was going to the horrible place that had produced Griffyn and Ysabel. Addie didn't let him despair for long. "That's why," she said, "when I walk out of here, I'm leaving the door unlocked. Don't expect any more help from me than that. You're on your own after this."

"What about my dad?"

"He's unconscious and under more guard than you are.

You can't help him. I'm only giving you this chance because we were friends when we were little—and because you brought help when the Dulacs had me. This makes us even."

"I thought we were still friends," Kel said bitterly. "I care about you, Addie."

Did he? Addie thought about Kel watching while Bran tortured her and how he did nothing to stop his father pinning her to the floor to break her wrist. She compared that to Evangeline binding herself to Griffyn for Addie's sake—and Jax coming to rescue her, getting stabbed, then returning for her with a really big sword.

"I don't think you even know what friendship means," she told Kel.

Addie didn't look back when she slipped out the door and into the brownie hole with Stink on her shoulder. She knew, guiltily, that she had no right to cast stones at Kel. *I ran away from the Carroways for selfish reasons and left them an ungrateful letter, too. I led terrible people to their doorstep and almost got them killed. I was as bad as Kel.*

But Dale still calls every week to find out if I'm okay.

Addie felt oddly hopeful. Maybe, in the company of her sister, her vassal, and their friends, she could learn to be a better person, too.

Why not?

39

EVANGELINE SUCCESSFULLY ARGUED a reprieve for all the Aeron children under the age of thirteen, although the Table required that they foster with Transitioner clans. The same went for the kidnapped orphans whose talents were useful in combat. Even though those kids had been coerced into fighting, cautious members of the Table didn't want to lose track of them.

What made Evangeline unhappy—and Jax, too—was that any Aerons thirteen and older were deemed "a risk" and condemned to Oeth-Anoeth along with the adults.

"That's when Riley proposed every member of the Table send a representative to Wales for the incarceration, to see for themselves where the prisoners are going and to make sure it's modern and humane." Evangeline looked up at Riley proudly, telling the story after the meeting. "It wasn't a popular idea with everyone, but majority ruled."

Sheila had voted against it, not wanting civilians

cluttering up her operation. She was joined by Sloane, Bors, and Sagramore. The rest had sided with Riley, although Riley said the new Pellinore leader was more interested in justice for his brother than inspecting conditions at the prison.

Evangeline had insisted on confessing her part in the death of Ash Pellinore in front of the Table, against the better judgment of Riley and Mrs. Crandall. "Luckily," Riley said, "it didn't start a clan feud." She hadn't been the one to deliver the killing blow, and the new Pellinore leader accepted her apology. "Not graciously," Riley reported, "but he appreciated her honesty."

"Does this mean I'm going to Oeth-Anoeth to represent Evangeline?" Jax asked.

"No," Evangeline said. "I was allowed to deputize Mr. Crandall to go, because my clan is composed only of minors." Jax felt disappointed *and* relieved. It would've been cool to visit a magic fortress from the time of Merlin and King Arthur, but he wasn't sure he wanted to watch kids his own age get locked up in it.

One Kin teen who would *not* be going was Kel Mathonwy. Even before the Table meeting was over, it was discovered that Kel had escaped from his cell. When Jax heard, he immediately looked at Addie. *I left you alone for ten minutes!* Addie stared back at him with the kind of innocent expression that only an extraordinarily guilty person could make. However, before anyone else could jump to the same conclusion, A.J. took responsibility. "The ward on his cell was sloppily done," A.J. said. "I made too many in too short a time. It's my fault."

Addie's changing expression was priceless. Surprise to elation to guilt. "That's Riley's vassal," Jax whispered. "He's got our back. Always."

Addie looked at Jax, then at A.J., who winked at her. Slowly, she broke out in a grin, as if she couldn't believe her luck—not luck in getting away with something, but in landing among people who'd back her up without question.

More worrisome than Kel Mathonwy's escape was the fact that Ysabel Arawen was still at large. Also, Bran's body had been recovered, but Griffyn's had not. When the Transitioner forces had finished transporting the live prisoners and went back for Griffyn, his body was gone. "Are you sure he was dead?" Addie asked.

"Yes," Jax insisted. "Evangeline wouldn't be free of him if he wasn't." Then he grimaced. "But Ysabel can talk to the dead, and she was Griffyn's girlfriend, right?"

Addie made a face, too. "Griffyn was awful enough when he was *alive.*"

"Leave it to a Kin girl to drag her dead boyfriend off for company," said a wry voice from behind them.

Addie whirled around, scowling, but Jax knew Tegan was only yanking his chain and figured he could give as good as he got. "I see you're wearing your grandmother's

honor blade." Jax had noticed it earlier and had been waiting for the right moment to comment.

Tegan's hand fell to the hilt of the dagger sheathed at
her side. It seemed like a surprisingly high-quality blade,
judging from the engraved hilt. Jax could see it was an
antique. "Just for help with the scrying."

"I also heard that *somebody* provided a whole bunch of
emergency supplies for the Normals driven out of their
homes—water, propane, canned goods—and wouldn't
take any money for them. Very *honorable*." Jax knew that
carrying an honor blade had nothing to do with behaving
honorably, but he couldn't resist teasing her. "What'd your
dad think about that?"

Tegan glared at him. "You want to make fun of my
dad? He risked his life out there tonight. Him and Thomas
both."

Jax got serious. "Yeah, I know they did. Sorry, Tegan
I'm just joking with you. Thanks for everything your family did. We couldn't have pulled this off without you."

"Well, you've got your two blondies back, safe and
sound. That's all that counts, right?" She looked Addie up
and down.

"Don't worry," Jax said. "Addie's my liege and my
friend, but not anything else."

"What do you mean by *that*?" Tegan's freckled face
flushed to almost the same color as her hair. "What makes

you think I care how you feel about *anybody*, you conceited jerk?"

"I . . . uh," Jax backpedaled.

"If you'll excuse me, *Mr. Aren't-I-the-Center-of-the-Universe*, I need to see if my father and brother are all healed up from the injuries they got when they did what I asked them to do. To save the world. Not *you*."

Jax's mouth flapped open and shut like a fish while Tegan stomped away.

"Is she your girlfriend or something?" Addie sounded amused.

"Not exactly, but I thought . . ." Jax scratched his head. "Okay, I have no clue."

"She doesn't seem very nice." Addie grinned. "I think I like her."

By the evening of that day, Jax and his two liege ladies were more than ready to leave Bedivere's and head back to the mountain cabin. They'd had no sleep the night before, and all three of them were practically dead on their feet. But there was one last surprise in store for them.

After the Table meeting had ended, but before the participants had dispersed, Uncle Finn requested a formal audience with Sloane. His injuries had been healed, but he still looked awful. As for Aunt Marian, she'd lost a lot of weight and sleep in the last two weeks, and she leaned against Dorian's shoulder as if unable to stand alone.

Sloane appeared annoyed by the request. "All right, Finn. I can meet with you in half an hour."

"No," Uncle Finn said. "I'd like to do this in front of the Table members and my family."

Sloane glanced around apprehensively, as if suspecting Finn had something unpleasant to say and not wanting everyone to hear it. But she composed her face and asked the Table members to return to the meeting room.

Dorian followed his father, and to Jax's surprise, Aunt Marian motioned for him to come, too. "You're family, Jax." While the Table members filed back into the room, Jax grabbed Addie by the arm and towed her along. Who knew what she'd get up to next if he left her alone?

Inside, Uncle Finn went down on one knee in front of Sloane, who turned very pale. "Everyone here knows my daughter was taken by the Morrigan," Finn said gruffly. "She's presumed lost by most of you. But witnesses saw Lesley overcome the Morrigan to save her brother, even if it was only for a few seconds. I refuse to believe my daughter is beyond hope. Therefore, I ask to be released from my vow of vassalhood so that I can devote myself to tracking down the Girl of Crows and rescuing my daughter. If the Morrigan is using other people for the Old Crone and the Washer Woman, I mean to free them as well. Additionally, I ask that this task be appointed to me as an official Quest of the Table so that I can carry the strength of all of you with me."

Confronted in this public manner, Sloane didn't have much choice, but she still made a token protest. "Finn, I don't want to let you go. I need you."

Uncle Finn looked up at her bleakly. "As much as my daughter does?"

There was no way for Sloane to answer that. She glanced around at all the watching people, then placed her hand on Finn's head to release him from his vow to her and the Dulac family.

One by one the other members of the Table approached Finn as he knelt on the floor, tapped him on both shoulders with their honor blades, and charged him with the Quest of "seeking the Morrigan and freeing her captive human hosts." Aunt Marian stood silently by with tears on her cheeks. Dorian put an arm around his mother and watched the ceremony with an expression Jax had never before seen on Dorian's face in connection with his dad.

Pride.

When Riley took his turn, Finn looked up at him and asked, "You'll make sure my nephew is safe and happy?"

"Yes, sir," Riley replied. "On my honor, I will."

Sloane went last. She laid her dagger on each of his shoulders, appointed him to the Quest, and added fiercely, "Go get her, Finn."

40

JAX SLEPT FOR SIXTEEN hours straight on Thursday and woke up sweaty. It was August—something he still couldn't wrap his mind around after jumping forward a week in that mountain house, bound to Kel Mathonwy—and the cabin wasn't air-conditioned. Even in the normally cool mountains, August was humid and sticky.

After grazing on everything he found in the refrigerator, he checked his phone and computer. Billy had asked for an update approximately six million times via voice mail, text, chat, and email. The only thing missing was a video.

While Jax was glancing through the messages, Riley stumbled past with nothing but a grunt in greeting. He returned from the kitchen a few minutes later, looking more cheerful and carrying a bowl of Cap'n Crunch, a Mountain Dew, and a plastic container of Jell-O pudding.

"You should have some sugar with that breakfast," Jax said.

Riley flung himself into a chair. "Any news?"

"Billy wants a report."

Riley heaved a sigh. Jax was sure he'd gotten his own texts and calls from Billy. "I'll call him later. His mom, too, 'cause we've got to make plans for you to move in with them," Riley said around a mouthful of cereal. "School starts in, what, two and a half weeks?"

Ugh. Eighth grade. "Do I really have to go? They have schools around here, and we're not in hiding anymore."

"True, but I doubt we'll stay here long. The house is too small already, and now we've got Evangeline *and* Addie. I'm not sure where we'll end up, and I don't think it'd be good for you to change schools again, maybe more than once. You need to go back to a place you know, with a friend like Billy. Also . . ." Riley paused for another mouthful, then continued casually, "Michael Donovan mentioned that he wanted to pull up roots and start over someplace where he wasn't so notorious, but Tegan vetoed it. She wants to finish middle school where she is. So, she'll be there too."

Sure. Tegan was having *way* too much fun confusing Jax to move away. But if Riley was fishing for how Jax felt about it, he was going to be disappointed. Jax changed the subject. "When are you and Mr. and Mrs. Crandall leaving for Wales?"

"Sunday. We'll be gone till Thursday or Friday. You and A.J. will have to watch out for the girls while we're gone."

"No problem," Jax said. "I bet they'll sleep most of the day."

They'd all arrived back at the cabin around eleven p.m. last night, exhausted. Evangeline had thrown herself facedown on the sofa and refused to move. So Jax had led Addie to Evangeline's normal sleeping spot. At the sight of the closet under the stairs, Addie had made the exact same Harry Potter joke Evangeline had made when *she* first saw it before crawling in and collapsing. Tired as he was, Jax had laughed silently to himself. The sisters were a lot more alike than either of them would ever admit.

"Your uncle's coming," said Riley. "To Wales, I mean. It's impossible to tell where the Morrigan will turn up next, but the transportation of three dozen Kin to Oeth-Anoeth might be hard for her to resist. You never know."

"I hope he finds her." They'd had casualties on their side of this conflict, but Jax didn't want Lesley to be one of them. And that reminded him . . . "About the Sword of Nuadu. I thought I was the one who was supposed to use it. Not that I *wanted* to kill anyone, but didn't it have to be me?"

Riley had moved on to the pudding. "That's the problem with prophecies and magic artifacts. You can't count on 'em. Prophecies are vague, and magic objects are tricky.

You invoked the Sword against Griffyn and brought it into his presence. You drew it on him, even. The Morrigan was probably the only creature on earth who could hold it besides you. The Sword killed Griffyn, and Lesley's body did the deed—thus fulfilling the *innocent hand* requirement. Remember, Bran Llyr had the Spear of Lugh, and it wasn't supposed to let him fail. But somehow Addie got it away from him."

Jax wanted to know how she did that, but getting the story out of her might take work. The girl was even more prickly and secretive than Tegan.

"Anyway," Riley continued, "regarding our living arrangements, if you pass eighth grade with a better average that you had in seventh grade—and I bet Mrs. Ramirez will make sure of that—we'll reevaluate the situation. The Crandalls need to find jobs, and we want to settle close to New York so Evangeline and I can attend to Table matters. If we land in a place with a good high school, you can live with us next year. Assuming you still want to."

The Crandalls were going to need jobs, but not Riley? Jax nodded to himself. It was just like he'd thought. "Do the Crandalls know yet?" he asked.

Riley swigged from the Mountain Dew. "Know where we're going to live?"

"No. What you plan to do to keep from aging seven times as fast as Evangeline."

Riley choked on a mouthful and put the bottle down.

"I should've guessed you'd figure it out."

It hadn't been very difficult. Evangeline couldn't live on *his* timeline, but Riley could live on *hers*. He'd proved that when he duct-taped their wrists together in an attempt to pull her into the seven-day world. Instead, he'd jumped to the following week with her, just like Jax did when he was tied to Kel. If Riley bound himself to Evangeline on a semi-regular basis, he'd stop racking up seven times as many days as she did, equalizing their aging rate. Not completely—but enough to make it tolerable.

He'd also skip over weeks at a time. Jax felt a little sad about that, which was weird, considering how much he'd despised Riley not that long ago. But if it made Evangeline happy, Jax would get used to it.

"Gloria figured it out, same as you," Riley admitted. "She disapproved at first. Said I'd be foolish to throw my life away for a girl. So, I told her that without *this* girl, it wouldn't be a very happy life."

"And she—"

"Started bawling. Like in a cartoon. The tears practically flew off her face." Riley illustrated with hand gestures. "She gave me her blessing and went off to blow her nose."

He'd made Mrs. Crandall cry? Jax was impressed.

Riley, however, looked apprehensive. "I haven't said anything to Evangeline yet. It's . . . awkward. We haven't

376

even had a *date*. How do I ask her to drag me through time with her?"

"You don't count fighting the wyvern as a date?" Then Jax realized Riley was serious. He was actually afraid of getting rejected. "Riley, you idiot. Just ask her. Or do you want me to pass her a note that says, *Do you like Riley? Circle yes or no?*" Jax ducked the empty pudding container Riley threw at his head, then frowned as another thought suddenly occurred to him.

"I'll be around," Riley assured him. "Once every eight days. Plus the other seven any time you need me. I'm not abandoning you."

"It's not that," Jax said. "It's just—I read a lot of King Arthur legends this summer, trying to catch up on what every other Transitioner knows. Some of them say Arthur didn't die on the battlefield—that he went into a suspended state where he could return and help his people when they needed him."

Riley put the empty soda bottle aside. "So what?"

"So, that's going to be you now, isn't it? You're going to jump into the future, a week at a time. Your aging will slow down. I'll get older; you won't. And if I need you, you'll be there. You're the new King Arthur."

Riley's mouth fell open. "No. Way."

"Yeah. Way." Jax grinned.

A second later, Jax was yanked from his chair, Riley

had him in a half nelson on the floor, and Jax was getting a noogie. "Stupid legends," Riley growled. "What a bunch of crap."

Jax wriggled uselessly. "You know, it won't be long— by your counting—that I'm as big as you are. Then we'll see who's getting the noogie. What d'ya think of that?"

"Looking forward to it, Squirt."

ACKNOWLEDGMENTS

I WROTE THE FIRST draft of *The Morrigan's Curse* in the winter months of 2014 while I was still teaching full-time. I had plenty of days off to work on it because Pennsylvania was hit that year by an astonishing number of snow and ice storms. When my fellow teachers heard I was writing a book with weather gods in it, they of course blamed me for the bizarre wintry mix—freezing fog? really?—which didn't break until I'd finally defeated the Llyrs. Coincidence? I think not. Despite the weather, my colleagues never failed to express their support for my writing, and I want to thank all of them, especially the "purple" team: Nichole Brown, Matt Krykew, and Kelly McGuffin.

I owe thanks to my agent, Sara Crowe, and my brilliant editors, Alexandra Cooper and Alyssa Miele, who helped me take the early drafts to the next level. The design team at HarperCollins and the cover artist, Mike Heath, deserve my unending gratitude for the eye-catching covers on all the books in the series.

I also want to thank my family, Bob, Gabbey, and Gina, for their enthusiastic support and my beta readers: Krystalyn Drown, Marcy Hatch, Katie Mills, Susan Kaye Quinn, and Maria Ann Witt. My reading students of the 2013–2014 school year—the very last fifth-grade students of my teaching career—talked me into reading them the first draft of this book so they could give feedback (and get their names listed here). Many, many thanks to my awesome students and devoted fans: Nik, Edson, Evelyn, Julian, Ava, Jasmine, Annie, Jack C., Kimberly, Omar, Brisa, Brandon, Belinda, Yareli, Aidan, Michael, Dylan, Jenny S., Tori, Liliana, Jenny B., Jacqui, Kate, Emma, Reece, Marley, Max, Jacob, J.J., Jimmy, Ethan, Rachel, Michelle, Erik, Chloe, Jackie, Lucy, Lauren, Sophia, Maggie, Matt, Joey, Caleb, Victoria, Ricky, Caitlyn, and Jack T.

DIANNE K. SALERNI attended the University of Delaware, where she earned her bachelor's degree in elementary education, and then went on to earn a master's in language arts education at the University of Pennsylvania. She was an elementary school teacher for over twenty years and has also written several books, including *We Hear the Dead* and *The Caged Graves*. *The Morrigan's Curse* is the third book in the Eighth Day series. Although Dianne knows there's not really such a thing as a secret Eighth Day, discovering one would explain all the food that disappears in her house. Until then, she'll continue to blame her husband, Bob, her two teenage daughters, Gabrielle and Gina, and her dog, Sorcia. Dianne lives in Chester County, Pennsylvania. You can visit her online at www.diannesalerni.com.

CATCH ALL OF JAX AUBREY'S
HEART-POUNDING ADVENTURES IN THE
EIGHTH DAY SERIES!

HARPER
An Imprint of HarperCollinsPublishers

www.harpercollinschildrens.com